NIGH

WINSTON GRAHAM is the author of more than thirty novels, which include *Cordelia*, *Marnie*, *The Walking Stick* and *Stephanie* as well as the highly successful *Poldark* series. His novels have been translated into seventeen languages and six have been filmed. Two television series have been adapted from the *Poldark* novels and shown in twenty-two countries. *The Stranger From the Sea* has now also been televised. *Tremor*, Winston Graham's latest bestseller, is also available from Pan Books.

Winston Graham lives in Sussex. He is a fellow of the Royal Society of Literature and in 1983 was awarded an OBE.

By the same author

ROSS POLDARK
DEMELZA
JEREMY POLDARK
WARLEGGAN
THE BLACK MOON
THE FOUR SWANS
THE ANGRY TIDE
THE STRANGER FROM THE SEA
THE MILLER'S DANCE
THE LOVING CUP
THE TWISTED SWORD

NIGHT JOURNEY
CORDELIA
THE FORGOTTEN STORY
THE MERCILESS LADIES
TAKE MY LIFE
FORTUNE IS A WOMAN
THE LITTLE WALLS
THE SLEEPING PARTNER
GREEK FIRE
THE TUMBLED HOUSE
MARNIE
THE GROVE OF EAGLES
AFTER THE ACT
THE WALKING STICK
ANGELL, PEARL AND LITTLE GOD
THE JAPANESE GIRL (short stories)
WOMAN IN THE MIRROR
THE GREEN FLASH
CAMEO
STEPHANIE
TREMOR

THE SPANISH ARMADAS
POLDARK'S CORNWALL

WINSTON GRAHAM

NIGHT
WITHOUT
STARS

PAN BOOKS

First published 1950 by Hodder and Stoughton Ltd

This edition published 1997 by Pan Books
an imprint of Macmillan Publishers Ltd
25 Eccleston Place, London SW1W 9NF
and Basingstoke

Associated companies throughout the world

ISBN 0 330 33906 0

1 3 5 7 9 8 6 4 2

A CIP catalogue record for this book is available from
the British Library

Typeset by CentraCet Limited, Cambridge
Printed and bound in Great Britain by
Mackays of Chatham plc, Chatham, Kent

To A. Gerard East

BOOK ONE

CHAPTER ONE

WHEN THE shell blinded me they sent me back to a base hospital for some weeks so that skin could be grafted on my hand. Every now and then a surgeon would come by and look at my eyes and say, well, it's too early yet to be sure, and the nurses would say how lucky I was not to be disfigured.

Blindness takes getting used to particularly in the mornings: at night you go to sleep and accept darkness as natural, it's the mornings that are the trying time, when you wake and want to lift something off; pull the curtains, so to speak. And in the night sometimes when you try to look at your luminous wrist-watch. Once you're properly awake your mind can take control and argue things out. Seeing isn't everything. There's likewise a wind on the heath . . .

After a month or so they began to talk about an operation and shipped me back to England. Rachel came over to see me almost at once, but it was all rather stiff and formal, and never got down to anything. It was bad knowing she was sitting beside me and not seeing her face or her hair or her eyes, or what she was dressed in. I'd been thinking a good deal about Rachel, having had plenty of time for thought.

But it somehow wasn't right plunging in at that first meeting for over six months; and the next time she had her mother with her, and the time after that was just before the operation and it seemed inappropriate to talk about the future when everyone was so hopeful and sold me the idea that in a few weeks I should be as good as ever.

Once or twice I wondered if this was the tin hare designed to get the dog to run.

They did things to my left eye, this being the least damaged, and it was a success. At least, it was a success so far as it went. I'd been able to get a few glimpses out of this eye when allowed to for the last week or so, and when they took the bandages off I could make out things fairly clearly again. Admitted it still wasn't much of a view, but small change is riches to a beggar.

They said something about blood in the eye and inflammation and that these would clear up as time went on. It was a question of patience and good behaviour now. I wasn't so sure.

Anyway, I'd had leisure to think things over thoroughly before Rachel came this time, and I was glad to see that she was alone. Yes, *see*. I saw her blurred and misty and grey, like one of those tactful screen close-ups done to disguise the fact that the heroine is long in the tooth.

But Rachel was twenty, and I knew her colour from memory.

'Is it – really all right, Giles?'

'It's all right.'

'. . . Sure?'

'You've got a new hat on, and you're doing your hair differently – and *where* did you get that brooch?'

'Well . . . thank *Heaven* . . . When did they take the bandages off?'

'Yesterday.'

She said doubtfully: 'How good is it?'

'Pretty good.'

'It doesn't look much different.'

'It is different, believe me.'

She sat down abruptly. 'I've had nightmares. To think of you, so active and vigorous . . . groping your way through life – twenty years, forty years. We can talk of it now.'

I could see myself doing a certain amount of groping, but I thought I'd save that bright thought until after tea. Nurse Rylands, who was a stone heavier and a foot taller than I'd imagined, pushed over a trolley, and after a few minutes we were alone again. It was then that I began to notice the differences in Rachel were not only in her voice. She talked, as she'd talked before on these visits, a bit feverishly, and now that I could see and she might have expected me to be watching her she seemed to want to avoid my gaze. I'd already assured myself that the nurses in Normandy had been telling the truth and that I was no worse to look at than usual.

I listened to her, but didn't say much. I knew it was time I started talking, because the longer it was left the

5

worse it would get; but I'm not the stuff heroes are made of, and there was the awful temptation to let things slide.

I knew there'd be argument because she was that sort. She'd want to stick by the contract, and it's hard arguing against your own interests. Anyway, if I wanted to be even moderately honest I had to make it clear to her that I wasn't going to be in good shape for getting married just yet. It seemed to me that the field was wide open. If in a month or six months or twelve months I found I could see as well as ever, I'd claim all the privileges going, but until then she must be free. The present state wasn't good enough. You can't earn your living and do any good with a wife and family on about a quarter of an eye.

Presently I lit her cigarette and one for myself, and carefully noticed that the flame which should have been amber was a sort of delicate mauve.

'I don't know what these damned surgeons have done,' I said, 'but they've taken the technicolour out of life. I shall probably do pretty well as a solicitor now – seeing everything in field grey. No danger of glamour distorting the judgment.'

'Shall you – go back to that? I mean, you're still a partner, aren't you?'

'Yes. I expect I shall go back.'

'You should take a long holiday first. It would be crazy to plunge straight back into it.'

'Maybe. It depends.'

There was a short silence.

'You'll go on wearing glasses, I suppose?'

'If they help. D'you mind?'

'Of course not.'

There was another pause. This was obviously the point to begin, but something in her voice made me wonder. She was nervously fastening and unfastening the second button of her attractive blouse.

'It's marvellous that you can see again. Wonderful.'

'Well, don't sound so miserable about it, darling.'

She got up.

I said: 'What's the matter?'

'Nothing.'

'Yes, there is.'

'Oh, God, I'm so unhappy, Giles.'

I got up too, and picked my way round the table, careful not to get my legs tied up with any obstructions on the way.

'What's troubling you?'

'I don't know. I feel I must tell you today, and yet I can't.'

'That's helpful. I've had a feeling for weeks that you were corking things up.'

'Have you? Sit down. It's – not right for you to be standing.'

'I'll not faint on you. Don't worry.'

'No, it's all that height. It makes me uncertain. Always did, you know.'

She smiled a bit, and I sat down to please her. She drew at her cigarette.

'I've wanted to tell you from the first. But I couldn't.

7

That's what makes me so thankful you've got your sight back . . .' She stopped. 'That makes me sound like a bitch, doesn't it. You see—'

'Suppose,' I said, 'you sit down and begin in Basic English. I'm all braced up now.'

She did as she was told. I folded my legs and waited. We were the only people on the veranda just then. It was a veranda partly enclosed in glass, and across the other side of the gravel path was a tennis court on which a couple of men, convalescents, were playing singles. You could hear the soft plop-plop of the tennis balls.

She said absolutely nothing at all.

'Does all this mean,' I said, 'that I've got a rival?'

She glanced up quickly.

'Yes.'

'Oh,' I said. It looked as if my *Traviata* scene wasn't going to come off as billed.

'I've been in hell, Giles. Really, I have. It was absolutely out of the blue. It was three months ago. I tried to fight against it, not see him, etc., do all the usual things. But it wouldn't work. It doesn't work if you feel like that.'

'Who is he?'

'A man in the navy. A lieutenant.'

'Out of the blue, as you remark.'

'I was going to write to you, and then I heard you were wounded. I thought I'd wait. Then I heard the rest.'

'So what?'

'I couldn't tell you anything or do anything until

8

you'd got your eyesight back. I had to help you to keep going. It was all there was to do.'

'And if I didn't see again? What then?'

'I hadn't got that far.'

Hadn't she? I wondered. I lit another cigarette and thought all round it.

She said: 'You *must* think me a bitch. I know that. I don't make any excuses, except what I have made. To-day's been awful. When I phoned this morning and knew you were all right I was so delighted for your sake. But I knew then that I'd got to tell you today. It was now or never.'

'Can I take your tray, Mr Gordon?' said Nurse Rylands, billowing up suddenly from behind.

I stared at the grey sunlight falling across my hands.

'Listen, Rachel,' I said, when Nurse Rylands had gone, 'we joined up nine months ago. Out of that we've had a weekend at your place, a week in London, and a couple of nights out in October. It's not a lot, and it's no good flogging yourself if something's happened to make it seem unimportant. It's not a good break for me, but at least I can see again; and just at present that's like the Gates of Heaven. I shall get over the rest.'

'I do feel absolutely awful,' she said.

'Thanks for sticking by me while I was – as I was. I suppose if this thing hadn't been a success you'd have felt bound to – go on sticking, eh . . .?'

'No. Not bound.'

'Not bound, but as good as. I think your naval bloke has done well for himself. Was he in on this?'

'More or less.'

9

'All the prayers there must have been for my recovery!' I paused. 'Look, darling, stop mucking about with that button. You'll spoil your blouse.'

She said: 'It isn't as if I don't care for you. I do, a great deal—'

'Suppose you leave the analysis for another day; we'll only get all tied up. Just at present everything's straightforward and clear. I've been jilted and I'm still on my feet. Metaphorically anyway. Why worry about the rest?'

'I think,' she said, 'you're the grandest person I ever met.'

'No, Rachel, if you only knew, I'm full of rage and bitterness. But I'm trying very hard to be the little gentleman. Don't elevate it beyond that. I'll see you again?'

'Of course – if you want to.'

'I want to.'

The tennis players had stopped and were doing something at the net.

'How long have you got to stay in here now?'

'A fortnight maybe. Then I'm free to go out into the brave new world. I'd like to meet your lieutenant. Perhaps we could get together and have a dinner or something.'

'Of course. If you want that. You know how I feel.'

'Good. That's settled, then. Now tell me about London. I haven't seen it for so long.'

Later when she left we kissed like old friends and I watched her walk into the encircling fog. It was right that she should go that way, even though later I should

10

have to write and say I'd changed my mind and that it would be better if we didn't meet again after all.

I'd been done out of my grand renunciation and now must make do with a small. Obviously it was best to keep her from knowing how little I could see. There was no point in our both being unhappy about it.

CHAPTER TWO

I WENT back to work. Somewhere about this time the war ended, and those who felt like it danced in the streets. I was too preoccupied forgetting Rachel and making a little daylight go a long way.

The eye improved a lot, and it was surprising how much I got around to.

Driving a car was rather an ordeal from the beginning, because, apart from the bad vision, it isn't easy to judge distances with one eye. But golf was quite possible, and I did a lot of walking. My eyes showed no sign of injury (except that the good one kept getting bloodshot) and this fooled most people into thinking I could see as well as they could.

Certain things had to be avoided. The cinema was out altogether, and bright lights hurt. I could read well enough, but not for long periods; and for the office work I found a gem of a girl called Marigold who was only fifteen and read slowly and with the precision of a parson. I was inclined to drop things, and in the end I never accepted a cup and saucer by hand if I could avoid it. Perspective was difficult, as it was bound to be, and there were good days and bad.

The family firm welcomed me back all right. Parker was in the Far East, but Hampden was still bending his grey head over the torts, and Cousin Lewis had managed to go on getting deferments until they were no longer necessary. There was plenty for me to do, and I put in as much work as I could at the courts, since Marigold could help me to memorise the details, and it saved a lot of reading.

The first Christmas of peace I spent with my sister in Oxford. Caroline is nine years older than I am and nearly as tall. She'd married a Fellow of St Peter's, and was a theosophist and a vegetarian. People said she ought to have been the lawyer. She always had the effect of making me feel about fourteen and slightly sheepish.

She said: 'Well, Giles, it's nice to have you at our table again. I'm glad you've recovered so well. We were so anxious for a time, weren't we, Hugh?'

'We telephoned every night,' said Hugh. 'They passed on our messages?'

'Yes.'

'Let's see, d'you take soda or water, I forget?'

'Soda, please.'

'What exactly did they do?'

I knew Hugh's interest in operations, his own and other people's. I said: 'Took an X-ray first, of course. Next day they stuck an electro-magnet round my head like a steel halo, so that I was the centre of a magnetic field. Then they pointed metal rods or something at my eye. After a bit of messing about something moved in my eye, and I said "Ugh?" and they said, "There it is."

13

Then apparently they manoeuvred it round till it came into a favourable position – then they cut the eye and took out a bit of steel from Krupps.'

After a long minute Caroline said: 'Yet you can see perfectly well with it now?'

'Not perfectly well. I get along.'

Hugh brought the drink. 'I shouldn't have known there was anything wrong at all.'

Caroline said: 'Of course, Giles always has walked and moved as if he'd got an inward preoccupation and wasn't really concerned with what he was doing at any particular moment. I used to try to cure him of it, make him more practical.'

'My dear Carrie, I'm intensely practical, always have been. Look how well I've settled back into the family firm.'

She sipped her barley water. 'I'll give you credit for that. I was afraid – well, after four years away . . .'

I said to tease: 'Did you expect me to go back to Paris?'

'No, dear . . . But one never knows, does one? Things have been very difficult for you lately.'

I didn't answer. She had never met Rachel, so there was nothing to be gained from discussing it.

Hugh said: 'You must be lost in that big old house. Can you get staff?'

'I'm thinking of selling it and taking a small flat somewhere in the West End. It'll save the journey and I shall be handy for concerts and things. That's if Caroline has no objection.'

'I think you're very wise,' she said. 'I never see any

advantage in clinging to things for their sentimental value.'

I looked at the table. 'One thing I'm always glad about when I come here and that's that Hugh isn't a vegetarian as well.'

'I only wish he were! He'd be so much healthier.'

Hugh looked apologetic but flickered a slow eyelid. '*Ad omnem libidinem projectus homo*. A man abandoned to every lust.'

It wasn't long after this that things began to go back a bit. Several days the eye looked red and inflamed and it watered a good deal, and I couldn't stick lights at all. So I went round to see Halliday who'd done the job. He was non-committal and grunted at me as he put his mirror thing back on the table.

'Hm. Yes. The Keratome incision has caused a scar which isn't quite as satisfactory as it might be. However, I shouldn't worry about it. Your colour values are all right now, aren't they?'

'Oh, yes.'

'No headaches?'

'No headaches.'

'I'll change your glasses and give you a little protection against the light. In the meantime take things easily. Plenty of fresh air and not too much hard work. Try to consider yourself convalescent still.'

'I'll try.'

Presently I heard Rachel was married and had gone to live in Portsmouth. I hadn't seen her since, but I

thought it safe enough to relax now and sent her some
Georgian silver as a wedding present. Probably if I had
been able I should have salved my pains by finding some
other girl to go about with, but that didn't seem to
make sense in the circumstances. I got to dining out and
playing cards after. For the first time in my life I began
to appreciate bridge and to take an interest in poker.
Then one day I woke up to the fact that I could see
definitely less than a week ago.

At first I put it down to the weather; but after a bit
of careful testing I realised that the rain wasn't to blame
for this.

I took a taxi and drove round in a panic to see
Halliday.

As was to be expected I had to wait half the morning
until he could fit me in between his appointments. He
grunted and nodded through what I had to say and then
took me in and did the same sort of things he had done
three months ago.

When he'd switched off the last light and made all
the necessary notes on his card index he looked at me
and said:

'Of course you're quite right, Mr Gordon. Your sight
has deteriorated since February. The cause, as I told
you, is the scar of the earlier operation, which is
contracting, and pulling the pupil up slightly towards
the top of the eye. Normally, this would not happen,
but for some reason that we don't know, perhaps
because of the foreign body we had to take out of the
eye, the scar became entangled and has been drawn up.'
He grunted and turned to make another note. 'It's very

disappointing, because it is reducing the value of the eye to you. I can only give you the advice I gave you before. Don't worry, take things easily. You're able to live a fairly normal life at present, aren't you, and it may never get any worse.'

There was something in the tone of his voice that I didn't like.

'Or it may?'

'There's really no reason why it should.'

'And if it does?'

He grunted again and shut his drawer. 'If the pupil gets further drawn up it will restrict sight further and – it would be necessary to adapt your life accordingly.'

'Can't operate again?'

'I should be afraid to with an eye in that condition. But why meet troubles before they come?'

I got up, feeling slightly sick, and looked for my hat. He passed it.

'Thanks,' I said. 'I'll keep you up to date.'

He'd evidently expected the thing to be rapid because when I went again in six months he showed no surprise. In the meantime I got about as usual.

I sold the family house in the end and found a smallish flat in Portland Place which suited a lot better. There were a few disadvantages, of course. I'd thought of pottering about with music again and it was a wrench to sell the piano, but I couldn't imagine myself doing much with it in the flat. Anyway I was in the centre of things.

Spare evenings now were mostly spent at my club, and I began to make money at poker. I gave up golf, said it was a strain, and nobody apparently suspected the truth. This slow loss of sight was quite different from the first go; all sorts of things helped: hearing, smell, touch.

I developed a low cunning too. It became a sort of game, a matter of pride not to get caught out. I knew where everything was in the office, had my own table at the club. When at last it got so that I couldn't read small print I depended more than ever on Marigold, and kept other people out of my office while the first business of the day was gone through.

Then after a time it wasn't a game any more but deadly earnest. I thought I'd go on as long as I could. After that it was anybody's guess. I hated the thought of becoming helpless, an object of sympathy. And I'd had one taste of complete darkness. I couldn't seem to see myself there again. But what was there to do about it?

One day I saw old Hampden and Cousin Lewis, and told them I was giving up. I think by now they suspected a good bit because they didn't jib much but only argued pacifically over the use of the leisure I was going to take and the amount of the allowance they were to make me. Cousin Lewis said he thought a sea-trip would put me right, and old Hampden advised salmon-fishing, but I left them saying I'd let them know where to send the money later on.

I didn't go to see Caroline and Hugh but dropped them a letter. It saved trouble. At that point it was hard to decide where to go, except that I'd a vague hankering to sit in the sun and let things slide. Then I thought of the Wintertons.

The Wintertons had reached England with other refugees from the South of France in 1940. Because they knew my father they came in to our office and I had been able to help them with credits and recommendations, and also to get a passage to America in the following year. When the war was over they went back to their villa in Beaulieu near Monte Carlo, and since then had sent me three letters asking me out.

It seemed worth trying. I had memories of hot sun and mountains and bathing in the Mediterranean when I was a kid. Too many of these precious months had dribbled away in offices and the courts and among the fogs that had nothing to do with my eyesight. I wanted the sun.

I wrote them and got a wire back: 'Delighted. Come and stay the winter.'

Walter Winterton was a Europeanised American of about fifty. Tall, graceful and grey-haired, he was supremely modest over most things but could never meet anyone fresh without telling them in the first ten minutes that he'd been to Eton and Cambridge, and that an ancestor of his had been one of the first governors of Boston. Once you got past that you were all right.

Claire was an indefinite forty-five, half French and half something else, I never knew what. She was small and rather plump, had a tired caressing voice and liked her hair in vivid colours.

They met me at the station in an enormous car – I could just recognise their figures on the platform – drove me to their white Italian villa overlooking the beach, and entertained me like a king. I stayed two months, browning in the winter sunshine, driving with them into Monte Carlo or Nice, talking endlessly and pleasantly on the veranda, sipping champagne cocktails, or taking up a corner at one of their sherry parties. Claire's hair changed with the seasons, from a luscious mahogany to a glamorous primrose yellow. Walter talked about cars and Wall Street and winter sports and radiograms and the international situation. Claire talked about the ballet, shopping, food, her friends, the latest novels and sometimes, to please her husband, cars. She said that cars were Walter's middle-aged vice. When he felt restless or discontented he took a new car the way other men took a mistress.

To a man with a mission they would have been supreme time-wasters, but just then it was ideal company for me. There was always something of interest happening, plenty of new society, no responsibilities or worries, and very little opportunity of being alone. I had my glasses changed into the fashionable pale rims and so looked exactly like everyone else.

But in the end I tired of it. The deterioration was going on all the time. The pupil was becoming more or less the same colour as the iris. That wasn't the way Halliday would have described it, but that was how it looked. My eyes are pretty dark so the change was hardly noticeable, but I could tell that by the time the change was complete I should no longer be able to see. And there was nothing to do to stop it. The eye was clear now and had stopped getting inflamed, but the damage was done.

So I wasn't very good company inwardly, and after a time the constant entertaining and idle talk began to get on my nerves. I *wanted* to be alone. I wanted time to think and reason it all out and face up to it. Early in the new year I told them I was leaving for Théoule, which is the other side of Cannes. There were the usual regal protests, the motions gone through of sweeping my resolutions aside. But this time they wouldn't be swept.

'It's no good, both of you,' I said. 'I've booked my hotel. There's no escape. I must go.'

'*Impossible*,' said Claire. 'The hotels at Théoule are beyond belief. You'd be dead with ennui in a week.'

'Then I must die. I can't sponge on you for the rest of my life.'

They didn't reply. 'I can't see you very clearly,' I said, 'but I believe you're both looking offended, as if I'd said something rather vulgar.'

'So you have, darling,' said Claire.

'I can't help it, it's true. And I can't begin to thank you for the wonderful time you've given me for more than nine weeks. You've both been simply grand.'

'One *gaffe* after another,' said Claire.

'What will you live on?' asked Walter. 'You can't get by on seventy-five pounds and what you can sell.'

'I took a chance and brought a good bit over. Thanks to the way you behave I've only succeeded in getting rid

21

of about a quarter of it, so I shall be in the clear for some months.'

'They ought to give you just as much as you want,' said Claire. 'Anyway, you can't possibly leave here. Please change the subject.'

'I want to go,' I had to say. 'Even if only for a few weeks. D'you know what it is? I want to see how I get on by myself. I'm afraid of getting too dependent . . . It's – psychological. That ought to appeal to you, Claire. You ought to understand.'

She sighed. 'But Théoule. No amenities. Not even a casino . . .'

'I'll be back,' I promised. 'In time for Walter's new car.'

Claire got up. 'You're very difficult, Giles. I will go and see what Marie has for dinner.'

So I went to Théoule. It's a good centre for exploring the Estérels, and I stayed at a little hotel-restaurant and got some satisfaction out of it because they never guessed more than that 'monsieur was a little short-sighted'. I bought a Victorian reading-glass and with it was able to write letters and transact ordinary business.

But I didn't stay long. Claire had been right in one respect. The change was too drastic. After all the company and the chatter, and the driving about to concerts and the social amenities of the villa, an entirely solitary life in my condition was insupportable. So in a few weeks I quietly moved back to Nice and took an apartment off the Avenue de Verdun.

I let the Wintertons know, but by now they realised I had to work the thing out for myself and they couldn't help. There was one other man I knew in the district: John Chapel who was attached to the British Consulate. We'd been at school together, and when he heard I was staying in the town he phoned asking me over to meet his wife. But in the mood I was then in I made an excuse and the thing lapsed.

Nice is a pleasant town. It's got fun if you want fun, it's got the quaintness of the old streets and the quiet; there's industry and miles of shops, and fishing and the rest. I settled down, or tried to settle down, to live out the remaining months until I grew completely helpless, until I took to a white stick and a dog and people began to help me across roads and exchange pitying glances and be self-consciously kind.

CHAPTER THREE

I'VE NEVER been able to count the number of shoe-shops in the Avenue de la Victoire. Anyway I met her in one on the right-hand side going up from the sea.

I'd gone in to buy a pair of walking shoes, having worn out three pairs during the winter.

A young thin girl served me. I didn't take much notice at first, as I was feeling pretty low, and anyway she was only a blur at two feet.

When people's faces and figures shimmer about in the shadows and only come into focus now and then at close range like fishes in an aquarium, one grows to have all sorts of new ways of summing them up. But to-day things were so bad with me that I only remembered afterwards that I'd liked her voice from the start.

She brought me some shoes and I had to ask her what colour they were.

I did catch the surprised upward glance of her eyes.

'Brown, monsieur. A dark brown like the leather of books. They are made in our workshops and hand stitched. They will wear better than most. That is not saying much, is it?' She gave a short laugh.

'The last pair I had were reinforced paper.'

'From here?'

'No, I got them in Juan.'

'Ah, that explains it exactly.'

'Professional rivalry?' I said.

She laughed. 'Really at present everything is bad. In a year or two it will be altogether different. The Germans took all the leather, as you will realise.'

I tried them on.

'These are good English shoes you are wearing, monsieur. Brogues, don't you call them?'

'Yes, I had them before the war. You know the English term, I see.'

'Oh, it's a technical term. My English is very poor.'

She went briskly away and came back with another clutter of boxes.

'There are these of a lighter shade. But no, I think not, do you, monsieur? And these are very strong. Possibly you will find them a little hard. Have you a fancy for the crêpe sole? Many people wear these now. Built into the heel, here, though you can't see it, is a metal rim. Very soon the top crêpe wears away. That is why we all go tap – tap.'

'You don't go tap – tap,' I said.

'Oh, no, in the shop it would be terrible. I wear sandals, as you see.'

I stood up. 'I'll try these.'

A few steps across to the window and back. Anyway, I turned to come back, and then suddenly didn't know which way to go. It was the first time in almost

25

all this time that I'd gone wrong in my sense of direction. I had always been too canny and so busy cheating other people that I'd partly been able to cheat myself.

I took two or three steps and then stumbled over a footrest and went slap on the floor full length.

When I was a boy I'd fallen on the ice with much the same result. All the breath went out and nothing came in, until I found myself sitting up and the slim girl had got her arm around my shoulders and about eight other women were crowding round chattering like birds.

I got up and they found me a chair, and somebody brought sal volatile, and it was some time before we got back to the business of shoes.

When eventually there was just the one girl left as before I said:

'I'll take these I have on. How much are they?'

'You would be very welcome to stay and rest a while longer if you want to.'

'I'm all right, thank you. How much are the shoes?'

'Two thousand, eight hundred, fifty. Will you keep them on?'

'What?'

'Shall I pack the new shoes or the old?'

'The old.'

She hesitated again, and then moved off. I got up to show them how fit I was. It was only a question of making a dignified exit.

She came back with the change and the parcel, and I thanked her for her kind attention.

'Very welcome,' she said formally. And then, 'I do hope you will be no worse for your fall.'

'Thanks. I'll be getting along. Good day.'

I went out.

It was near lunch-time but I couldn't do anything about that. I went across to the café on the opposite corner and ordered a drink and sat listening to the sound of the traffic and the passing bubble of people's voices. Overhead the wind was making a noise like a waterfall in the great plane trees. An old woman was going from table to table selling lottery tickets. When she came to my table I waved her away and just said *aveugle* and left it at that. No use disguising it any more. There was a wireless playing somewhere, jigging out a cheap dance tune. A man whistled it as he went out. The waiter came across and wiped over the vacated table; I heard the slur of his cloth and the scrape of the ashtray.

My ankle was beginning to ache.

Since leaving the Wintertons' I'd been avoiding company, living within myself waiting for the crash, and now it had come – literally, only by chance, to symbolise the rest.

I drank my wine and wrestled with the devil who'd been conjured up in loneliness and was only waiting to pounce. I thought I wasn't real any longer. I might be a ghost, I thought, kicking around in the old haunts, just passing the time until some summons came from another world. All the warmth and the light and the noise was going on as usual but I'd no longer any share

27

in it. Somebody'd shut the glass door. Inside, the symphony – or maybe it was a cacophony – blared away, but I was out in the cold and the dark. Better to be really dead.

And suddenly it seemed to me that that *was* the way out. Till now it had been just a thought, a threat, a promise with a hint of bravado. Now it leered at me like a challenge to my own integrity and guts. You can't be so very sorry for yourself if all the time it's in your own hands to do something about it.

And it seemed to me just then that hesitation would be admitting you were beaten. If you hesitated, all the weak comforting thoughts would creep in and you'd never have the courage again. Now. Now. Make a move while the anger is there.

Someone took the other seat at my table.

The girl from the shoe-shop said: 'Forgive me. But you *are* ill.'

I peered at her. I felt a bit of a fool, as if my inmost thoughts had been surprised.

'I'm all right, thanks.'

'I came out for lunch and saw you here.'

'I'm all right.'

She didn't speak for a minute, seeming to weigh me up.

I said with a sort of casual irritableness, to throw her off the scent: 'Do these winds ever get on your nerves, or are you all immune?'

'We don't like them, of course.'

'First you get the Mistral – and now it's something else.'

'The Tramontane. It will drop tomorrow.'

'Then I shall be better tomorrow.'

She said: 'Do you want to be left alone? You have only to say.'

'I think I do.'

She didn't move. 'You're blind, aren't you.'

I rapped on the table for the waiter but didn't answer. I was angry now – not so much with her as at that weak part of myself which was trying to be glad of her interest.

'It's the war, isn't it. I know the signs so well. The war-injured are different from other people – afraid of showing themselves, afraid of sympathy. Well, I'll not give you sympathy if you don't want it. But . . . I thought you were a stranger in a foreign country. I thought it was the least I could do to come and see . . .'

'Monsieur?'

'Bring this lady something to drink. What will you have, mad'moiselle?'

'Nothing, thank you.'

'An aperitif for mad'moiselle.'

He reeled off the usual list, and after a minute she chose one, I don't remember what it was. The waiter went away.

She said: 'Have you been in France long?'

'Since November.'

'You speak the language very fluently. But your accent is bad. What has made you so ill today?'

The waiter came back with her aperitif.

'It's good of you to be interested, but I'm not ill. Only a little under the weather.'

'. . . I'm sorry. But I mustn't be sorry, must I? At least I'm sorry that you fell in our shop.'

'Your carpet was commendably clean.'

'It – upset us all very much . . . What are you going to do now?'

'Have lunch, I should think. Perhaps you'll join me.'

She moved her chair. 'No, thank you. That was not what I meant at all.'

'Does it matter?'

'*I* think so.'

Quite suddenly now, having got its way, the resentment began to go. 'Sit down. I thought you wanted to help me.'

'I thought perhaps I could be of some use if you were ill.'

'It would help me if you saved me from a solitary meal.'

'That wasn't what I intended.'

'Well, it's the only way you can be of assistance.'

'If that is all you need . . .'

Two women sat down at the next table and began arguing noisily.

I said: 'Talking of accents, yours is not the local one.'

'No . . .'

'Do you come from Paris?'

'No, but I was at school there for a time.'

'During the war?'

'Before.'

I said: 'I studied in Paris for a year just before the war. I was hoping to go back there sometime but it hasn't turned out that way.'

'Perhaps you will yet.'

I shook my head.

She seemed to think that out for a minute. 'Did you go back to England when the war came?'

'No, the year before. Or, at least, a man with my name did. I doubt if I should recognise him now.'

She said sombrely: 'Should we any of us recognise ourselves.'

'Ah. A fellow feeling. But you at least are not among the throw-outs, redundant war property within the meaning of the act.'

She hesitated, seemed about to say something, stopped.

'I will lunch with you if you want me to, monsieur.'

'It's the least you can do, mad'moiselle.'

'Madame,' she said.

We went up the street to Biffi's. I felt rather ashamed of being boorish. She'd had every excuse to drop the thing and walk out, and I didn't really want a nasty taste in my mouth. It's very hard to deceive a near-blind man, and I was sure she'd interfered only out of kindness of heart. You couldn't hold that against her. After all, I thought, forgetting my earlier feelings, there's not all that hurry.

Her voice was low-pitched and quick-speaking – you didn't need to see her to know what her wits were like – it was eager and faintly humorous, and often she'd end her sentences with an upward lilt which was like a laugh without quite being one. It was an extraordinarily

31

'round' voice, capable of all sorts of changes of tone. She sounded very young – most of the time.

Well, it was true I didn't want her sympathy; but the meal was a change. Her name was Alix Delaisse and she lived in an apartment in a street off the Rue St-François-de-Paule. She tried to get me to talk, as if knowing that was really the way to help. She seemed irritated about the way I'd come to France to stay with friends and then chosen to go off alone just when they were most needed. What were friends and relations for if they couldn't be of use now?

'They could be of use if they could help me to see.'

'But they *can* help you to see. That's just how. Companionship's a way of seeing, isn't it? Aren't we all blind if we haven't any friends?'

We argued about it, and I listened to the sound of coffee being poured. The whole thing had suddenly come down off its pinnacle, become matter-of-fact and ordinary again. For the time being at least, melodrama was out.

'Without being personal,' I said, 'you're hardly the type one expects to find – where you are. Have you been selling "brogues" for long?'

'Oh . . . nearly two years.'

'And before that?'

'Before that was – the occupation.' She was not encouraging me to inquire into it.

'Does your husband work in Nice?'

'No. It's nearly time I went back.'

'You're – young to be married.'

'Oh, I'm not all that young.'

'Would you do me the favour of moving to this chair? I can see nothing from there and I'd like to make sure.'

After a minute she laughed in slight embarrassment, but she moved over.

'You are young. Not more than twenty-two.'

'Twenty-three. That can be old. It depends where you have lived.'

'And the colour of your hair?'

'Brown.'

'A dark brown like the leather of books?'

'Lighter than that. And not made in our own workshops.'

'Just as good as pre-war, I've no doubt.'

Feeling had swung the other way now, to the other extreme. A sort of reaction. It would have been silly if it hadn't been natural.

'Did I deceive you coming into the shop; or did you think here's a silly fellow pretending he's like other men?'

'You deceived me.'

'Until I fell over your foot-rest. Have you ever thought what death-traps those things are for the stiff-necks of the world?'

'I was afraid you had hurt yourself.'

'I did hurt myself.'

'But badly. You're so tall. That makes it worse.'

The slight scent she was using wasn't exactly a cheap one. I guessed it came from the Schiaparelli or Chanel stable.

'So you advise me,' I said, 'to go back home.'

'Now you're poking fun at me.'

'No, I'm not.'

'Well, yes. Or return to your friends here. Or make other friends.'

'How can I make friends with people I can't see?'

'You should find it easy.'

'Only with those who make it easy.'

We got up to leave.

I said: 'D'you think your husband would mind if I improved on this friendship?'

There was silence. 'I don't think so,' she said shortly.

'May I meet him sometime?'

'. . . Perhaps.'

'Will you dine with me tomorrow night?'

'Not tomorrow, I'm afraid.'

'Saturday?'

'Thank you.'

All right, I thought, that's settled. I'll stay around till then.

CHAPTER FOUR

THAT WAS the way it began. I've often thought if I'd
picked another shoe-shop not any of the rest would
have happened. Or part of it would have happened
anyway but I should have had no share in it. By the
Saturday I might have solved all the mysteries by
opening a vein in my bath. Instead of that I was giving
some thought to the best way of spending the evening
out.

Of course I knew I was most probably running into
trouble. In a few days there would be an excited young
Frenchman round at my apartment wanting to do the
blood-letting trick for me. Or perhaps Delaisse would
be a blasé intellectual who'd want to talk the whole
thing out on the existentialist plane.

While I waited for her I thought this was the first
time I'd taken a girl out for nearly three years. The last
one had been Rachel on that London leave. (Rachel
married now and with a son.) One or two of Claire
Winterton's younger guests had made on-coming re-
marks, but I'd had a complex about the whole business.
In this new mood it seemed objectless to have been so
stuffy. Perhaps this was one way of getting back on life.

I stood and waited on the corner of the Place
Masséna and listened to the rickety old trams thumping
past. Under the portico an old woman was shouting in
a monotonous metallic voice: '*Samedi Soir. Paris-Presse.
Samedi Soir. Paris-Presse.*' She might have been calling
the faithful to prayer. There had been only a light breeze
today, and this had dropped with evening. A bite in the
air now the sun was gone.

I heard her come up before she spoke, in fact I knew
she stood a few moments looking at me, but I didn't let
on.

'Good evening, Monsieur Gordon.'

'Madame Delaisse.'

We shook hands formally in the French way and
then we got a taxi and drove to a place I knew on the
front.

'This is very expensive,' she said as we went in.
'Can't we go somewhere cheaper?'

'One of the drawbacks about going out with a man
like me is that there's nothing much to do in the
evening except talk and eat. This is a good place to do
both.'

'There are cheaper places to do both. Less smart. I –
shall feel a little out of my depth.'

'I don't think I quite believe that.'

She looked up quickly.

'What do you mean?'

'Oh . . . just that.'

'Just what?'

'I can't put it more plainly because I don't know

36

myself. I've an instinct that you won't really feel – out of your depth. Or should have no need to.'

She didn't say any more until we were seated. When we came to order the wine I left it to her and after hesitation she chose a good one.

I said gently: 'My guess is that you come of a good family and that the war has made all the difference. Right?'

She said: 'What is a good family? My father was good. My grandfather was good. Is that what you mean?'

'All right,' I agreed. 'What are your views on the fall of the Government?'

'No. Talk about yourself. Where were you wounded? I want to know that. Was it in France?'

'D'you think it tactful to bring up the subject?'

'I think it would be too tactful if I avoided it.'

I said in surprise: 'Maybe you're right . . . Though I don't want to go on about it.'

All the same I found myself telling her about Normandy and the tank battles round Caen and how the shell had burst much nearer two other men who had only got scratched up a bit . . . I went on about the rest, and didn't realise till afterwards that it was practically the first time I'd told anyone the whole thing.

We put in most of the evening there. I sat near enough to make out the light in her eyes sometimes and the glimmer of her teeth. She had a pleasant laugh, self-deprecating and a little husky. She was wearing a tight velvet bodice of some sort with a white brooch at her throat. I think she was more frank and open and more quickly companionable with me because I had this drawback. I wasn't as other men: ordinary standards didn't apply.

She had a queer way of looking at things. She wouldn't talk about her own experiences, but it was plain enough they had been bitter. Underneath her liveliness, her self-chiding humour, her youth, was a layer of bitterness, or resentment or grief, I couldn't tell quite what. It was like wandering through flowery fields and stubbing your toe on a stone.

For the first time for months my own interest was drawn out and away. I wanted to know about her. The change from a week ago was enormous.

We sat on through the coffee and the cognac and the cigarettes, getting more friendly all the time, till quite suddenly she stiffened in her chair and then went on talking one per cent faster than before. I took no notice until a man stopped at our table and she looked up as if seeing him for the first time.

'Good evening, Alix.'

'Oh, good evening, Pierre.'

'Strange, our meeting like this.'

'Yes, isn't it. Monsieur Gordon, may I introduce M. Pierre Grognard.'

We shook hands. He was a biggish man, plump and fairly young. His hands were manicured and had never done hard work. His grip was just a contact, as if he'd passed you something over a counter.

'I hope you didn't feel tired after last night,' he said to her.

'No, of course not. It was fun.'

'If we'd come away when you said, I should have been fifty thousand francs richer.'

'Oh, well . . . that's the way of things.'

'Next time I'll respect your judgment, Alix.'

'It wasn't really judgment. I always like to seize my winnings when they're there.'

'Good principle. I shall take it to heart. You are visiting Nice, monsieur?'

'Yes, I've been here since February.'

'I hope you find it agreeable.'

'Very pleasant, thanks.'

'In the summer, of course, it gets too hot.'

'I like the heat.'

'Do you? I always try to get up into the mountains. One can breathe there. Well, I must go. *Au revoir*, Alix. Tuesday?'

She hesitated a second. 'Yes, Tuesday.'

'Good. *Au revoir*, monsieur.'

'*Au revoir*.'

As I sat down I thought it wasn't only a husband who might resent my being about.

She fidgeted a minute rather uncomfortably, digging in her handbag for something and generally trying to be busy. I waited.

At length she said: 'I think soon we should go.'

'Why?' I said gently. 'D'you feel in need of an early night?'

'That,' she said, 'is presuming a little, Monsieur Gordon.'

'. . . Would it also be presuming a little to suggest that you call me Giles?'

39

After a minute she said: 'Very well – if you wish it.'

There was another silence.

'You must agree,' I said, 'that it's a trifle unusual to meet someone who works in a shoe-shop during the day and at night goes to the Casino and wins – and loses – fifty thousand francs. It—'

'Oh, no, don't make that mistake. It was Pierre who gambled. It is his money. I stood and watched.'

'And advised him.'

'And advised him.'

'And you are going to do the same next Tuesday?'

'Oh, if he wants to go I shall go with him, I suppose.'

'Who is he? May I ask that?'

'I don't think I want to discuss him, please.'

'Fair enough.' I thought the thing out. 'All right,' I said. 'I'll tell you. Pierre Grognard's about thirty-three or four. He's come up in the world. Began life as a school teacher or – no – more likely a lawyer's clerk, somewhere in the north. Don't think he's in law at present, but knows enough about it to get round it when he wants. He's in commerce some way, probably owns a big shop or hotel. Thoroughly respectable now. Knows how to do things at the right time with the right people. Fond of women, and conceited about his successes. Smokes Havana cigars and very fond of garlic and probably shell-fish. Still a bit nervy and unsure about something in spite of all his prosperity.'

She didn't speak for a while. The waiter came, and I got the bill and paid it.

When he'd gone she said in a queer voice: 'I'm troubled.'

'Why?'

'Tell me why you're interested in Pierre?'

'I'm not interested in him.'

'Has someone been talking to you?'

'I've never heard of him till tonight.'

She sat back in her chair. 'How do you know all that?'

'When you can't see you rely on what you hear, what you touch, what you smell. They all grow twice as keen. And other things. I don't know. One gets into a bit of an old maid, all sensitised plate and impressions. Positively no witchcraft.'

'You swear you have never heard of Pierre before?'

'Certainly, if it helps you.'

'I am still disquieted.'

'Why?'

'I wonder how much you know about me.'

I laughed. 'I've told you.'

'All?'

'Well, nearly all. I had a feeling just now that you really don't like Grognard as much as you try to.'

'That's quite wrong,' she said with a first glint of anger. 'He's a friend of mine.'

'Well, that's fair enough, too.' I wondered if it was just her loyalty that was ruffled. 'I was thinking – are you doing anything Monday evening?'

'I am busy Monday evening.'

'Wednesday, then. Come and gamble with me on Wednesday.'

'No, I don't like to gamble really. It's very dull.'

I drove her home in a taxi. When we got into the old

town she stopped the cab and said she would get down here.

I said: 'Anyway it was a nice gesture coming out this once. Thanks for the sympathy.'

'I didn't come with you out of sympathy,' she said with that glint again. 'I came because I wanted to come.'

'Well, that's pleasant to know.'

'If you can read people so well you should have known that.'

'There's always the danger of reading into people what you want to read.'

'Nasty things as well as nice?'

'Nice things as well as nasty.'

'That's very modest.'

'It's better than being pig-headed.'

I used the word *entêté* and didn't realise until after I'd spoken that it could mean infatuated as well.

After a minute she said: 'Perhaps I'll come again sometime.'

'On Wednesday?'

'. . . Very well, then. If you will ask me.'

'What do I say: "Please, Alix"?'

'Thank you – Giles.'

'And you'll come because you want to come?'

'I'll come because I want to come.'

On Wednesday I met her in the same place. She was ten minutes late and out of breath, and explained she'd been kept at the shop, and had only had a few minutes to rush home and change. First, before we were quite

42

free, she had a note to deliver. It was a few minutes'
walk, along the Boulevard Carabacel and then up the
Rue St-Laurent-du-Var. We stopped at what appeared
to be a shop, but she led the way in at a side door and
up a flight of stairs.

She said: 'I will just knock in case the servant is in,
but I know Pierre is in Monte Carlo.'

We waited. If I'd known where we were coming I
should have stayed downstairs.

She said: 'I'll push it under the door, then.'

As we went down I said: 'So that's where Pierre
lives.'

'Yes, it is a nice flat. It goes right over Mallard's
bookshop. The shop isn't his, but he finds it a con-
venient place to live.'

'A bachelor ménage, I suppose.'

'Yes. He has been married but is divorced. That is
almost the only thing you didn't guess with your
witchcraft.'

I wanted to ask more but decided not.

Tonight we did most of the opposite sort of things,
dined in a cheap restaurant in the old town; then, since
the night was cool but still, walked round the harbour
and out towards Mont Boron. She guided me with a
touch or two on my elbow. (Some people steer a man
as if he were a farm tractor.) She chatted most of the
time in her low, lively voice with its humorous
overtones.

'Someone once told me,' she said, 'that Englishmen
don't really *like* women. Is that true, d'you think?'

'Was it an Englishman who told you that?'

'No.'

'Ah.'

'But he was a Frenchman who had lived long in England. He said what Englishmen were *really* interested in was golf and gardening and dogs and *men's* company. And of course sometimes their work – but that more often in the upper classes than the lower.'

I said: 'And what do you think about that?'

'Oh, I . . . I have had no experience of them until I met you – and you are one by yourself.'

'Every man is one by himself.'

'Yes, but some people fit in more than others. You for instance I should not have guessed as a lawyer.'

'What, then?'

'When you came in that morning you looked . . . tall, a little untidy, preoccupied, a little aloof. Then when you sat down I found that was just a – shell . . . for protection – a thin shell. It didn't even last through buying a pair of shoes.'

'Very ineffectual. And what does a lawyer look like?'

'Oh, that's not easy to say. I should have thought you lived by your brain, but something more creative perhaps.'

'Gracious of you. I expect we all have two sides; the "be" and the "would be".'

'Yes,' she said, and seemed to mean a lot by it.

We stopped under a lamp and leaned over the wall. The frogs were croaking in the quiet night.

'Tell me what you see.'

'Oh . . . it's very dark. The moon won't rise for another hour. Down there, that way, is Nice: two

hundred – three hundred thousand people, lights twink-
ling, casinos, big hotels, poor streets, poverty, slums,
pleasure steamers, fishing boats, dredgers and coal
barges. Beyond that, though you can't see it, are mountains. This way, straight ahead, it is nothing, all black.
That way, to your left, the coast goes in towards
Villefranche then out again at Cap Ferrat. Beyond that
is the Tête de Chien and Monaco. I often go to
Villefranche. I have relatives there.'

'Good opening,' I said, 'but even the guide books can
do better than, "Villefranche. I have relatives there".'

'I am not a guide book. I couldn't write one. To
write a guide book you must have a flat mind. Mine is
hilly.'

'I believe you. Somebody once said: "The vigorous
mind has mountains to climb and valleys to repose in".'

'Did they?' She was pleased. 'Someone thinks like
me. Who was it?'

'Hazlitt, I believe. Or Emerson.'

'Shouldn't there be a difference?'

'There is. But not in my memory.'

'And,' she said, 'did he add: "The vigorous memory
has mountains to look back on and valleys to dread,
and – and beacons to keep alight!"'

'No. He didn't say that. Do you believe that?'

She didn't answer, and after a minute I said: 'Don't
you think there might be a risk in keeping too many
beacons alight?'

'How do you mean?'

'Well, it isn't much of a profession for a young
person. I've met confirmed fire-feeders in the past.'

She said: 'Some day I will tell you.'

'Good. The sooner the better. I'm in rather a fog at present.'

'A fog?'

'Well, I've only the slightest idea what you look like – that one glimpse at Biffi's. And I've hardly begun to know you yet.'

'Isn't it a little ambitious – so soon?'

'Perhaps we can go into that sometime . . . Just at the moment I get a sense of being let in to the ground floor and welcome. But there's a basement marked "Staff only" . . .'

'So?'

'Well, I don't know anything about that, but I get glimpses of things. Something seems to be sprouting down there, and I'm sure it's not sweet brier.'

She laughed. Somewhere not far away music had begun. It was only radio from a house but it sounded romantic in the night.

She said: 'Can I quote back to you, Giles? Don't we say: "Physician, heal thyself."'

'Someone did.'

'Well, then, forgive me, but aren't we perhaps in the same boat? Yes, I'm unhappy for things that have happened to me. Sometime I'll tell you. I'm young; I like life; I'm greedy for it all. But when I remember what I do remember, then some of that feeling shrivels up.' She shook back her hair. 'Well, isn't that how you are? Didn't you feel you couldn't go on that day we met? Now you're better, but aren't you still unhappy about what's happened to you? You think, "Life's

played me a dirty trick. All right. The Devil take it!"
Don't you?'

I thought a minute. 'Yes, I suppose I do. Now the
cure?'

'Ah, I don't know it.'

The radio was playing a rumba. The thumping beat
of the thing and the tinkle of the castanets came through
the giant palm trees behind us.

'Yes,' I said, 'but you know the cause of my
complaints.'

'Well, I will tell you about mine, but not now, please.
I don't want to think of it now.'

'I'm sorry.'

'As to the other fog,' she said. 'Is there nothing to be
done?'

'Apparently not.'

'You've had, of course . . . lots of advice.'

'Lots of advice.'

'It's very hard.'

'Let's talk about the weather.'

'Anyway,' she said, 'sometime, if it would help, to
see the person you're going out with . . . you have a
little sight at close range?'

'You're very obliging.'

'Not at all.'

I said: 'There's no time like the present. This
lamp . . .'

'Oh, it would be better in the daylight.'

'It's not the sort of thing that should be done in a
public street.'

She laughed a little. 'Nor perhaps here.'

All the same she didn't move when I bent to look at her.

Her eyes were narrowed in the light of the lamp, her lips turned in a faint smile that wasn't absolutely free from shyness.

I said pleasantly: 'And in the night-time I shall not forget.'

'What do you say?'

'. . . You might be English.'

'Is that meant to be nice or not? I don't know.'

'It's a remark made in scrupulous detachment.'

'I don't think I want to be summed up.'

'Privilege of my profession.'

'Only surely for the judge.'

'Don't move, please.'

She turned a little away and then, defensively, back again. It was all rather light-hearted.

'Oh. Well . . . Haven't you seen enough?'

'It's not a view I should tire of easily.'

'I have got very accustomed to it.'

'But you'd agree that it has its points.'

'Oh, yes . . . It has its points.'

I touched her forehead, brought my fingers down her cheek to her chin.

I kissed her. After a bit the music stopped.

She drew back against the wall. 'Well, Giles . . . That is all very conventional.'

'Does it matter?'

She lifted her shoulders. 'I don't know if I am old-fashioned or new-fashioned. Perhaps I'm just Alix fashioned. One has one's fidelity . . .'

The music had started again. But this time it was a nasal tenor singing in Italian. The life had gone out of her. It was as if she had shivered.

'You mean to your husband? I can't advise you on that.'

'No . . . No one can. I'm – not very happy about this. I can't explain now. I think we should go home – forget it has happened.'

'As you wish.'

She took my hand. 'Come, we'll stroll back, perhaps stop at a café on the way.'

I turned to go with her.

'*Esser in prigione*' [sang the tenor,] '*e non poter
     fugire, Ed ammalato e non poter guarire.*'

Or it sounded to me like that.

CHAPTER FIVE

I SAW her about twice a week during the next month. Of course there was no future in it; but I wasn't going to be put off by that. Each time we met there seemed to be something new to do or to talk about. Even my eyesight didn't depress me the way it had.

She never mentioned her husband, and neither did I. Sometimes, by her movements and arrangements he seemed to be in the background; other times one hardly believed in his existence. When she spoke about the past it was usually about her childhood. Her father had been a country doctor near Dijon. She had gone to a convent in Paris until she was sixteen, and then on the fall of France had come to live with an aunt in Nice. Father and aunt were both dead.

I knew she went on seeing Pierre Grognard about as often as she came out with me – and though I didn't much like it there was nothing I could do about it. Her life was her own, and I certainly had no claims I could decently put up.

I used to think of Rachel sometimes and try to compare Alix with her. It didn't get far because there wasn't much common ground, but I did find that companionship with Alix brought up thoughts about that old affair. I dug out a snap of Rachel with some idea that it might help me to feel more clearly, but the face was too small for me to see.

By this time I was running short of money. It was awkward, because now more than at any other time I was anxious not to go to England; in fact I was determined to stay. I'd written Cousin Lewis on it, asking if he could see any way round the difficulty, but he hadn't been helpful. There was always the fathomless hospitality of the Wintertons to fall back on, but it was a hospitality not without some obligations. I couldn't go to them and then rush off to Nice twice a week on secret business of my own. So when I went to see them I was careful to keep right off the subject.

One morning I had a visitor. I was just writing to Lewis again with the suggestion that he might try to do something for me on health grounds, and had got the magnifying glass over the paper to see whether the writing was straight or whether it climbed all over the sheet, when old Larosse the concierge tapped at the door and said M. Grognard had called.

I was standing against the mantelpiece when he came in. We said good day in the usual way, but I noticed he didn't attempt to shake hands. When I offered him a chair he said no, he'd rather stand. So – ho, I thought.

After a bit he came back from the window and said: 'You have a pleasant flat here, monsieur.'

'Pleasant enough.'

'Nice is empty now. The summer season has not yet begun.'

'I hope it will be a good one.'

'On the contrary. The world is still very much upset. We have all suffered much from the war.'

'Of course,' I said sympathetically. 'Comrades in arms, and all that.'

I could tell he was eyeing me.

He said: 'You're blind, aren't you, Monsieur Gordon. You disguise it well.'

'I get along.'

'Yes,' he said, 'Alix told me. Women are sympathetic creatures.'

'I know. The surest way to their hearts is through a hard luck story.'

'Ah? You've found it so. A psychologist once told me that a woman is never happy unless she has something or someone to mother.'

'There's a profound truth hidden somewhere in that.'

He was ill at ease; I could hear him rubbing the shaved skin of his cheek.

'Of course,' he said, 'in a woman there are the two interests. There is the pity for a lame dog. And there is the love for a whole man. Unfortunately there are some who might confuse the two. That could lead to trouble all round.'

'Only trouble, surely,' I said, 'for the lame dog?'

He thought that one out. 'Yes. Trouble for the lame dog if you prefer it.'

'But supposing the lame dog has nothing to lose and is willing to risk it?'

'Everyone has something to lose, monsieur. Even if it is only his self-respect.'

It was a good reply. I offered him a cigarette, which he refused, and then lit one myself.

I said: 'The parable's so thin that the bones stick through. Can't we do without it?'

He flapped the table with something – his gloves, I think.

'Yes, we can. Alix belongs to me, Monsieur Gordon. I have come to tell you to keep your hands off my property.'

'That's rather a big claim, isn't it? What's your title: absolute, qualified, or possessory?'

'It will soon be absolute, since you choose those terms.'

'Does Alix know?'

'Naturally.'

'I congratulate you.'

'Thank you.'

He waited and scraped his chin again. 'And now . . .'

'Now?'

'I should like your promise to keep out of my affairs.'

'I don't understand. What have you to fear from a – lame dog?'

'Nothing. But I find your interference offensive.'

'I could say the same about your visit this morning.'

'I am sorry to be discourteous. But you have brought it on yourself.'

I drew at the cigarette but didn't get much fun out of it. Half the enjoyment goes when you can't see the smoke.

'Of course Alix knows you've come to see me?'

He hesitated. 'Of course.'

'She approves?'

'Well . . . naturally she is still sorry for you.'

'Well,' I said, 'you've made the situation quite clear, as you see it. Probably that's just as well. It saves misunderstanding.'

'I should like some assurance from you, monsieur.'

'I think you're a very lucky man.'

'That may be. But it doesn't alter the fact that—'

'It doesn't alter the fact that that's all the assurance you'll get. I think you're a very lucky man. Now good morning.'

He didn't like leaving on that, but I wasn't having any further truck with him. After he'd gone I lit another cigarette rather miserably and shoved the unfinished letter in a drawer. I didn't feel like doing any more at it just then.

A couple of days later I had the long-promised meal with John Chapel. As it happened his wife was indoors with a sore throat, so we ate by ourselves.

It seemed to me that John, with his special consular knowledge, might be the right person to advise on the currency business – also he might know something of Grognard. John was the sort of man who never lived in a town a week without knowing the right place to eat, the safest place to have your shirts laundered, the man to go to if you wanted seats for something that was all booked up, where to find the finest local wines and, probably, the best-dressed cabaret show.

Marriage, I thought, had toned him down. Or perhaps it was just that I hadn't met him since he was twenty-one.

After we'd talked over, rather unfruitfully, the flight from the pound I said:

'There was another thing I wanted to see you about, Johnny. D'you by any chance know a man called Pierre Grognard?'

'Grognard?' he said. 'It's not a common name. Is that the fellow who's in the catering business?'

'It could be . . .'

'The bloke I'm thinking of has three restaurants: one here, one in Monte Carlo, one somewhere else.'

'What sort of age?'

'Oh, about thirty-five; very good-looking if you like the type. A bit on the plump side, or soon will be.'

'That's the man. D'you know anything about him?'

'Precious little. I've seen him sometimes at the Casino playing boules. A mug's game, boules, old boy. The odds aren't worth taking.'

'You say he runs a restaurant?'

'Well, I imagine he's beyond that now. He *owns* them, supervises. Very select sort of places.' John chewed reflectively. 'The one in Nice is in the Rue Diano Marina. Beautiful food at fantastic prices. Soft lights, sweet music. The only people who can afford to go there are the war profiteers. I shouldn't think he's very popular.'

'Why not?'

'Well, are the new rich anywhere? Certainly not in

France. His restaurants were open all through the occupation, of course, and I've heard someone say that they were mostly full of German officers.'

'Is that sort of thing remembered?'

He filled my glass and then his own. 'Good Lord, yes. And will be for years.'

'Have you ever seen Grognard with a girl?'

'What sort?' His voice showed a connoisseur's interest.

'On the slim side, rather tall, light brown colouring – poise but no show, quick on the uptake – oval face, pretty.'

'Uh-huh? I did see him with a young woman about a month ago. She was quite a looker. It might fit. Remember thinking she can't be as young and innocent as she looks if she's with Grognard.'

'Yes.'

'Yes, what?'

'You ever heard of anyone called Delaisse?'

'No . . .' He waited. 'What's all this leading up to, Giles?'

'I wish I knew.'

Next day was Monday, and Monday was Alix's day off. We'd arranged to hire a small cutter and spend the afternoon fishing, and I wasn't going to be put off by Grognard's visit. There'd been clouds over the mountains all morning but about noon it cleared and we left the harbour in bright sun.

There were all sorts of things I found I could still do

with Alix's help, and sailing was one of them. In fact it only needed an occasional word from her to set me right. Sometimes she seemed to see for both of us, and quite often I could anticipate what she was going to say. It was queer the way it had grown up between us in so short a time.

Once we got out I'd intended telling her about Pierre, but I just hadn't the heart to begin it.

Perhaps I was flattering myself, but it seemed to me that she'd changed as well in these few weeks. She'd grown younger and more light-hearted, and the flashes of angry cynicism were rarer. I tried to see her in my mind sitting there in the bows, the breeze blowing her hair back from her face. She was wearing a silk frock that slithered when she moved; and she was carrying a big leather handbag with a strap over one shoulder and a zip fastener.

About two the clouds came over again and it began to rain. We were off Cap Ferrat and it meant tacking back all the way, so Alix suggested we should run into Villefranche. We could make use of the freshening wind, and we could get shelter there until the rain cleared.

As we came in, and I followed Alix's directions, I thought of the Villefranche I had seen when I was a kid, and how it had looked so old and so Moorish and so inscrutable. I remembered the cafés and the little shops along the quay set out to attract the sailors when their ships came in; and behind the quay the old town brooding up the hill with its slit alleys and its tunnels, its broken flights and its secretive gateways, which all looked as if they'd grown into the hillside and stood a thousand years. I remembered being in the town once after dark when the few lonely lamps were lit and black shadows stood in the long cobbled streets and cheap music tinkled through the café curtains.

We got in safely enough and ran for shelter. But Alix's frock was soaking, so after waiting a bit to see if the rain would ease she suggested we should go up to her friends and get coats and perhaps a change of clothing.

She said a bit doubtfully: 'They are my husband's relatives and friends, you'll understand.'

'There's no need for me to go along. I can stay here while you nip up.'

'No,' she said. 'I would like you to come.'

I followed her along the quay and then up a rising street that ran under an archway and broke into steps. We turned and climbed a few more steps, then over a narrow bridge and along a street which ran parallel with the quay.

'This is the Rue St-Agel. On the corner is the Café Gambetta, where we are going.'

It was the quiet part of the afternoon, but there were four men playing cards in a corner of the café as we went in, and a boy of some sort was in charge behind the bar.

The four men stopped playing, I could tell because the cards no longer moved, and the boy came forward, greeting Alix with a reservation in his voice that was no doubt due to me. Where was Mère Roget? asked Alix. Resting, said the boy; it would be worth his life to disturb her till four. She had come with her friend for shelter and dry clothes, said Alix; was Gaston in the kitchen? Yes, Gaston was in the kitchen, and we went through some bead curtains into a sort of inner dining-room and from there into the kitchen.

Gaston, a middle-aged man with a wooden leg, was rattling pans about, but spoke to Alix warmly enough. He seemed uncertain what to make of me, yet I was pretty sure from his manner that he'd already heard of me. The warmth of the kitchen was welcome after the rain. Alix left me there for a few minutes while she went upstairs, and when she came down I could tell that she'd changed her frock. She also brought me a coat of some alpaca material and made me change.

'It is Armand's,' she said. 'My brother-in-law. It will be a little short but it will do.'

We went back into the dining-room and Gaston brought us coffee.

'Let's drink it out here,' she said, and we moved out on to an open veranda with the rain drumming on the roof.

There was a good deal of space all round us, and I didn't need to be told that we overlooked the bay.

I said: 'I don't think you can expect your husband's family to take to me like an old friend, Alix.'

'Oh, that's all right. I'm rather glad you are going to meet them.'

'Do they know about Grognard too?'

'Oh, yes, of course.'

I said: 'I ought to tell you. I've been going to all day. Pierre came to see me last Friday.'

She was startled. 'Pierre? Where? At your flat?'

59

'Yes.'

'What did he want?'

'He wanted to warn me against the dangers of trespass.'

'Trespass?'

'Poaching and trespass on his property. The property being you.'

'Oh . . .' She picked up her bag and unzipped it, rustled about inside. 'How silly of him. How childish . . . He has no right to interfere.'

'That's what I thought.' But I should have been happier if she'd sounded more decided.

'What did he say?'

I told her what had gone on.

'And you didn't – ask him about my husband?'

'No.'

'You're very trusting, Giles.'

'Not specially so. But I trust you. Why shouldn't I?'

'I have to tell you,' she said, 'that Jacques, my husband, is dead.'

The rain was stopping now; the spots overhead were intermittent, but it was still gushing off the gutter.

I said: 'I half guessed that. Or that you'd separated. Of course I wasn't sure.'

She said in a flat unemotional voice: 'He was in the Resistance. He was one of the leaders although he was only twenty-three. He was a journalist; it helped him to get about. Even during the occupation they were allowed some freedom of movement if they pretended to be – not unfriendly. He volunteered for active sabotage work. He was a man without fear – full of high spirits, reckless. Just being with him was an adventure. I met him in February three years ago, and we were married in the April. Six weeks afterwards he was arrested. In May they hanged him in the public square in Nice. They left his body hanging there for a week . . .'

I said after a bit: 'I'm so very sorry. I'd no idea.'

'They left his body hanging there for a week. Every day I used to pray, dear God, may they have cut him down – but he was still there. I used to tell myself it wasn't the Jacques I knew and loved, that Jacques had gone, was far away. But it didn't work. He was still *there* . . . moving when the wind blew, changing colour . . .' She put up her hands to her face with a defensive movement, but checked it. 'You understand then why people have to be buried – before your image of them is destroyed.'

I didn't say anything. Now that the rain had stopped you could hear the stir of the sea down below.

'I still dream about it,' she said. 'I wake up sweating all over. That's funny, isn't it . . .'

I said: 'You were very much in love with him.'

'Yes. I was very much in love with him.'

Neither of us said anything then for a long time. There was a canary somewhere chirping in a cage.

'Oh, well,' she said. 'We had six weeks – though he was away half that time. It's as much perhaps as you can expect, isn't it?'

'I don't know. I don't know the answer at all.'

'Father Mathieu talks about resignation to the will of God. I spoke of that to – to someone I know – and he said the will of God is the priest's name for anything that looks like the will of a stupid ape.'

'It's a point of view.'

'Well, hasn't it been so in your case too? Doesn't everything seem wanton, aimlessly wicked?'

'. . . You should have asked me six weeks ago. I'd have cheered for your friend then. Now one feels faintly less – worked up. That's your doing.'

After a minute she got up. 'Have you a cigarette, please?'

I lit one for her and knew that her lips weren't quite steady. I said: 'God knows, I'm completely uncertain about everything. We all are these days. But it's all much too difficult to put in simple terms.'

'Can it be put in any terms?'

'I don't know . . . As for you . . .'

She stirred her coffee, which must have gone cold. 'As for me?'

It was on my lips to say, 'There's Pierre Grognard,' but I knew somehow that it wasn't so. She might be going to marry him, but he didn't make up for the man she'd really cared for.

'Something may work out.'

'Yes,' she said. 'Something may work out.'

I turned at a sound in the doorway behind us, and Alix said:

'Ah, Mère Roget, this is my English friend, M. Gordon.'

Mère Roget had a deep voice and a hard hand. I pictured her as a woman of about sixty, formidable and untidy. She wore carpet slippers.

'Gordon is a French name, monsieur.'

'Is it? It's also English and Scottish.'

'There is a village near here called Gourdon, which is also known as the Eagle's Nest because it is high in the mountains.'

'That is Gourdon, mother. Giles's name is Gordon.'

'Nevertheless it is said it was the birthplace of the Gordons. Have you ever been there, monsieur?'

'No. But I shall go.'

'A wonderful view. But pardon, of course, I forgot.'

So she also had heard of me.

'We were out sailing, mother, and got caught in the storm.'

'Well, it is over now. In an hour you will be able to start back.'

Later we went into the back room, and Armand, the brother, came in; and then two more men. All the men were a bit surly, Mère Roget polite with a hint of reserve. I wondered if they were pro-Grognard or merely anti anyone who threatened to replace Jacques. I would have liked to go, but couldn't leave without Alix.

There was a piano in this room, and someone started strumming on it, while the place filled up. It's always more difficult to pick out things when there are a lot of people in a room. A fisherman with the agreeable name of Roquefort began to sing the choruses, and several of the others joined in. Alix was in the kitchen talking to Mère Roget, and I felt rather out of it.

Eventually the pianist gave up and noisily refused to do any more. He slumped over to a table nearby and I could hear him gulping his wine.

63

They were a queer bunch, more mixed than one expects to find even in a French café. Two people at the next table were discussing the effects of inhaling chloride of ethyl. They were the first cultured voices I'd heard except Alix's.

Alix said: 'You play yourself, don't you, Giles?'

She had come in unnoticed in the din and had evidently been watching me.

'I used to know "Bluebells of Scotland",' I said shortly.

I might have guessed that that wouldn't register.

'Would you play something now?'

'Good God, no!'

'Please. To please me.'

'It's high time we went! It'll take us two hours to get back.'

'Never mind. Just a little tune. Do you know anything French?' Some of the others were listening.

I said: 'You're embarrassing me very much, Alix. I haven't touched a piano for three years. We'll go now and say goodbye to Mère Roget.'

She put her hand on mine. 'Please, dear Giles.'

It was silly to get hot and indignant, but I couldn't help it. The last thing I wanted was to be made conspicuous.

'Hell!' I said, and got up and groped round to the piano. Somebody clapped politely.

I'm not a good pianist by any respectable standards – partly because when I was ten I found I could play any tune I could whistle without learning the notes. But in the old days, I'd been able to make a show among friends.

Now I wasn't among friends. I sat on the chair in embarrassment and couldn't think what to play. Quite a lot of the people had stopped talking.

I thought of a thing my mother had played and that I'd learned from her, a short thing by Liszt which ends up with a whole pianoful of octaves and is generally the sort of showy piece that fits a bad temper.

Anyway I went crashing into this, desperately out of practice and playing a piano for the first time without seeing it. But perhaps annoyance helped, and I got through the whole thing with only about six miss-hits.

When it was over quite a lot of people clapped and I heard them say: '*Très bien!*' and '*Bravo!*' and '*Ecoutez-le donc!*'

I wiped my hands down the sides of Armand's alpaca coat and tried 'Gardens in the Rain'. Debussy is a good starter in most company, if the company isn't shi-shi, and he went over well here. I dropped three bars in the middle, but nobody seemed to mind. Everyone had stopped talking.

'Go on, please,' said Alix, who'd come round to the piano.

Then I suddenly thought of those Provençal songs I'd learned here twelve or thirteen years ago. By this time I was feeling better about it all and gathered the company was feeling better about me. Half-way through the first song Roquefort the fisherman came up to the piano, and after a bit of coughing and shuffling he joined in.

Others followed him. But they sang quite decently, not shouting each other down. When I'd played four, someone handed me a glass of wine and Gaston patted me on the back, and they all crowded round asking which others I knew.

In the end it was dark before we left, and we had to leave the cutter in the harbour and go home by bus. They said they would phone up the man who owned it – they all knew old Gros-Jean – and put it right with him. They'd have it returned in the morning.

In the bus Alix said, delighted: 'It was just on the impulse. I had a feeling that something, *something* was needed to make you feel at home and make them . . . accept you. Then when I saw your expression when Vallon was playing I remembered you said you could play. But of course I didn't guess it all . . .'

I grunted, feeling a bit ashamed of myself after the show-off.

'I know you were angry about it at the time,' she said. 'But not now?'

'Absolutely unpardonable.'

She patted my hand. 'Now you're a friend there. You will always be welcome.'

The crowded bus roared and swayed madly towards Nice, full of talking, laughing, arguing passengers.

When we got out I said: 'Friday, as last week?'

'I'll try.'

'Promise.'

'All right. I promise . . . But it may not be for very much longer, Giles. I wish I could say different.'

'You wish you could say different.'

'Well . . . In a *way* . . . You understand.'

'You mean you wish you could say different – for my sake.'

She didn't speak. Some of the bubble had gone out of her.

'Whether I understand that or not,' I said, 'there's one thing I find hard to take in. Your husband being what he was – and you thinking of him as you do – doesn't it make it specially hard-going for Pierre?'

'Why?'

'Well – he made money out of the occupation, didn't he?'

'Who told you that?'

'Someone I know.'

'Well, it's not true . . . or it's only half the story.'

'I'm glad to hear it.'

She stirred something on the ground with her toe.

'Pierre kept his restaurants open and was much patronised by the Germans. Of course he made money out of that. In fact he openly collaborated. But he really used his restaurants to pick up information from them and pass it on to the FFI. In fact he was a member of the same Resistance group as Jacques. He was arrested soon after Jacques and only escaped death by a miracle. He was decorated for his work. He was Jacques' closest friend.'

CHAPTER SIX

I RECEIVED a letter from Cousin Lewis.

'DEAR GILES' [it ran].

'Thanks for yours of the 19th. I saw a Treasury
official about your case yesterday, but he was not
too hopeful. Permits can only be issued on health
grounds if it can be shown that the condition of the
patient's health necessitates his going or staying
abroad. The most obvious case is that of a man with
tuberculosis needing to winter in Switzerland. But
his view was that the condition of your eyes was
something which would remain the same anywhere
and therefore there were no grounds for a permit
being issued.

'Of course we shan't leave it there, but I don't
know if it will be possible to get the decision altered.
My own suggestion is that you should come home
and consult Halliday again; he should be able to
pull strings that we can't, as you're a war victim. If
you are set on remaining, perhaps there is some
possibility of your earning some money out there. I
don't know if Chapel could help you in this, but

there must be occasional legal work to do with the consulate.

'I had a letter from Parker the other day, and he has definitely decided not to rejoin the firm. This is a disappointment, and his place will be difficult to fill.

'You don't mention the condition of your eyes, but your letter suggests they are not good. It may well be that the constant bright sunshine is bad for them and that a little London fog would rest them and bring about an improvement. But then no doubt you know best how you feel. Mother is keeping well, thank you, and sends her kind wishes.

                              'Yours sincerely,
                                  'LEWIS.'

The typing was double-spaced, but I had to get Old Larosse to read it to me.

I took John and his wife out to a meal.

John said: 'All the information we've got, old boy, is that things will get worse instead of better. What's going to happen when sterling becomes convertible I don't know. The rosy-faced boys in Westminster seem to think it won't make any difference. But my guess is that every country in Europe – as well as some outside – will demand payment in dollars the minute they're entitled to it. Then there'll be a crisis and all the Westminster boys will have to eat their words. Obviously it's going to be more and more difficult for

Britons to live abroad or travel abroad unless they can earn money as they go.'

'I don't know why everyone is so anxious to come away,' said Kay. 'I long to see a bit of England.'

'Those who are in want to get out, and those who are out want to get back. That's the way it comes, old dear. You shouldn't have married an empire builder.'

She gave a little laugh. 'Is it builder or liquidator these days?'

John said to me: 'There are some still carrying on the old Max Intrator trade. I expect you've discovered that?'

'The barman at the Bouquet d'Or hinted as much.'

'Did you swallow the bait?'

'Not yet.'

'Well, I shouldn't. If you want to fiddle, do it with pound notes, not cheques; you haven't got to sign 'em.'

Kay said: 'Are all consular officials as helpful?'

John shifted in his chair. 'I'm only giving sensible advice to an old school friend. I wouldn't give it to every good-time playboy. They don't need it anyhow ... Of course everything's heading for chaos. The war's put Europe in the crazy situation of needing a non-European currency to keep the wheels going. By the way, Giles, if you want to spend your time in France, why don't you get tied up with our export drive. If you can only do that a grateful government will lavish sterling on you. Aren't there any strings you can pull?'

'I've never been much of a string-puller.'

'Get Cousin What's-it to go through the family

clients for you; there's sure to be one these days who's exporting typewriters to Belgium or bottled pickles to the Alpes-Maritimes. It's only a question of getting to know.'

'Weren't those somebody's famous last words?' Kay said.

But by now the wine was warming John to his theme. 'Of course to do the thing properly you should get Lewis to find a family with a skeleton in the cupboard. Once you've proof that the second marquis was born out of wedlock you can practically go and demand anything you like.'

Kay said: 'You'll have to excuse John for being so out of date. He doesn't realise yet that it isn't the marquises who can pull the strings. And the people who *can* wouldn't be frightened of a family skeleton. They probably take it with them every day to sit beside them in the House of Commons.'

I said with a grin: 'I wonder if we export tin cups and mouth-organs.'

There was a faint embarrassed pause.

John said: 'My dear old boy, blindness is a minor disability compared to what some of the people I meet are suffering from.'

'But John told me you could see a bit,' Kay said.

'I can see a lot,' I said, sorry now to have brought the thing up, even as a joke.

They went on for a while, asking what specialists I'd been under, etc. I had a feeling they were glad to get on a topic where there wouldn't be any sparks struck, so I

71

let them plug away. There was an air of strained cheerfulness about them tonight that suggested unmistakably a squabble not long blown over.

Later we went along to the Municipal Casino and gambled a bit, and I met a slim-built, sophisticated youngish man called Charles Bénat whom John said I ought to have much in common with, seeing that he was one of the most successful lawyers in Provence.

Bénat said: 'If your friend has been a lawyer he'll know that isn't difficult. It's always a matter of deciding at the outset which of two litigants is the bigger rogue.'

'Or has the more money,' I suggested, in the same tone.

'But never I suppose,' John said, 'taking into account the merits of the case.'

'Absolutely fatal,' agreed the Frenchman. 'It's entirely a matter for the judge, who of course decides solely on the legal technicalities . . .'

We chatted amiably for a few minutes, and then he left. I could tell they thought him pretty important, and when he moved away John said:

'Don't be deceived by his flippant way of talking. He's a big shot around here. Everybody knows Bénat.'

We went on into the baccarat room, where John lost three thousand francs and I won a hundred and fifty. Not an auspicious evening.

Twice more to the Café Gambetta in Villefranche.

The first time everything was fine. Mère Roget still kept her distance – she was very much the martinet in her own home – but the others welcomed me practically as one of themselves. Among the friendliest were Roquefort the fisherman and a man called Scipion. Scipion had fought with the Free French in the invasion of Normandy and had lived two years in England, so that made us virtually blood brothers. He fancied himself as a military strategist, and I could hear him moving wine bottles and ashtrays about to illustrate his points. He had a duodenal ulcer, and all the fight went out of his voice when he told me about that. Roquefort was a specialist in butterflies, and spent nearly all his spare time watching them or catching them. It was a queer hobby for a fisherman, and they pulled his leg about it, but he was in deadly earnest; and someone said his collection was worth a hundred thousand francs.

Alix seemed to get something out of seeing me welcome among her friends and relatives, otherwise I shouldn't have gone again. I knew the strength of family ties in France. The more I saw of them all, the more I felt that the Delaisse family was at the back of the Alix–Pierre arrangement. Right at the start I'd thought Alix's feelings for Pierre weren't really quite as warm as she tried to make them. Our own friendship couldn't have gone on if they had been.

Altogether I seemed to be working my way out on a limb, and no decent way of retreat. If a marriage on the grounds of convenience had been arranged between her and Pierre Grognard – not so much to blot out Jacques's memory as to perpetuate it – my showing up on the scene could only complicate life for everyone. To the

73

Delaisses I was an obstruction and a pitiable nuisance, to Alix I was an unsettling influence plucking at her affections when they were better buried, to Pierre I was an object of bitter jealousy just because I was unsettling Alix that way. The only reasonable thing really was to cut the entanglement right out and go back to England.

But so long as there was a chance of going on as we were, I hadn't the courage to do the operation for myself.

The third visit to Villefranche was quite different from the other two.

It was Alix's idea as usual. We'd walked out from Nice about two miles, and suddenly she said why not go on to Villefranche, have a drink there and catch the last bus back. I said all right, if she felt like that. The place was busier than usual, it being a Sunday, and as we turned into the Rue St-Agel there was the sound of singing from the bistro on the opposite corner. At the Café Gambetta someone was playing a concertina. The rusty music and the babel of voices met us as we went in.

'Go on into the inner room,' Alix said. 'I'll tell Mère Roget we've come.'

I went in, pushing through the jingling bead curtains, and Gaston, who happened to be there, stumped across and led me to an empty table. Now from the first Gaston had been one of the friendliest. Last week he'd stood for ten minutes leaning on an empty chair telling me how he lost his leg; a customer had had to bang on a table three times before Gaston would move. Tonight I could hardly drag a word out of him. It was 'Yes, monsieur,' 'No, monsieur,', and 'But certainly.' As soon as he could he hobbled away.

The inner room was much quieter than the outer one to-night – in fact there were only four people in the room: Uncle Henri Delaisse, a fellow called Dramont, another called Jean Roux, and a new man addressed as Rastel. None of them spoke to me, but I soon picked out each voice for myself. I wondered what the devil was wrong. They'd all been talking freely a minute before I walked in.

The boy Maurice came in, and I ordered the usual *café filtre* and lit a cigarette and waited for Alix. After a minute or two the conversation loosened up, but it was self-conscious stuff, about a cycle race that was going to begin in a couple of days.

Then the concertina stopped in the outer bar, and I suddenly realised that there was someone else in this room.

It's surprisingly hard to cheat a blind man. He comes to hear and identify the slightest sounds, for no one ever stays quite still. He almost always knows when someone is near him and what they are doing.

But this was the stillest sitter I'd come across. He could hardly have moved a muscle, and certainly wasn't moving now; it was only because the concertina had given out for a minute that I heard his breathing, which was quiet enough but with a just detectable and distinctive tick-tick sound at the back of the nose.

At first I thought of saying something, but decided against it. If somebody didn't want to be sociable it was really not my affair.

Gaston came limping across from the kitchen. 'Mère Roget has some special wine to offer you, monsieur, and would like you to come into the kitchen to take it.'

'Very well.' The inner room wasn't for me tonight.

As I got to the kitchen door someone came out and stood on one side to let me pass. I thanked him, but he didn't speak, so I couldn't be sure that it was Armand Delaisse.

Things were a bit distant in the kitchen too, and we left fairly early. On the way home Alix, for the only time ever, talked too much. She was bright and lively, but the brightness didn't ring true, and there was a jarring note somewhere.

In the end I said: 'Look, Alix, dear, you don't *need* to be the life and soul of the party. In fact there's no party, and I'd rather have you in your depressed mood than – this way.'

She stopped. 'This way?' she said. 'I don't know what you mean by "this way".'

'Oh . . . faintly over-anxious to convince yourself that you don't care a damn for anybody.'

She was silent, faintly whistling through pursed lips. 'Why should I have to convince myself of what I know to be the truth?'

'Why indeed? If it is the truth.'

We walked along some way. She gave a little irritable flick at her skirt. 'I don't think you understand me as well as you think you do.'

'I don't think I understand you at all.'

'You find me – unreasonable?'

'Rarely, if ever.'

76

'. . . If so I wonder you trouble to come out with me.'

I said: 'You know why I come out with you. That's not at issue . . . If tonight for some reason you'd like to find something to quarrel about, go right ahead, but don't expect me to help you.'

'I think you're helping me very well.'

I thought it out. 'Yes, I suppose I am.'

We both laughed, but it was still a bit half-hearted. She said: 'When you are angry the shell comes back – but much thicker. Truly aloof then.'

'Very far from it, believe me. More than ever painfully involved.'

'And when I'm angry . . .' She sighed. 'Oh, I don't know. I think the world is rather a mess, don't you?'

'Let's forget it.'

'Yes, let's forget it.'

We changed the subject then, and there were no more sparks; but there was something different about her all the rest of the evening.

CHAPTER SEVEN

WE'D ARRANGED to meet on the Monday, but she rang up making an excuse. We put it off till the following Monday, and I think she would have got out of that if it hadn't been a long-promised date to go to Monte Carlo. I wondered how we should meet, if the mood of Sunday night would carry over the eight days between. But when we met there was no sign of it at all. She was a bit subdued but at her nicest – and that was saying something.

We went by train in the afternoon – one of those diesel trains with the driver in a raised cabin in the roof. When we halted at Villefranche she said:

'Giles, I think I must stop meeting you.'

I'd been expecting it, but it was a jolt all the same.

'Think so?'

'It isn't fair to you.'

'I'll look out for that.'

'No. It's not fair to any of us. I have told Pierre that I'm not seeing you any more. If he finds out there will be trouble.'

'Don't you want to go on seeing me?'

'Should I have lied to Pierre if I hadn't? But it can't

78

go on for ever. There must be a break, Giles. Perhaps in a—'

She stopped.

'What were you going to say?'

'Nothing. It's for the best that we should give this up.'

'I suppose nobody's suggested that you should give Pierre up instead?'

'I have had feelings that way.'

'Then . . .' I swallowed. 'If you can say that . . .'

The diesel engine started with that sound like the tired battery of a motor car, and we moved slowly out of the station.

I felt happy and miserable together. I said: 'Listen, Alix.'

'Yes?'

'I'm no use to you. I can't expect any woman . . . But at least there's no compulsion to throw yourself away. Pierre doesn't make the grade. There are other men in the world – plenty of them. Don't sacrifice yourself just to please your first husband's friends—'

'Why do you say that?'

'It's pretty plain, isn't it? You don't really love the man. The marriage is tied up with the Delaisse family: they look on Pierre as an old comrade of Jacques, a rich man, a comfortable and seemly match for little Alix.'

She said after a minute: 'Well, aren't those all good reasons?' It was as if by saying over their arguments I'd strengthened their case instead of my own.

'No, they aren't if the man is a man like Pierre.'

'What's wrong with him?'

I shrugged. Facing it, what was there? A mild personal antipathy. 'You loved Jacques Delaisse, you say?'

'I still do.'

'Then don't spoil his memory by taking a man you don't care for.'

'That can't spoil his memory.'

I said, suddenly angry: 'You told me the other night I didn't understand you as well as I thought. Well, I tell you again: I don't understand you at all. I'm crazy about you – you know that – but I don't understand. You've got me completely beaten.'

She didn't say anything. There was no anger in her today. The train stopped at another station, but I didn't know which it was and didn't care.

I said: 'Surely, there's someone of your own family to advise you? You're not really one of the Delaisse family.'

'I'm proud to belong to it.'

'Aren't there any of your own blood alive?'

'I've told you. I have a brother in Dakar. There is no one else. I am a Delaisse.'

Off again, gathering speed with a deepening dynamo hum, the sound pressing back upon itself as we drilled into the mouth of a long tunnel.

'You mustn't be crazy about me, Giles,' she said in a softer tone.

'At least you can't stop that.'

'No . . . Perhaps I don't want to stop it. But I hate to think of hurting you.'

'I'll take care of that too.'

'I am sorry I had to tell you this now. It will spoil our day.'

'. . . Whatever else, I'd like to finish up this business between you and Pierre.'

'Let's not talk about it any more. It is something I have – made up my mind to. You can't alter it, dear Giles. None of us can alter the past.'

'We can change our *view* of the past – according to circumstances. If we don't it may push the present out of shape.'

'Oh, well . . . we shall see. Forget it now. Let's try to be happy as we have been other days.'

We tried to be happy. When darkness fell we were sitting on a seat in the garden of the Casino. It was the warmest evening there had been for some time, and the smell of mimosa was everywhere.

Alix was sitting with her legs curled under her. She said: 'I don't think today has been as good as the others. Let's go home.'

'So this is really goodbye?'

'. . . It must be.'

After a while she said: 'What shall you do?'

'I may have to go back to England, anyhow.'

'. . . Perhaps that will be for the best.'

'Like hell it will be for the best.'

'Go back home and forget me.'

'Should I swim the Channel on the way?'

'I know. I know. It won't be easy. Perhaps you are not the only one.'

'I'm the only one without the remedy in my own hands.'

There was silence. 'When shall you go home?' she said.
'Pretty soon.'

'And some day you might come back?'

'Unlikely. A burnt child, you know.'

She touched my arm. 'I don't know if I've done harm
or good by interfering in your life. If it's harm, then I'm
sorry.'

I put my hand over hers. 'What's a broken heart
among friends?'

'No, I don't want you to joke. Tell me.'

'I don't feel like joking. Believe me. All I can tell you
is that I don't want it to end like this.'

She said after a minute: 'Let's go and eat.' But she
made no move.

I said: 'Oh, of course it's been worth it. Every time.
You owe me nothing, my dear. It was good while it
lasted.'

'. . . More than good.'

'And more than friendship.'

Her hand was half clenched, and I slowly unbent the
fingers and kissed the palm.

She said: 'How would you expect it to be easier
ended if it ended any other way?'

There was a sudden silence. 'I don't want it easier
ended.'

'Then ended . . . No, Giles: it wouldn't . . . make
sense.'

'Nothing could be worse than it is.'

'Perhaps you think that I . . .'

'I don't think anything at all.'

She uncurled her legs and sat up. I offered her a

82

cigarette and she took one. Her hand fumbled as I lit it.

'I think perhaps I haven't played quite fair with you,' she said. 'But I didn't expect this. I didn't expect any of it.'

'It's nothing to do with fairness or unfairness. There aren't any Marquess of Queensberry rules . . .'

'What?'

'Any rules. Life isn't well brought up. It just shoves us about as it pleases.'

'. . . I'm only trying to be reasonable, sensible, to see it all from outside ourselves.'

'And are you succeeding?'

'No. All the craziness, you know, is not on your side . . .'

I got up. 'Let's go.'

'Where?'

'Anywhere. Home.'

She stood up slowly with her back to me. I laid my hands on her shoulders and she leaned against me. I put my face in her hair.

'When I was a little girl,' she said, 'I threw a doll that I loved and prized more than anything else at another girl I was angry with. It didn't hit the girl but fell on the floor and the head broke to pieces.'

'Well?'

'I don't want to damage, to upset what is good between us for the sake of a gesture. To make something ordinary and – perhaps trivial in your memory out of what has been . . . up to now—'

'Trivial!' I said. 'Good God!'

She gave a little laugh.

'You blow my hesitations away with great broadsides. D'you think they need all that?'

I said: 'I'm terrified of even one being left.'

We went back by bus, there being no train at that time.

It was the usual crazy journey, more crowded than ever being evening and no passengers ever turned away. By the time we got to Monaco there were twenty-three standing, and the conductor kept shouting '*Avancez dans le couloir, s'il vous plaît!*' in a tired chiding tone as if he were a schoolmaster with a bunch of children. At Eze station five passengers got off and eight climbed volubly in. Parcels and baskets and dirty notes and good temper and ill temper and the smell of garlic and a baby crying.

I got separated from Alix by two fat talkative women, and every time the bus stopped I tried to reach her again. It would have been all right if I'd been able to see her, but once she was out of touch she seemed to disappear from reality.

The whole thing had suddenly gone off into something not quite earth-bound. I kept gripping the back of the seat I was clinging on to and saying to myself: This is real. Alix loves you. Just for the moment, just for to-night nothing else counts.

When at last the bus drew up in the square at Nice and evacuated its chattering contents I waited till she came up to me and then gripped her arm.

'Why do you hold me like that?'

'I was afraid.'

'Of what?'

'That you'd disappeared.'

She slid her arm into mine. 'No.'

'Where shall we go? To my flat?'

'To mine. Mme Colloni is away till tomorrow. I can cook a bit of supper and . . .'

We turned down towards the old town.

I said: 'This comes of being kind to a strange man in a shoe-shop.'

'Now I have to cook his supper.'

'What to eat? Something nice?'

'Snails, I expect.'

'My favourite dish – so long as they're fresh killed.'

She said: 'We are both quite mad now, Giles.'

'It's a mad world. We meet it on its own terms.'

It didn't much matter what we said just then. What mattered was a one-ness of feeling and decision. Just for the time we were ahead of reason and common logic. I thought, may it stay so; not for tonight only, perhaps for ever; perhaps it will last; tomorrow's sunrise is ten hours away; if it lasts until then. I thought, supposing she came to England; have I the wantonness to be selfish? But she wouldn't come, she's only being kind.

I said: 'Are you only being kind?'

We crossed a street, threaded our way among some empty stalls. There were a few leaves underfoot and what felt like an occasional crushed blossom as from a flower market.

I said: 'I'm sorry, I shouldn't have asked that.' I could have kicked myself.

She said quietly: 'We're nearly there.' There wasn't anything more for either of us to say.

Her apartment was on the fourth floor of a tall house. There was no one about. When we got inside the door I said:

'It's dark here, isn't it?'

'Yes.'

I pulled her quietly into the recess behind the door and kissed her.

'Darling Alix. Darling Alix. I love you so much.'

She said breathlessly after a moment: 'I like it when you speak to me in English.'

'I'll speak often to you in English tonight, then.'

We went up the stairs.

At the top of the first flight I said: 'Someone's coming down. Shall we go up separately to avoid talk?'

'No. It can't be anyone important.'

We went on. At the turn of the second flight she stopped. There was a creak of wood as someone leaned over the banisters.

'So there you are,' said Pierre Grognard.

I could have murdered him. Alix had dropped my hand, drawn a bit away. It was instinctive but it meant a lot.

She said: 'We've just been to Monte Carlo. I was coming to get a book Giles had lent me.'

He came down two steps.

'So that's how you spend your day off.'

'Not always – as you know. Did you want me for something, Pierre?' She was cool, trying to carry it off.

'I thought you were spending the day with Armand.'

'It couldn't be arranged at the last moment.'

'I called you up twice but couldn't get a reply. I left a note under your door about Wednesday.'

'Thank you.'

'I thought you had promised me not to meet this . . . *goujat* again?'

'I'm not married to you yet, Pierre.'

'Instead I find him sneaking up to your flat late at night – a private apartment from which I am always excluded.'

She said: 'I think you'd better go now, Pierre.'

'Not until I see this man out of the building.'

I didn't speak. It seemed to me that the only way to help Alix was to do nothing to make things worse.

She said in a low voice: 'Will you forgive me, Giles?'

'. . . Of course.' I didn't move. With a feeling of black bitter hate and disappointment I heard Alix move from beside me and go towards the third flight.

'Good night, Giles,' she said. 'And thank you.'

'Good night,' I got out.

She went slowly up the third flight.

'Good night, Alix,' Pierre said.

'Good night.'

'I'll call for you on Wednesday. You'll find it all in the note I left.'

She didn't reply but went on. There was silence until we heard a door open and close far up. All the spell of five minutes ago was gone. The swine, I thought. (But wouldn't you behave like that in his position?) At least, I'd not suggest insultingly to a girl like Alix that ... (But wasn't that precisely what had been going to happen?)

'Well?' he demanded. 'What are you waiting for?'

I said: 'I was interested to see how offensive you really could be to her.'

'If you're so considerate of Alix's feelings I wonder you put her in a position inviting insult.'

'I should think almost any excuse would do for you.'

He came down the remaining steps and came up to me.

'Go on,' he said, 'before I kick you down the stairs!'

I said: 'I don't feel in much danger of that.'

'No doubt you're aware that it's difficult to strike a cripple.'

'I should have thought it very easy. Anyway don't let that stand in your light.'

After a minute he turned away. 'This man is blind and takes advantage of it.'

I'd been aware of two other people coming up the stairs who had heard all this and were waiting to get past. I felt too sick and fed up to carry on the schoolboy stuff any more.

A man said: 'What is it, monsieur? What is wrong?'

I didn't know which of us he was addressing, and Pierre answered him.

'This foreigner comes to Nice and plays upon the sympathy of my fiancée. He prevails upon her—'

I said: 'If you can't keep your girl faithful without

outside help, why don't you go to the mayor and ask him for a distraint order—'

I had half turned to go, and he gave me a shove in the back that sent me against the wall. I turned and swung out with my fist but didn't find anything.

Then someone had me by the arm.

'Please, monsieur. If there are differences they should be settled in a manner—'

'We cannot have fighting here!'

'*Mon Dieu*, this is a pretty scene!'

Evidently somebody was restraining Grognard too. There were about four people there now who'd been brought by our voices, and one woman spoke with authority, as if she had something to do with the flats. She badly wanted to know whom we'd been visiting, but Pierre had at least the sense to keep that to himself.

We went down the stairs and were shown out of the front door. The woman stood on the top step talking after us. 'Brawling on the stairs. *Mon Dieu*, some people have no idea. They should go and cool their heads in the harbour! If my husband was here! There are those who cannot hold their wine. They will be sick as dogs before the night is out. For two pins I would call the police!' I heard Grognard go off and then stop a taxi and get in. Raging and humiliated and sick of it all, I began to make my way home.

CHAPTER EIGHT

JOHN CHAPEL rang me up next day and said:

'Look, old boy, I've got a fellow coming in this evening; might just be your cup of tea; a Scotsman called McWheeler; let's see, you still play bridge, don't you?'

'No, not these days.'

'Oh, sorry. He's frightfully keen, I thought we might have had a foursome. Anyway, the point is he's over here on business, and it occurred to me you might be of use to each other. What?'

It was on my tongue to say, 'I've changed my mind, Johnny; the south of France means nothing to me at all now; I'm going home next week and staying there.' But it seemed a bit curt after he'd gone to the trouble of thinking something up, so I said: 'All right, Johnny. Many thanks. I'll be along.'

From his voice I pictured McWheeler as a stout chap with a bald head and black eyebrows, but possibly that was just my fancy.

He said: 'Actually I'm in the biscuit trade, Mr Gordon, but that's really beside the point. I'm in France at present representing our Chamber of Commerce and over thirty Scottish export interests. You *have* made a special study of commercial law, I understand from Chapel?'

'Yes,' I said, and thought: to *hell* with commercial law and exports, and with Alix, who meekly takes that arrogant fool's dictation and hasn't even had the decency to phone me . . .

'Well, since I came over here I've been very much impressed by the need for someone who can advise us generally on the French scene – someone particularly with an expert legal background. This big expansion of exports has brought up all sorts of little problems in its train – I'm over here about a case of infringement of designs, for one thing – and it comes hard on some of the smaller firms who have had no knowledge of the export trade until last year. Of course we can get help from government sources, but often that hasn't the *personal* interest behind it. A man on the spot who could advise in an expert way could be of considerable value.'

'Yes,' I said. And to *hell* with myself for getting out on a limb, for being in a rage of jealousy, for taking myself too seriously and pushing Alix into an impossible position where she couldn't behave straightly with anyone.

'I understand,' said McWheeler, 'that you are short-sighted, but able to conduct business affairs quite ably. You know something of French law?'

'Very little, I'm afraid.'

'Oh. But you studied in Paris for a year?'

'. . . I wasn't studying law.' John had evidently been putting over a sales talk.

McWheeler seemed a trifle thoughtful. 'Well, the man I envisage will have to become acquainted with it. Not that I look on this as work which would be purely legal in character. We've men we could send over who could do that. But when Chapel mentioned you and your wish to live in France it seemed worth discussing the matter . . .'

'That's very good of you.'

'. . . I'm not here, of course, to make any appointment – I'm not empowered to do that – I'm not even sure that it would be a full-time job yet. But we certainly feel the need of someone and some such representative, someone who understands France and the French from the inside. It's the psychological approach, you know – to avoid the legal channel rather than to seek it. A personal interview, a few words explaining a point of view – that's the important thing, which can't be done from a thousand miles away. There's any amount of good will over here so long as it isn't frustrated by petty misunderstandings and surface differences in methods of doing business.'

'Oh, there's any amount of good will,' I agreed. Do you understand France and the French from the inside? What about Pierre? What's the psychological slant on him?

'I confess,' said McWheeler, getting confidential over the third drink, 'that I find the Continental approach to things a little unbees-nesslike. I'm speaking as an outsider, mind you. But they often seem to be optimistic – or the reverse – without being *logical*. That is, they don't seem to see the future in terms of hard fact. You either have pessimistic irrelevances brought in, or else you are gratuitously assured that "everything will be all right" without any apparent effort having been made to envisage the difficulties.'

I said: 'Nothing's working properly yet. The government's torn between the extremist groups and is afraid to give a lead. The ordinary business man just shrugs his shoulders and lives from day to day.'

'Aye. But I'm not sure that that quite answers my complaint, because isn't any government composed of ordinary individuals? Isn't putting the blame on the government an easy excuse for avoiding the responsibility yourself? Mind you, I don't know. I'm asking you these things.'

We talked for about half an hour. He seemed decent enough, and I felt an impostor (a) because he evidently didn't realise what a total write-off I'd become, and (b) because the incentive was gone which might have made me anxious to do something for him. Yet because I couldn't *quite* make up my mind never to attempt to see Alix again, I stalled and let the thing move on, so that when he finally left we'd arranged a further meeting in a fortnight's time when he got back from Italy.

I didn't realise then how much else would have moved on in a fortnight.

I was listening to the radio when the telephone rang. It was three days since the meeting with McWheeler.

I lifted the receiver, and someone said something I couldn't catch.

'Wait,' I said, and switched off the set. 'Yes?'

'Madame Colloni?' said a woman's voice.

'You've got the wrong number,' I said, and then stopped. Alix's voice. 'Hullo!'

'Madame Colloni. I've phoned to say I'll not be back tonight. I thought you might be worried if you didn't hear.'

I said: 'Is that Alix?'

'Yes. This is Alix Delaisse speaking.'

'What's the matter? Where are you?'

'At M. Grognard's flat. I can't say exactly when I shall be home, but I'll let you know. Don't bother forwarding any letters.'

I said: 'This is Giles. Are you playing some sort of a joke?'

'Of course not,' said the voice casually. 'I thought I'd ring you just to let you know.'

'Let me know what? What's wrong? D'you want me to come round?'

'Yes, please do. It will be much better if you do that.'

'Is Pierre with you?'

'Thank you very much,' said the voice. 'Goodbye.' The line went dead.

The conversation was like an overheard one on a crossed wire. Yet the voice had seemed to answer some of my questions. And the voice was Alix's. I felt irritated and put out. Grognard's flat was the last place. But she must have known that; it wasn't in her interest to provoke a rough house – perhaps Pierre was away. Then . . .

I'd never heard Alix speak like that before. I found my shoes, put them on and laced them, picked up my stick. By a piece of luck Old Larosse was fiddling about in the hall, and I sent him for a taxi and waited in the doorway, blowing on the handle of my stick. He didn't come back. After a while I began to fume. It would have been a bit of an awkward walk for me, but at least I should have been well on the way by now.

Just as I was about to go off, there came the clip-clop of hooves on the road.

'It was difficult, monsieur. In the end I had to bring a fiacre.'

'Rue St-Laurent-du-Var,' I said to the cab driver.

As I climbed in I tried to remember the name of the bookshop. Something to do with a duck. We clip-clopped off into the night.

It seemed a long way.

'What number?' he said presently.

'The bookshop. Mallard's.' That was it.

'*Et voilà.*'

I got out, paid him his outrageous charge without argument and crossed the pavement. For a minute I wasn't quite sure where I was, then realised he'd brought me just past the shop. I turned back and it wasn't long before my fingers found the door leading upstairs. I could tell that the stairs were lighted, but that was about all.

At the top was the door of his flat. I fumbled about and found the bell.

No one came. I rang again. Someone was singing or humming in the flat. A man. I caught English words.

'You found I was true, Although you knew You'd broken your date with love . . .'

The wait for the taxi had made me more impatient than usual. I groped for the knocker but there didn't seem to be one. But slight pressure showed that the door was ajar.

I pushed it open an inch or two and said: 'Anyone at home?'

Nobody answered. It was the radio that was on – but not the station I'd been listening to.

'It's all very fine To take that line, But no one can ask for more than I give In keeping a date with love.'

I went in.

It seemed to be one of those flats where the front door opens straight into the living-room. The light was on, and I got a definite feeling of space. The radio was on very low, in the far left-hand corner.

An awkward situation. A call over the phone – either designedly or by way of crossed wires – had brought me to Pierre's flat, where I certainly wouldn't be welcomed by its owner. Perhaps Alix and Pierre were in another room having a meal or the servant had gone out for something and left the door ajar. But if Alix wasn't here I'd better get out again quick. She'd been here: I could tell that at once from the faint scent.

Perhaps at this moment Pierre was sitting by the wireless sneering at me. I cursed not being able to see.

After a bit I began to walk into the room feeling the way with my stick and moving towards the wireless. I got round a small table and a chair, nearly came to grief over a tiger-skin rug, found the wall and then the wireless.

'*Ici Radio Paris. Vous avez entendu—*'

I switched it off.

There was no one in the room. Could tell that at once now. The only sound was an electric fire over to my left.

Work it out. You came in at the door, and the hearth and electric fire were to your right. The radio was left corner.

There were probably a couple of doors to the other rooms, one in the left wall, one in the far wall, not a long way from where I was standing. Perhaps it was Alix and Pierre who had just gone out and would be back in a minute. Perhaps Pierre was in Monte Carlo and it was just Alix. Wait a bit and see.

I waited.

It's a quiet part of Nice, and there was only an occasional car passing outside. A clock was ticking over above the electric fire. In the distance a train whistled. Occasionally a piece of furniture 'cricked' slightly. The bookshop was shut and the staff had gone home. I wondered if there was another flat above this. If so no one moved in it.

Somebody had been smoking a Turkish cigarette recently, and there was a faint stale smell somewhere like stale water.

The clock began to ping suddenly. Ten.

The sound got me impatient again. I began to feel

along the wall beside the wireless set. Expensively framed picture; ornament like a mask; door. Just about where one would have expected it.

I lifted my stick and gave a sharp rap: one, two, three, on the panels.

Nothing happened. Surprising how startling a noise you make yourself can be.

I felt for the handle, turned it and the door opened. A step in. Darkness and I didn't bother to put on the light, because again I could tell the room was empty. Unmistakably a man's bedroom: you could smell the hair cream, the sheets, the shoes and suits, the toothpaste. I backed out and shut the door.

That was that. Now was the other hunch right, that there would be another door in the left wall? Back to the wireless and then move off along the left wall. Bookshelves, a cupboard with glass handles; probably drinks. Contact with the tiger rug again. More wall. No, wrong. No door there.

I turned about and wondered whether to leave. Not comfortable. Yet Alix had been here. And the more I thought of it the more likely it seemed that she'd deliberately telephoned me. Old Larosse and the fiacre.

Try the opposite wall, between the fire and the main door. I went back to the main door and moved across in the other direction. Soon I should have completed a circuit of the walls.

Ah . . . A door here. My sense of the plan of the place had been wrong. Knock again. Again no answer.

Open it.

A kitchen. The light on here, but empty. Go in a few

paces. Smell of herbs, eggs, raw steak, coffee, one of the cream cheeses, probably Chèvre; it all smelled clean; there had been no cooking done there today. What servants did Pierre employ? Never heard. Probably one man. Anyhow, the servant was away or out.

Back into the living-room again. There was only one small corner now unexplored, and that didn't seem worth bothering about. There was also the large central space of the room not quite furnished in my mind.

I passed in front of the fireplace and felt the heat of the electric fire, turned away from it and touched the end of a cretonne-covered settee. Negotiating this, I moved across in the general direction of the glass-handled cupboard. If there was to be a wait, a drink would help to pass the time.

At that moment my foot trod on something, which crunched lightly under it. I bent down and found a carnation on the carpet. The head itself was wet, and in a moment the tips of my fingers were wet as they touched the floor. A dozen other carnations and then a glass vase. It had evidently been knocked over or had fallen over, but it wasn't broken. I stuck the flowers back in the vase and felt around for a table, found one and put the flowers on it.

Hands on the glass handles of the cupboard, I paused. I certainly hadn't tipped over the flowers. Whoever had done so must have been very untidy or in a devil of a hurry. Open the cupboard.

Disappointment here. China ornaments of some sort instead of bottles. The cupboard doors were of glass: Pierre evidently collected pieces of Doulton or Sèvres.

His display cabinet. Shepherdesses and peacocks and cottages and dogs, and little men and women sitting on chairs. Careful not to knock any down. Fine work.

Put them back. Well . . . stay or go? I'd already been here a good ten minutes and no one had come in. The flat was obviously empty. *Yet Alix had telephoned from here.* I moved back to the settee. Wait another five, or as near as could be gauged. I sat down on the settee and lit a cigarette.

Once sure that the place was empty, and with the general lay-out in my mind, I'd begun to feel better about the whole thing; but now, for no particular reason, I began to grow uneasy again. Perhaps it was just the silence. Twice I fancied footsteps coming up the stairs, and once a car stopped nearly outside, and I half got up expecting to hear someone come in. Then after a bit I began to have the idea that someone was creeping up behind the settee. This was just silly because I should have heard the slightest sound.

The clock was ticking away like anything. There might have been an urgency about it, as if it wanted to get to the end of the day and start again. As if its hair-spring had slipped and it was racing, trying to tell me . . . For something to do I put my wrist-watch up to my good eye but of course it was no use. There'd been a general deterioration again this month. Whatever the outcome of my affair with Alix I should never see her face again.

Yet in a way the blackest mood of all had not come back. However sick and resentful, the experiment in suicide was off.

There were various faint smells in the room I couldn't pin down; and perhaps they were at the back of the added feeling of unease. Or perhaps it was the over-turned flower vase. Or perhaps it was the continued silence, coming into the flat of an enemy, where the lights and the fire were burning, the radio on, finding nobody, and sitting here listening and waiting. And not being able to *see*.

I began to feel convinced I was being *watched*. There were six of them, sitting in different parts of the room, all watching me and waiting. A Chinaman with a knife; a grinning lunatic. And the man I'd seen in the ditch near Caen, and that girl with lupus . . .

Careful. That way . . . I alone was in darkness, that was what it amounted to. There was danger some-where and I didn't know of it. There was a gun pointed at my head, a knife lifted . . . I had to move, to duck, or . . .

'Who's there?' I said, turning my head swiftly. Just the same silence.

I got up.

At least – I began to get up, and in doing so put my hand down further along the settee. My hand touched a man's coat sleeve.

I got in a hell of a panic and grasped the man's arm in self-defence, putting my other hand up to guard my face. He moved across the settee to attack me, but I struck at him and jumped up, nearly fell, backed away.

I backed into a table and it went over with a crash, the vase of flowers with it – and this time the vase broke.

I stumbled back over the tiger rug and fetched up against the wall.

The sweat had broken out all over my hands and arms. I waited for him to move, but he didn't again.

I said: 'Is it you, Grognard?'

Couldn't see – and now somehow mustn't be able to hear. I rubbed my eyes instinctively, trying . . .

Couldn't hear the man breathing; my own was noisy enough. I stumbled back to the settee. He'd fallen full length across the seat of it, one hand touching the floor. The smell of his clothes told me it was Pierre Grognard; he was dead.

CHAPTER NINE

IT TAKES a lot to make me tremble, but I was shaking from head to foot. I groped for a chair and sat on it and nearly vomited.

First thought was: get out of here. Put a distance between you and your companion on the settee.

But I was too shaken up for a minute, and by the time my legs were holding, other thoughts were cramming in. From somewhere I got the idea of a suicide pact. Perhaps because of me things had gone amiss between Alix and Pierre, and in his temperamental way he'd decided to finish them both. It fitted with Alix's attempt to tell me something while pretending to speak to someone else. Perhaps she thought I would be in time to stop it.

'Alix! Alix!' I shouted, getting up and beginning to grope about, dreading now that I should stumble across her body. I flung open the bedroom door and went in, switching on the light from habit, felt across the bed, beside the wardrobe, by the window, moving my feet like mine detectors across the floor.

'Alix! Alix!' I shouted, going into the kitchen, knocking over a chair, feeling about the floor. There was another door beyond, but that led out of the flat. I came back wiping the sweat. The silence was unbearable. Steady, steady! Think. The whole thing's got a perfectly natural explanation. Pierre and Alix were sitting smoking, listening to the radio; Pierre had a heart attack, died suddenly; Alix panicked, ran for a doctor. Any minute she'll be back. But why not phone for the doctor? And why that oblique call?

There was one way of finding out something more, but it wasn't the way I wanted to take. It's one thing to look at a dead body for signs of the cause of death; it's another to have to feel over it.

The telephone bell rang.

It was close beside me and jerked at my nerves. I felt for the phone; stop it at once. Another table, books, telephone. But if I answered it . . .

Well, the thing couldn't go on ringing in that silent flat. I took off the receiver.

'Yes?'

'Monsieur Grognard?' It was a man's voice.

'No,' I said, and cleared my throat. 'M. Grognard is not in.'

'Oh . . . Very well. I'll call him later.'

'Who is it speaking, please?'

But the man had rung off. I put the receiver back.

My cigarette had got lost long since. I took out a new one and lit it, standing there in the middle of the room, hoping it would steady my nerves. My voice must have sounded like a frog's. I had to think quickly, reason it out. Suppose something had happened between Alix and Pierre, they had quarrelled and Alix had left for good. Must get in touch with her. She would be back at her own flat. Ring now. But she had no phone in her own flat – it would mean her coming downstairs, talking in semi-public. Better to go round.

The cigarette was helping a bit; I thought, well, whatever else, Pierre can't hurt you now. I may be unpleasant, but it's only superstition, an instinct. I went over to the settee, and by a touch here and there made out how he was lying. He'd been sitting more or less straight with his head back when I took hold of his arm, and the pull had been enough to topple him over. Now he was lying on his face across the length of the settee and a jerk would probably overbalance him on to the floor. In spite of reason, that was something it seemed better to avoid.

I stubbed out the cigarette. His head was under my hand. Sleek black hair, I let my fingers travel over it: quickly took them away. The hair was sticky with something beside pomade; a deep wound along the top of the skull.

So not much examination needed. I wasn't specially grateful. I'd wanted some comfortable, reasonable solution to pull it all back to normal again; not this.

I turned and made for the outer door, in a sudden hurry now to be gone. As the door opened I realised I'd not got my stick.

Back again, groping on the floor about the settee. Not there. God only knew what had happened to it. In that first panic it might have been dropped in any of the three rooms. I went back into the kitchen, then into the bedroom. The infuriating thing was that it might have come within an inch of one of my groping hands and still have been passed by.

A car went past outside, seemed to be stopping, accelerated away again with grating gears. That settled it: the stick would have to be left. I went out, pulling the outer door to behind me but not catching it. That was as it had been found.

The air was cool, even cold; in the flat it had been overheated, the electric fire burning away. I went down the steps with shaky knees, found myself in the quiet street. The breeze was like a tonic. I could think straight again, my mind not pushed askew. I began to walk down the street.

'Pardon me,' I said. 'It's Mme Delaisse on the fourth floor I want. I don't know the number.'

'Number forty-two, monsieur. All the doors are marked.'

'Thank you. Unfortunately, I'm too short-sighted to see the numbers. Would it be possible for someone to come up with me?'

'I will come up with you.' She said it grudgingly, but I was thankful it wasn't the woman who'd shouted after me last week.

'Are you – Madame Colloni?'

'I am, monsieur.'

'Have you had any phone call from Mme Delaisse tonight?'

'No. Nothing at all.'

We went up and she showed me the door. I thanked

106

her and knocked but there was no reply. I knocked twice more and found a bell and rang that. Alix wasn't at home. She hadn't got back. I waited a quarter of an hour and then gave it up. It wasn't until I was nearly home that I realised what a corner I might be in myself.

Supposing Pierre hadn't fallen in the hearth or slipped from a ladder – in fact supposing appearances were what they seemed – whom would the police be likely to suspect as a murderer? Surely a semi-blind Englishman who'd had a quarrel with the murdered man a few days before, whose stick was found on the scene of the crime, who'd probably got bloodstained hands or bloodstained clothing – which might already have been noticed – and who had obligingly left finger-prints on practically every polished surface in the flat.

I got home and went up and mixed a stiff brandy. I needed it. I couldn't hold the glass steady.

Ought to have rung the police. As soon as I found Pierre I ought to have rung the police. Because of Alix I'd hardly thought of it. All the time I'd felt, she'll explain, she'll explain. Well, she hadn't. If she didn't ring or come soon . . .

I went to bed about one. Through the night I kept thinking I heard the telephone or someone knocking. Twice I dreamed Pierre Grognard was sitting in the chair by the bed waiting for me. I kept waking up in a sweat saying: 'God, it's dark!' Then I'd rub and rub at my eyes, trying to see.

It was bad to get tangled up in a thing like this when I was at such a disadvantage. If Alix wanted my help I wanted to be there, not groping about in the darkness half a mile away. She might still be somewhere in the flat, dead like her fiancé. This was the worst thought of all. Once I nearly got up and went back to the flat to see if the door was still ajar, to see if there was still time to make another search.

It came light at last, and I got up and had a bath and shaved. It was still early, but I couldn't rest and picked up the receiver to try Pierre's flat. But I put the phone down again. By now almost certainly the police would be there. No point in tying myself up still more. Whatever had happened one ought to go slow. After all, my stick was not an unusual one, it carried no name or initials; the quarrel and the fingerprints might just not connect up.

Breakfast and the morning papers. It had all happened too late for these. After the meal I went out, bought another stick and went round to the shoe-shop.

She was not in her usual corner.

'Yes, monsieur? Can I help you?'

'I'm looking for Mme Delaisse.'

'Our assistant? I'm sorry, Mme Delaisse is on holiday.'

'Holiday? How long for?'

'I think it is ten days. It started from Wednesday, I know.'

'She wasn't here yesterday?'

'No, monsieur.'

'Oh . . . Thank you.'

Stand in the street for a minute in the sun. She hadn't been here yesterday. I walked slowly across the town to her apartment. After trying the fourth floor and getting no answer I found Mme Colloni again.

She said: 'No, monsieur, Madame Delaisse is away.'

'Oh, you've seen her since last night, then.'

'No, monsieur, she wrote to me. She has gone on a holiday.'

'I should be very much obliged if you could tell me where she has gone.'

'I don't know, monsieur. She writes from Grasse.'

'You mean the letter was posted from Grasse?'

'Of course.'

'When you last saw her she didn't tell you she was going on a holiday?'

'Oh, I knew she was thinking of it. She has gone away to get married, you see.'

'Married . . .'

'Yes. She was a widow, you understand.'

'Oh, yes, I know that.'

The woman didn't say any more, but I couldn't leave it like that. I let her see that they were hundred-franc notes in my hand.

'Does she mention the name of her husband?'

'No, monsieur.'

'When was the letter posted in Grasse?'

'Yesterday afternoon.'

'And it was delivered here this morning?'

'Yes, this morning.'

I couldn't make the thing out at all. 'If she should come back unexpectedly, would you ring me at this number? It's specially important. I'll make it worth doing.'

'Very well, monsieur. Thank you very much.'

*

I waited till the afternoon and then sent out for the evening papers. Old Larosse read them to me. Because I couldn't tell him what to look for I had to sit patiently while he went through the French government crisis and all the other stuff. He drew a complete blank.

I said: 'But is there no local news? No murders, suicides, weddings, or births to make it all more interesting?'

He chuckled and went on picking out bits; but it was perfectly plain by now that there was nothing about Grognard in the papers.

I waited in then until seven o'clock, hoping against hope for a message of some sort. *Had* she phoned last night? How could she have phoned if she was in Grasse? Had I mistaken the voice or the message? At seven I went out and had a meal, then walked to the square where the buses start. One left at eight-thirty for Cap Ferrat. This would do, as it would pass through Villefranche.

CHAPTER TEN

I HADN'T been to the Café Gambetta on my own, but it was easy enough to find. The bus stopped on the main road, and you went straight down towards the quay, took the second on the left and followed straight along till you came to the steps.

It had been a lovely day, though I hadn't been in a mood to appreciate it. Now in the evening a nightingale was beginning to warble. The scents were particularly clear: the hot sun had warmed the earth, and in the cool everything was fresh and fragrant. One could picture the harbour glimmering and glinting in the evening light, the long curve of the bay, the mountains behind.

I went along pretty cautiously because Villefranche is a death-trap for the non-seeing or the unwary. You're always coming to a step or two or a sudden dip in the cobbles or a sharp angle in the streets. It must have been about nine or just after when I walked up to the Café Gambetta. It was quieter than usual, and in the outer room there was only the usual four in the corner playing cards and two or three men at the bar.

'Monsieur?' said the boy behind the bar.

It didn't sound the usual voice.

'Is it François?' I said.

'No. My name is Raoul.'

'You're new here, aren't you?'

'No, monsieur. I've been here for some time.'

'Is Mère Roget in?'

'Mère Roget, monsieur? Who is she?'

The four in the corner had stopped playing. I put my hand gently on the bar.

'Go and tell Mère Roget that Giles Gordon wants to see her.'

He sounded puzzled. 'But monsieur, I know no Mère Roget. You are mistaken.'

I said: 'Go and fetch Armand Delaisse, then. Ask him if his sister is here.'

He said again, but in a more impatient tone: 'You've made a mistake, monsieur. No one of that name lives here. Can I get you something to drink?'

I turned to the men playing cards. 'Isn't this the Café Gambetta?'

'No, monsieur. This is the Café des Fourmis.'

A couple of them said it together. Strange voices.

'This is the Rue St-Agel?'

'No, monsieur. The Rue Carnot.'

What a fool. To think yourself so clever getting here. 'I beg your pardon. I've mistaken the street.'

I moved away from the bar. Even the floor seemed familiar.

I said to the men at the table: 'Could you direct me to the Rue St-Agel. Is it the one below this?'

There was silence. Then one of them said: 'I've never

heard of the Rue St-Agel, monsieur. Is it in Villefranche?'

'It certainly is. The Café Gambetta is on the corner.'

Another said: 'I've lived in Villefranche all my life and never heard of either.'

'Thank you very much.' I turned into the street.

Just for a minute my head swam. It all seemed so lunatic. That people shouldn't know of the Café Gambetta, people who were natives of the place. In a bit I should be asking if this was Villefranche. They were lying – it couldn't be anything else. A clumsy device, and not hard to show up. I walked away a few yards, bit at the handle of my stick, then walked further off, to the other end of the street. There I drew back against the wall and waited. When perhaps five minutes had passed I came out again and listened for the next passer-by.

Two women were coming up from the direction of the harbour. They were talking away at a great rate about the price of meat.

I said: 'Forgive me, I'm short-sighted. Could you tell me the name of this street?'

They stopped in mid-spate. One said: 'Rue Carnot, monsieur.'

That shook me.

'And the café down there on the corner?'

'The Café des Fourmis.'

I said: 'Could you please tell me, then, where the Rue St-Agel is?'

'Rue St-Agel? In Villefranche? Do you know it, Netta?'

'I've never heard of it.'

'Or the Café Gambetta?' I said.

'No, monsieur. Are you sure it is in Villefranche?'

'It is owned by Mère Roget.'

'No, monsieur. I'm sorry. We don't know that at all.'

They went on.

John said: 'And when did all this happen?'

'A couple of days ago.'

'What did you do then?'

'Not very much. What was there to do? I hung about at the end of the street for a time and then went down to the quay to see if there was any sign of Roquefort. That was a fisherman who'd been specially friendly at the Gambetta. But nobody seemed to have heard of him, so in the end I came home. Yesterday I stayed in most of the day. I felt pretty queer; especially as Larosse hasn't been able to find anything about it in the papers.'

'No, there's certainly been no mention of Grognard.' John re-lit his pipe. 'I really don't know what to make of it, Giles. If it were anybody but you I'd think . . .' He paused. 'Of course, not being able to see . . .'

'I know. It makes every statement suspect, doesn't it?'

'I wouldn't go as far as that. But there might be a flaw somewhere in the story which isn't detectable to *me* because I have only your account, and which isn't detectable to *you* because . . . For instance, are you sure this man you found was dead?'

'Certain.'

'And are you sure it was Grognard's flat you went to? You say you'd only been once before.'

'It was the one I'd been to before.'

John grunted. 'There's one possibility – I don't know if it's occurred to you, but it's one that ought to be considered. That is that there's been an attempt to frame you.'

'It had occurred to me.'

'You could be in rather a spot, you know.'

'I know that.'

'Were you invited there for that special purpose? A murder was planned and someone imitated this girl's voice. You obligingly went along and stuck fingerprints all over the walls. What more could they want?'

'Nothing at all.'

'As for the girl, on the face of it, I agree it's not very likely that she should have anything to do with the murder . . .'

'I've been meeting Alix for nearly two months. One does get to know a bit about a woman in that time.'

He was still unconvinced. 'This Villefranche business is all in keeping too.'

I said: 'You know those jigsaws where you pick up a piece that looks exactly right for a particular hole, but when you try to put it in it just doesn't fit. That's the sort of piece you've got hold of now.'

'Well, where is the right piece?'

'I wish to God I knew.'

He was silent. I could tell that his brain was going all round the thing.

'Anyway we agree that if that body is found you're in a nasty position.'

'Yes.'

'There's one thing I'd certainly advise you to do here and now.'

'What?'

'Get out.'

'The criminal flees from his crime.'

'Right enough. But you'll be a lot safer in England all the same. There's a plane leaves Nice every day. You could be in England tomorrow.'

I shook my head. 'We all ask advice and then don't take it. How should I ever settle at home with this thing turning over in my head?'

'Go away and come back in a month if the coast's clear. I'll keep you up-to-date.'

'I *can't*, Johnny. Not at this stage. I feel I ought to go to the police.'

'Over my dead body. Sorry, perhaps that's the wrong simile. But can you imagine telling the story you've told me to a Commissaire or a Juge de Paix?'

'If I hang on for a day or two, can you make any inquiries for me?'

'I'll do what I can, of course. In a private capacity, that is. I'll check up.'

There wasn't anything in the papers the next day. I stayed in most of the day, trying to forget the sort of frame-up John had suggested. In the afternoon I went to sleep, tired out with thinking, and woke up full of discontent and anxiety. If Alix were still alive, why hadn't she let me know something somehow? Either she was dead or ... I felt surrounded with lies and deceit, and no means of telling where the truth ended and the falseness began.

That evening I went round to the Chapels' again.

John said: 'I've told Kay. I hope you don't mind.'

'Of course not.'

'We haven't found much. First, the easy thing: Pierre Grognard lives at the address you visited. Second, Kay went round there this afternoon; the door of the flat was locked and no one answered the bell.'

'It's been found, then.'

'By someone. Third, I rang up his restaurant here and was told he'd gone away for a fortnight. Fourth, there's no café called the Café Gambetta in Villefranche. That's all we've done.'

'Thank you. You've helped a lot. Did you by any chance ring his flat?'

'No.'

'I did this morning. There wasn't any answer. D'you mind if I try again now?'

'Go ahead.'

I got the number and heard it ringing. For a second I had the queer feeling that I was back there at the other end of the telephone in that silent room with the electric fire still burning. And Pierre Grognard still lay face downwards on the settee. The broken flower-vase was at my feet and the carnations were crushed and fading ...

There was no reply. I hung up.

'Now what?'

John said: 'Look, Giles, McWheeler will be back here next Wednesday. Meet him again and go back with him to England. Once you're there you'll more or less be out of danger, and anyway you'll have time to think the whole thing over in perspective. Then if you still feel you want to come back here you can talk business with him. In the meantime I can keep in touch with things and let you know. Obviously if Grognard doesn't turn up in a fortnight, there'll be a hue and cry. That's the time for you to be absent.'

I said: 'Do you know more than you're telling me?'

'No . . . Far from it. My advice to any British subject I saw drifting into a mess would be the same: cut it out and go home. Even more so when it's an old friend. The other and more particular reason is to do with this place and time. A country can't be occupied and practically at civil war within itself and get over it in two or three years. Think what London must have been like two years after Cromwell died . . . Well, now, this thing you're concerned in may be just another eternal triangle. But there's a strong chance that its origins lie somewhere in the occupation. That might be dangerous. In any case, you're better out of it, far better. Believe me.'

'I grant you all that.'

'But you won't go?'

'No.'

Kay said: 'Do you think Charles Bénat could help us?'

'Um . . . It's an idea. He's got a finger in every pie.'

I said: 'The fellow I met that evening with you?'

'Yes. He's one of the most brilliant men of his generation. He was in the Resistance, too: one of the leaders. What he doesn't know about things in this area isn't worth knowing. Anyway, he could advise you.'

I said: 'I thought of going to the police and telling them half the story – that Alix Delaisse had disappeared and I was anxious to trace her. It might set them off.'

'Until we know what's been found in Grognard's flat I shouldn't go *near* the police. I mean that, Giles.'

There was a minute's silence.

'Where does this lawyer friend of yours live?' I asked.

'In the Boulevard de Normandie. But he's got a terrific practice; he's quite likely to be in Paris or Marseilles.'

'Why don't you ring him?' Kay suggested. 'Ask him round.'

Johnny said: 'I doubt if he'd come. But I'll ring him in the morning. Maybe you could go to his place.'

It seemed pretty hopeless, but, 'All right,' I said. 'Thanks. I feel a dead loss by myself. So long as there's something moving . . .'

John phoned me about eleven next day.

'There's still nothing in the papers, old boy.'

'No.'

'Well, I rang Bénat's office this morning. But he's spending the weekend at his villa above Vence, so I rang him there. He was very nice about it – of course I only hinted at the business – but anyway he suggested you could go up there on Sunday morning. He's leaving for Toulon on Monday, so it seemed the best thing to do.'

'Thanks very much. I suppose it's worth trying. You're not coming with me?'

'I think you'll be better on your own. Two lawyers together, as it were. You talk the same language.'

'How do I get there?'

'It's almost impossible except by car. I've got to go to Cagnes on Sunday morning, so I thought I'd run you as far as that and book a taxi to take you the rest of the way.'

'Very good of you. What time?'

'Call for you around ten.'

'Thanks,' I said again, 'that'll suit me very well.'

But as I hung up the receiver it seemed a forlorn hope. The knowledgeable lawyer with his wry dry wisdom – didn't I know the type! No doubt he'd give advice which was sound enough in principle, the outsider's view of the case. In the old days at home when I was just feeling my way in law, I'd been at such interviews between old Hampden and a client, when old Hampden had said exactly the right thing from a legal point of view and I'd seen the client struggling vainly to convey to him all the subtle nuances that were known only to the man who saw the case from within.

Well, I didn't fancy myself in that position. But the interview was arranged, and perhaps it would turn out better than one feared. In the meantime there was all Saturday to go through. Perhaps it would bring something to give us a new light on things.

CHAPTER ELEVEN

THERE WAS still no mention of Grognard in the papers. It rained heavily Saturday night but was fine enough Sunday morning, and the sun was breaking through as I tried to fold myself into John's little Fiat.

He said: 'I wonder what it feels like being as tall as you. I'm sure it doesn't serve any useful purpose.'

I said: 'It serves the purpose of keeping the species endlessly variable. Does this door shut?'

'Only when the hinges are free of clothing. Let me.'

I was grateful for his cheerful talk on the way to Cagnes. He'd never been able to stop talking at school, and it had got him into endless trouble. As I sat there listening to him I could fancy the years had never happened and the war had never happened and that everything was as it had once been.

I should have been glad enough to see this morning after I said goodbye to him and got into the taxi, because, although I'd never been to Vence, I knew it was well up in the foothills with the mountains rising sharply behind it, and the views would be fine.

In Vence, Maurice, the taxi driver, stopped to ask the way. Then we branched off and began to climb again. I sat in the front seat with him, and he talked as much as John and smoked incessantly.

I said: 'Is this one of those roads on the edge of a precipice?'

'More or less, monsieur. There is a fall but it is not a very big one. The road winds up the valley, you see. I have never been this way before. On the other road the bridge was blown by the Boche, but I am told they have put a trestle bridge across.'

We took two double hair-pin bends that destroyed my sense of direction entirely. I said: 'I often wonder they don't build bigger parapets on these mountain roads.'

He blew a cloud of cigarette smoke over me. 'Oh, there is very little traffic up here. A bicycle or two. The corners are nothing. Of course I have never been this way before.' We swung carelessly round again and back, and then began to drop slightly for a change.

'Do you know when we are there, monsieur? I wonder if that is it?'

'What?'

'There is a villa of some sort on the other side of the valley. It is the only house to be seen.'

'No. I haven't been before.'

The road deteriorated, and for a few restful moments Maurice slowed down while we bumped over it.

'They are repairing the road,' he said. 'And not before time. The rain has brought down a lot of loose stones from above. They will find extra work when they come in the morning.'

After a bit we came to a stop.

'What's the matter?'

'A fork. There has been a signpost but it has been broken off. No doubt the Maquis did it.'

'I should make for the villa.'

'It has disappeared. But I should think if we take the left fork.'

He swivelled the car round and started off. 'Ah, there it is.' He blew smoke all over me again. 'We shall soon be there now. If it is the wrong villa we can at least inquire the way.'

But it was the right villa. Charles Bénat had seen us coming and was waiting on the steps, a big dog at his side.

Bénat's hands were slim and long, rather like a woman's; the grip firm but disinterested.

I said: 'I've heard a good deal of your beautiful house.'

'Oh, this. A fancy for Renaissance furniture; what else is there to do with one's money? Can I get you something to drink? Quiet, Grutli, the gentleman has come to stay.'

In the theatre there's a technique called 'throw away'; that's how Charles Bénat talked: quickly but casually, deprecatingly, off-hand. He discarded his thoughts, throwing them like a bone to the dog.

'This is English gin, of course. French gin is outrageous. You haven't been here before? One can see

Corsica on a fine day. Not that there's any special pleasure in detecting a smudge on the horizon. Why do people suppose there is.'

'I expect the general view is very good.'

'Agreeable. You can see across the nearer valleys to the green hills which stretch down to the sea. I like generosity in nature because it's so rare in one's friends.'

We were in a large room. The chair I was in was of studded leather, shaped like a doge's chair. From the way the light fell, I gathered that the window was tall and narrow and latticed, running from floor to ceiling. The dog, a Great Dane, crouched on the floor, watching me suspiciously. Every now and then he would shift round and shake himself.

'This is an old house?'

'No. Oh, no. It was built in the twenties by a rich industrialist from Lille – in the forties he sided with the decrepit Marshal. When he was shot a grateful country gave me the first refusal of his property – charging me not more than three times what it cost to build. You'll stay to lunch, of course.'

I said I'd half promised to meet John in Cagnes at one.

'You should gave brought Mr Chapel. I like him, even though one feels there's something retarded about him, as if he's never quite grown up. Anyway, he can go home without you. A promise has become a convention no one takes seriously these days. I have American cigarettes but not English. Or do you prefer your own?'

We talked for a while, not getting anywhere in

particular; and then Bénat broke off in mid-stream and said: 'But we aren't here to discuss my affairs, are we? I understand you've been getting into trouble, Mr Gordon. I hope I can help. It won't be the first time I've helped one of your countrymen. The last one was a parachutist who misguidedly landed near St Jeannet.'

I said: 'You'll think I'm wasting your time.'

'That, of course, remains to be seen.'

And then he was silent. A few minutes ago I'd wondered when he gave his clients room to talk. But now he completely dried up. I couldn't see him, so could only suppose his attention.

'Perhaps,' I said, 'you know Pierre Grognard.'

'I do indeed. We worked for the same cause during the occupation.'

So that much was true.

'And a young woman called Alix Delaisse.'

'I know her by sight. Her husband was also under me in the Resistance movement. He lost his life.'

'Yes, I know.' I went on, not telling the story very well. I told him about finding the body and what had happened. He didn't speak. The only sound was the occasional movement of the dog. It's hard going through a longish story when you've no guide to the attitude of your listener, can't see the expression in his eyes or judge by a smile or a frown whether he's interested or bored.

When I'd finished he got up. 'Let me fill your glass.'

'Thanks.'

He came over, fiddled about at the table before sitting down. He had a slight limp, I thought.

He asked exactly the same question John had asked. 'Are you sure the man was dead?'

'Quite sure.'

'How?'

'By the feel of his hands and face.'

'They were cold?'

'No, but cooling.'

'And when did this happen?'

'Last Wednesday.'

'Supposing the man was dead, what makes you sure it was Pierre Grognard?'

'That's a—' I stopped.

'Have you ever seen Pierre Grognard?'

'Obviously not.'

'But it was his flat?'

I said: 'It was his flat, it was his hair-oil, his type of hands.'

'Yes, well, I'm afraid you're mistaken, Mr Gordon. It was not Pierre.'

'What makes you so sure?'

'Because I've seen him since.'

'Since Wednesday?'

'I saw him on Friday in Grasse.'

I frowned. 'Good God!'

'Yes, it's very strange.'

'Was he – all right?'

'He seemed very well. I only exchanged a few words with him because I had an appointment at the Mairie.'

'What was he doing in Grasse?'

'He'd gone up there for his marriage. He was to be

married yesterday, and then they were leaving to spend their honeymoon in Paris.'

'They,' I said.

'Yes, he and his new wife. You know her as Alix Delaisse.'

There was a smell of lavender in the room. I think Bénat had gone across to a vase and broken a bit of flower off to stick in his coat.

I said dully: 'But why Grasse?'

'I don't understand.'

'Why did they go to Grasse to get married?'

'It was his home town. His parents lived there. Yes, Grutli, you may go out if you want to.'

'But whose was the body I found in his flat on Wednesday evening?'

'That remains to be seen. I'm afraid I'm not very satisfied about it, Mr Gordon.'

I laughed briefly. 'You think the body wasn't there or that the body wasn't – dead.'

'I don't in the least doubt the evidence of the senses you still have. But there are one or two possible explanations . . .'

'I'd be glad to hear them.'

'Well . . . Pierre Grognard is a complex character. Though you might not think it, he has a malicious sense of humour. During the occupation he played at least one practical joke on Darnand's men which was a classic of its kind. That sort of thing grows on one.

You'd quarrelled with him. It's not impossible that this was some elaborate joke. Perhaps it misfired; perhaps you were expected to ring up the police.'

'And you think Alix Delaisse would join in it?'

He shrugged his shoulders. 'You know the lady better than I do.'

'And the café in Villefranche?'

'Again – you know the lady better than I do.'

'And if I'm convinced the man was dead?'

'That's up to you, what you believe. I can give you the address of Pierre's servant if you choose, and you can go to the flat together.'

There was silence. I said: 'How long will they be away?'

'I don't know that. You could find out at any of Pierre's restaurants. I think he said a month.'

Irrespective of anything that had happened on Wednesday night, it was hard to believe that Alix had gone off without a word. What I felt may have shown in my face, because he came across and touched my shoulder.

'Is it so unusual to be let down by a woman? Don't tell me you still have illusions, Mr Gordon.'

'It seems to me,' I said dryly, 'that I have practically nothing else.'

He laughed. 'Oh, those are a different sort.'

'Are they?'

'So I should have thought. What did Mr Chapel advise you to do?'

'Very much what I think you will.'

'You mean – go home ... Well, it's the obvious

thing, isn't it. You're not really in a condition . . . After all, whether this thing was a hoax or not isn't really the point.'

'What is, then?'

'I should say the lady in the case.'

'You're dead right.'

'That being so, there's still less you can do at this stage. Trying to interrupt a honeymoon – that would make you popular with no one. If I were you I should swallow my pride and go home for a year or so. Then, if you still feel like it, come back and take aim at the lady. She might welcome you. On the law of averages she will. It's really much more fun that way if one can bring it off, because one represents romance with none of the tiresome obligations.'

I said: 'You take a poor view of human nature.'

'Far from it. But one tries not to be sentimental. Sentimentality is the cause of so much trouble in the world, don't you think. It leads people to tell themselves lies – which is so much more dangerous than telling lies to others.'

I stayed to lunch. We had it in a low cool room with a tiled floor and pot palms which made a graceful rustling sound by the open windows. The meal was caviare, plovers' eggs, saddle of lamb, fresh strawberries and ice cream, Arabian coffee. The wines and liqueurs were in keeping.

I said: 'Do you live here quite by yourself?'

'Except for Grutli and the servants. Yes. Why not?

I'm away a lot, bothering with other people's troubles. When I come back here I like to relax.'

'You haven't married?'

'My God, I have not.'

'Preferring, I suppose, the romance without the tiresome obligations.'

'Women are all right in their place – and their place is pleasure. One enjoys good wine and good food, but who'd think of marrying them!'

I said: 'Food and wine as good as this are almost worth it.'

'The old man from Lille laid in a good cellar. But then he was a Catholic and believed in the mortification of the flesh.'

'You aren't fond of the Catholics.'

'How could I be? I was brought up one.'

The manservant padded across, put new glasses on the table and filled them.

When he'd withdrawn into the background I said: 'Perhaps the Communists have your sympathy.'

I think Bénat smiled. 'You wish to be knowing, don't you. If it's of interest they haven't ... I look on a Communist as only another sort of Catholic – an unfrocked Jesuit, so to speak. Don't you think that's true? People join the Communist Party now for much the same reason they joined the Catholic Church in the Middle Ages, because they are afraid. If they're stupid it's fear of intimidation. If they're intelligent it's fear of facing up to the spiritual consequences of standing alone. Down, Grutli, you may not move till we do.'

'An individualist, then.'

130

'I should use the word anarchist if it hadn't the wrong associations. Anarch is a little better perhaps – it's the same word in English, isn't it? The Anarch is surely a man who considers that all dogma exists only to be challenged and who admits no moral law beyond his own need – who sees his own judgment to be the equal of all men's and therefore fundamentally more important to himself, who's prepared to act alone and think alone and has the courage to face his own inevitable despair. More coffee?'

'No, thank you.'

'Good coffee's still hard to get. This came from Baghdad. The idea of an anarchist as a man of violence is rather silly. He need not be at all. The Catholics and the Communists have killed and tortured millions. An anarchist would torture none and kill only those who interfered irremovably with his own peace of mind – as the Italians and the Germans did with mine during the war.'

I said, smiling: 'You despise the law but live very well out of it.'

'You're a lawyer yourself. Don't we all do that?'

'Not to the extent of taking it into our own hands.'

'Oh, well, that was a little rhetorical. Most French-men are inclined to be rhetorical as most Englishmen are inclined to be literal. Naturally I don't advise a client to go and shoot his neighbour just because he disagrees with him. Any more than I advise you to shoot Pierre Grognard for disappointing you in the matter of his death.'

'I shall go back to England for a while.'

131

'It hasn't been a pleasant experience, I can see. Being duped seldom is. Fortunately most of the human race never realise their blindness.'

I said: 'It would be a pity to generalise too much from my experience.'

'I beg your pardon. That wasn't a very good remark.'

'Well . . . thanks for bearing with me.'

'I've enjoyed it. Come and see me again if you're in this district.'

'I will.' But I wasn't sure whether he meant it, because he suddenly sounded flat and casual. He came to the door with me, but reluctantly, as if he'd lost interest and wanted to get back to his own work.

Before I could go more than a few paces Bénat had moved away and was talking to his dog.

Maurice had been well fed in the servants' quarters and drove down more furiously than he'd come up. He chatted a lot, about what a great man Bénat was and how lucky I was to know him, but I was thoughtful and don't remember a lot of what he said. John, of course, hadn't waited, and I took a bus back from Cagnes.

Early on in my talk with Charles Bénat I realised I'd only known one man before who could sit as quiet as he could. It was probably just a coincidence, and I decided not to mention it to John. It would only confirm him in the view that I was imagining things.

BOOK TWO

BOOK TWO

CHAPTER ONE

THE FOLLOWING week I went back to England.

It's all right to talk about swallowing your pride, but it's hard enough when it comes to the point. But, as Bénat said, there wasn't much else I could do. If I went to the police I could only offer them my story, doubtful evidence at best. They would listen politely and put the statement away in a drawer. Or perhaps they wouldn't even listen politely.

Left to myself, I should have hung on the month to confront Alix and Grognard when they came back. I was on the spot, and it needed no initiative to wait. But it needed money, and I was down to my last five pounds.

Then at the crucial moment McWheeler turned up again, and his presence weighted the scale. Representatives of his Chamber of Commerce would be in London next month, and if I cared to meet them he thought something might be worked out between us. I wasn't at all sure I wanted his job, supposing it to be had; but looking after it seemed so much more active, so much more dignified than moving back to the Wintertons as a non-paying guest. So I argued with myself that I was sick of everything to do with Alix and

135

that a breath of English air would be a welcome change after all this unpleasantness. Altogether it would depend very much on the way the wind set when I got back to England whether I ever left it again.

London wasn't very welcoming to begin. The flat was gone, and hotel life is expensive and dreary. At home the disablement was worse, more conspicuous. Concerts were a help, and I went to as many as possible; but of course they only filled up a small part of the time. And time is an enemy when you can do so little with it.

I told Cousin Lewis of the Proposition McWheeler.

He said: 'It doesn't strike me as being your – hm – cup of tea, Giles. Mercantile law's one thing – French commercial law another. Lot of study would be needed. Could you do it?'

'There are ways.'

'Much better – hm – come back to your own firm. Business growing and I'm overworked.'

'There'd be a certain satisfaction in holding down a job that wasn't anybody's charity.'

'Nonsense, there's no charity in coming back here. You could pull your weight in all sorts of ways.'

'I shall have to fight it out. At the moment I just don't know.'

'I suppose they're aware of your disability?'

'I'm not sure. McWheeler knows I'm very short-sighted.'

'I suppose you'll tell them.'

'I suppose so.'

'Well, personally . . .' Lewis cleared his throat once or twice. 'Personally, of course, if I were in your position, I shouldn't want to leave England and my friends – it would be the last thing. But if for some reason I felt I had to go off again I'd be much more inclined to try to get over on health grounds. It's altogether different now you're here personally. I should think Halliday could put your case to the Treasury in such a way as to make it seem essential. My own feeling would be to go and talk it over with Halliday first.'

'Afraid it isn't mine. I'm sick of eye specialists.'

'Just so. You must be. Well, there it is. If you feel like taking on a job which is likely to be so exacting . . . always supposing you get it . . . then you must go ahead. I wish you well . . .'

During that week I argued it out – trying to settle whether I did want to go back or not – trying to decide as well whether there was any more than a chance likeness between Bénat and the man who'd been at Villefranche. Neither question got anywhere, and in the end I drifted with events. So I saw McWheeler's Chamber of Commerce after all. It was either funny or pathetic, I don't know which.

The meeting was in a room at the Savoy, and I couldn't move about as freely as in the Chapels' sitting-room. But I found the hands extended and the seat I was expected to take. McWheeler sat on the right in a deep armchair; a man called Beardmore was by the window and there was another called Newton who was more or less in charge of proceedings. From his hand I judged him to be a small, quick, dry little man of about sixty. On his left was Jeffery, another Scotsman, whose room this was.

Newton started the ball rolling, and from the beginning I took rather a dislike to him. It was clear he thought McWheeler had been unbusinesslike in talking it over with me as if it might become an arrangement between friends. In the first place Newton took care to point out that this was purely an exploratory meeting – it was early to talk of an appointment being made. The interests they represented were considering whether it wouldn't be to their advantage to have a legal and trade representative resident abroad – that was what it came to. That being so, Newton delicately implied, it wasn't so much a question of whether I was willing to take the post as, first, whether the post was to be created and, second, whether someone could be found suitable for it. What was my age? Parents? Married? Where educated? Legal qualifications? Yes, yes. Satisfactory enough so far as it went. Of course, this was work which needed not only a knowledge of foreign law but also experience in trade. He personally would have thought—

McWheeler said: 'I think what we have to consider is Mr Gordon's all-round suitability. It's not a question of whether we could get a better man to represent us in one respect but whether any one other person would combine the qualifications ... You'll excuse us talking like this before you, Gordon – Mr Newton only arrived back from America yesterday. But it's rather embarrassing for you.'

'Not at all,' I said.

'Well,' Newton said. 'Let's hear of Mr Gordon's all-round suitability.'

'He has the legal training; he wants to live abroad; he's British and will understand our views; at the same time he knows and understands the French.'

Newton said: 'Just what is your knowledge of France?'

I said: 'I've known the language all my life. I've spent several holidays there. I lived a year in Paris when I was twenty-one. I'm attracted to the country sentimentally and believe in its future.'

'Yes, yes, no doubt. No doubt.' Newton seemed to think this over. 'I confess I wish we had Smith here. I'm a little at sea when it comes to law ... Of course plenty of us are fond of France – would like a holiday there at this moment. *I'd* like to go. But the restriction on holiday money does make it difficult.'

I said with a smile: 'I don't want to take another holiday there at your expense.'

Jeffery made tufting noises. 'Naturally not. Er – this work as we see it is bound to cover a good deal of ground. It would probably extend to Belgium and possibly Holland as well. I suppose you'd be willing to make Paris your centre if that were thought most suitable.'

'I'd prefer to live in the south, but it's entirely up to you.'

Newton said: 'Why are you not practising law in England, Mr Gordon?'

'The close work tries my eyes.' I didn't really want to

start lying to them, but the interview had somehow gone downhill since Newton began putting his questions.

'Don't you think this work may be too close for you also?'

'I hope not.'

Jeffery said: 'I don't think the question of salary has been discussed at all yet. Perhaps it's premature, but personally I should like some sort of proposition in mind, and probably Mr Gordon would too.'

I said: 'It's not the most important point in the early stages.'

'Oh?' Newton was interested. 'Mean to say you'd be willing to work as it were on a piece-rate basis?'

'Within reason, yes.'

McWheeler said: 'I don't think we can expect all that of Gordon. Either we ask him to represent us or we don't. If he represents us then he must receive expenses and some fixed yearly salary which—'

'Which he's willing to have adjusted according to the amount of work he happens to have to do for us. That's what he says. That seems very fair. Something satisfactory anyhow.'

Beardmore spoke for the first time; he'd a voice like a professional bass singer. 'I think if the appointment is made, Mr Gordon, you should first spend a month or so in Scotland just meeting each one of the manufacturers and talking over his business with him. Then once you'd a firm picture of the situation in your mind you could return to France. It's the personal touch that counts – at this end as well as at the other.'

'That's perfectly reasonable.'

We went on for a few minutes. Newton hadn't anything more to say, and I suspected him of hatching some unpleasantness. Then McWheeler said: 'I'm thinking it's best now for us to talk this over during the week, and then let you know more on Saturday. Don't you think so?'

There was a murmur of agreement. I got up. 'Thank you. That will suit me.' I shook hands all round and left them there.

When I got out I missed the lift and wandered a good way past before knowing I'd gone wrong. So when I got back there I was annoyed to find Newton just pressing the button.

'Ah, Mr Gordon. We can go down together.'

'Yes.'

'Give you a lift somewhere, eh?' he asked as we left the hotel.

'No thanks, I'll get a taxi.'

'No need to do that. My car's just here.'

I thought, if I was really considering the job . . .

'Thank you.' We got into a large saloon. I was rather surprised to find he drove himself.

He said: 'You're very clever, aren't you?'

I said: 'What the devil d'you mean?'

'About your blindness. Fooled me for a time. Tackled McWheeler as soon as you'd gone. None of the others was sure.'

I didn't speak for a bit. 'And what did McWheeler say?'

'He told us all about it then. Must say I admire your pluck.'

We turned into the Strand, waited for traffic lights, moved off.

'I lost a son at El Alamein,' said Newton. 'Twenty-one. Just had a year at Cambridge before going in. Brilliant youngster. The clever one's been taken and the stupid one left. You should have told us at the beginning. McWheeler should have told us.'

'What effect would that have had?'

'More understanding attitude. I'm a hard-headed business man, pride myself on being no fool, no senti-mentalist. But admire pluck. And losing a son makes a difference . . .'

I didn't speak.

'Great thing when one has disability like yours is to be self-supporting. That's how you feel, I imagine. Self-respect. Well, it's up to other people to co-operate. Mind you, can't promise anything yet – whole pro-position, I think, needs more careful consideration – it's up in the air, nothing concrete. I like propositions I feel I can stand on – three-dimensional, see all round them, if you follow me. That's a matter of detail. But if it comes to an appointment no doubt you'd do good work for us over there. No doubt at all.'

'Thanks,' I said again.

'Where are you going now? Lunch with me? Rather a dull club, but passable food. And no waiting, that's the main thing.'

'It's very good of you. I'd like to another day, but to-day I'm booked. If you could drop me at the corner of Park Lane I can get a bus from there.'

'Sure you can manage? But of course, silly of me to

ask. You get about everywhere, don't you. Well, now, don't worry about the job. Mind you, I'd like to have Smith present on Saturday, have the legal side thrashed out. Get the details. That's what we need now. Hope we shall be able to get something fixed.' The car came to a stop.

'Thank you very much,' I said for the last time, getting down. 'Goodbye.'

I walked up Park Lane.

Newton had called me clever, but on the whole I was inclined to think myself a fool. I'd been flattering myself without justification. All this time I'd thought I was cheating McWheeler and all this time he'd known the truth perfectly well. It was pretty silly really. John had not only given him a sales talk about me but had also told him the truth. 'This poor chap, wounded in the war, very talented really, anxious to go on living in the south of France, etc. etc.' One could hear it.

The mistake McWheeler had made was not telling the others beforehand: then they could have kept up the tactful farce. As it was he'd tried me out on them and half-way through the interview they'd tumbled to the truth – as any normally observant person, I now realised, easily would. I'd been priding myself on being different from the other blind, able to carry on, look normal, be normal.

Newton wasn't a bad fellow really. Anyway, the thing had touched him on a soft spot. Support the war heroes. Poppy day and all that. I'd write to them before

Saturday, tell them how much I appreciated their gesture; it wasn't everyone who was prepared to subsidise an invalid with no claims on them.

Perhaps it wasn't as bad as that. I should have been able to do a good bit for them. Some of the qualifications they needed. Capable enough within limits. But if I couldn't get a job on the plain merits of the case I wasn't taking one at all. Perhaps it was silly but it was the way I felt. I somehow didn't feel I could take charity from anyone, however gracefully it might be put up.

CHAPTER TWO

IT DIDN'T come easy asking favours even of Halliday, but now there was no other way.

With the McWheeler job gone the need to go back had contrarily grown stronger. I just wasn't willing to forget what had happened in Nice. Not a minute or a syllable of it. Of course one could try to push money across and manage that way, but the heavy fines being dealt out all round just then didn't make it seem a healthy pastime. Besides, unlike Charles Bénat, familiarity with the law hadn't brought contempt. I kept putting off the visit to Harley Street and putting it off, but eventually after about a fortnight I made a date.

Halliday listened to what I had to say.

'Oh, I think something can be done about that. The health of the eyes is partly governed by the health of the body. Mind you, if you'd asked my advice before going last time I should have said the intense light wasn't what you wanted at all. However, all that low-grade irritability looks as if it's cleared up. Come round to-morrow and I'll have something thought out. After all, I don't think the Treasury can afford to be too mean. If it hadn't been for men like you there wouldn't be any sterling area left.'

'I leave it to you to make up the story.'

'I can see your eye has deteriorated a good deal since I saw you last. Sight isn't completely gone, is it?'

'Pretty well.'

'A great pity. You're sensitive to certain impressions still? It won't get any worse now, if that's any consolation.'

'Not very much.'

'I'll just examine you while you're here.'

I sighed in resignation and sat back in my chair. The usual thing followed.

'Ye-es. Can you see that?'

'As a flash of some sort, yes.'

'Um. You have no watering or redness now? This is the normal condition of the eye?'

'I haven't had any trouble of that kind for nine months. But the loss of sight's come just the same.'

'Oh, yes, it would; it would. I wonder if it might be worth your seeing Mr Coulson.'

'Who's he?'

'A surgeon who's done some remarkable operations during the last year or two.'

Not that again, I thought.

'What could he do?'

'Well ... as the eye was last time I saw it, no one could have done anything. Now, it's just possible he might think it worth attempting. There wouldn't be any harm in your seeing him, anyway.'

'No harm, perhaps.'

Halliday grunted. 'Definitely if I were in your shoes I should make the effort. I don't want to raise false hopes in the slightest—'

'You won't.'

'But in this case a second opinion ... Before you go abroad. After all, you've very little to lose.'

I'd had six or eight opinions while in hospital.

'Where does he live?'

'He has rooms just round the corner in Queen Anne's Street, but I should arrange for you to see him at the Vauxhall where he's consultant surgeon. Of course it's entirely up to you.'

A visit to the Vauxhall for another bout of head shaking. 'All right,' I said.

Coulson was a little man with a quick, rather nervous way of talking and warm light hands. He sounded more like a business man than a surgeon.

He said: 'The sight of the left eye isn't gone, Mr Gordon, it's *obscured*, d'you see. Mr Halliday will have explained, no doubt.'

'He did, but I didn't follow him.'

'What he proposes is that I should perform an iridectomy. Of course, in an eye with a history like yours it's so much a matter of chance what one finds behind. There might be any sort of disorganisation arising from the earlier injuries.'

'I follow roughly.'

'Well, it's like this. You know what the pupil is, don't you? It's the gap in the eye that the light goes

147

through. Like the iris diaphragm in a camera. It expands or contracts according to the amount of light it has to cope with. Surrounding it is the iris. Well, the operation you had two years ago left a scar which contracted badly, drawing the iris so much out of shape that it has now almost completely closed the gap. No pupil's left, d'you see. Little light gets in. What I should do if I attempted that operation would be to cut you a new pupil.'

I thought this one out.

'What then?'

'Then the eye would begin to function more or less normally again.'

'I should see?'

'Yes, if it were a success.'

'What's against it?'

'At any time it's an operation of great delicacy. The extra hazards in this case I've already told you.'

'And if the hazards turned up?'

Coulson blew out a slow breath. 'At present you can tell the difference between daylight and darkness; you can detect, though you can't identify, objects moved in the region of the eye. It helps you to live your life. There are three possibilities if I operated. One is full sight. A second is a great improvement in the light you would get but slight or no increase of vision. The third is complete darkness.'

'What are the chances?'

'It's almost impossible to say ... If I had to make some sort of estimate I should say three to two.'

'Against?'

'Against complete success, yes.'

'Well, that's frank anyhow.'

'There'd be no virtue in being otherwise. But I may be unduly cautious. I'm going somewhat on the history Mr Halliday has provided, d'you see.'

I got up and stretched my legs. 'Would you mind if I had a cigarette?'

'Of course not. Have one of mine.'

'Thanks.'

When he lit it I could detect the flicker of his lighter.

We talked holidays for a minute or two.

I said: 'There's one thing. This operation you're proposing: might it mean the same as last time? Sight for twelve months, then a tactful fade-out.'

'Not if it's successful. There's no reason why you should get any decrease of vision afterwards – provided you get the vision at all. But there's no hurry to decide. I'd advise you to go home now and think it over quietly. Discuss it with your wife – I beg your pardon, your family then. Try to weigh up the alternatives. For my part, if I were in your place, I should have it done, not because I was in any way certain of success but because the possible gain is so much greater than the possible loss.'

The cigarette was proving the customary disappointment.

'I suppose it would be the usual local anaesthetic?'

'Yes. You don't find that very unpleasant, do you?'

'Well, there are nicer ways of spending the afternoon.'

He said with a twinkle: 'I always operate in the morning.'

'All right. Thank you for your candour. I'll let you know in, say, a week.'

'There's no hurry. Goodbye.'

I went to Oxford and discussed it with 'my family'. After three years' delay Hugh had just received the proofs of his book *The Philosophical Content of Hegel and Kierkegaard*; and Caroline had broken a bone in her ankle coming down the steps from a lecture on Hindu theosophy. Aside from these preoccupations they were sympathetic and kind.

Caroline said: 'I should certainly take the chance. Personally I hate to be dependent on anyone in the smallest degree – I'm so thankful the new treatment allows one to move about with a broken bone – and I suspect you're very much the same, Giles. We're alike in very few things, but I believe that's one of them. I can bear invalidism in others but not in myself.'

'You're too intelligent to be conceited over most things,' Hugh said. 'But that's a form of conceit, you know. Or pride anyway. The I, I, cannot bend. Not as other mortals. That's why Giles feels his loss of sight so much.'

I said: 'You'll make us both pharisees in a minute.' It was strange to feel common cause with Caroline.

'In the normal way,' she said, 'I've very little faith in doctors. They'd be an anachronism in a society which lived the right sort of life and lived on the right sort of food. Except of course in this sort of case. Giles is blinded. If the knife can help him I'd say he should try it just this once more.'

I hadn't told them about the McWheeler job. Now I said: 'I've decided to go abroad again in any case. Halliday thinks he can get permission.'

'Have you ever tried to take up Braille?'

'No.'

'It's a mistake not to, I think, Giles. It helps one to keep up with things. There was a man sitting next to me at the lecture when I fractured my leg. He was taking notes in Braille. It's done by puncturing paper somehow. Makes a clicking sound. But I'm sure it does help. You should try it because it would be a new interest to keep up if the operation turned out disappointing.'

I saw that she perceived the issues more clearly than I'd been giving her credit for.

'I'll wait another couple of weeks. There'll be plenty of time to begin that – afterwards.'

That night I faced up to the reasons for still hesitating about Coulson, and now the thing came fairly clear. It wasn't the operation which stood in the way. What I was afraid of was failure. Since that first day with Alix, I'd grown more or less reconciled. Her company had done it. Even when she disappeared the old feeling hadn't quite come back. But Halliday and Coulson had put forward a new hope, however thin. Once let me accept it as a possibility – and going for the operation meant accepting it – then any failure would be the end. You can't go on offering the same carrot to the same donkey.

I looked all round it that night and thought: already it's taking you all your time not to get excited about it, not to start thinking what it would be like to see again, to go back perhaps to Nice, to know what Alix really looks like, to find out the truth about Pierre ... But above all to see Alix and discover whether your feeling for her is solid or sham. Coulson and Halliday have put the seed there whether you want it or not; it's there now stirring and sprouting. Caroline saw that this evening. That's what she was trying to guard against.

Perhaps there never was really any choice. Perhaps it was only fallacy to sit back and think I could do this or that. From the minute Halliday said, see Coulson, a movement inside me had begun, and without fail it would lead to the hospital and the knife.

It was all very well to say I'd very little to lose. In a sense I had my eyesight to lose over again.

The next morning I telephoned Coulson and made an appointment to go into the ophthalmic wing at the Vauxhall on the following Monday week.

CHAPTER THREE

THEY GAVE me a little room facing south in the same corridor as the general ward, but separated from it by the matron's room. On the Tuesday morning the sun fell across my bed, crept up to my hands, but by the time Coulson arrived clouds had blown up and the day seemed chilly again.

Or perhaps it was just his manner. I always think, however hard they try to be cheerful and kind, there's a faintly sinister air about the surgeon and the nurses when there's an operation in prospect. One gets a ha-ha-but-no-nonsense impression, as if they once had to deal with a hysterical child and have never quite forgotten it. Or maybe it's just the circumstances.

Eye operations aren't much different from other operations except that you know more about them at the time, which is no asset. They'd given me luminal and had been putting cocaine drops in the eye every five minutes for the half-hour before he came, so things were more or less ready when we got into the theatre. When I felt Coulson's warm hands on my forehead I thought, well, this is it.

They began by injecting more cocaine – into the

lower lid with a hypodermic – and then they pottered about for a few minutes while this also took effect. This part always reminds me of having a tooth out. Only the rest is different. I heard Coulson reject one of the instruments laid out for him, and another had to be brought.

The other doctor, Saunders, sponged my eyelid and surrounding face with some sort of oily iodine, and presently Coulson's hands were back again like warm butterflies; and he fixed in a speculum, which is a wire thing on a spring to keep the eyelids apart. Then he pinched a tiny bit of the eyeball between forceps to hold the eye steady and cut into the top of the eyeball with a knife.

'Now perfectly still, old man,' he said.

It was damned hot in the room and I could feel myself beginning to sweat. I thought about Mont Boron and kissing a girl under a lamp and a plaintive Italian singing, *Esser in prigione, e non poter fugire*. I felt like that myself.

They mopped up some of the fluid which had drained out of the eye, and Coulson said:

'Straight ahead, just as if you were looking at a football a few feet away: that's right. Very still. Don't *squeeze* the lids.'

At this stage I gather he inserted the iridectomy scissors into the eyeball. I tried to think about that last journey home in the swaying bus together and the walk to her flat with our fingers clasped; and the telephone call a few days after, and the clopping hooves of the horse taking me to Pierre's place. I thought, if this comes off . . .

Coulson said: 'Steady,' and he must have begun to cut the iris. I didn't think of anything then.

After a minute he said: 'Splendid. Quite still. Eye on the ball, that's it.'

Light fell on my eye. I said: 'Christ!'

He said: 'Perfectly clear lens, Saunders. Better than I'd hoped. Just a few seconds more, old man.' He withdrew the scissors.

I thought, here is the path to anonymity and here the signs . . . some poem. I must have gone a bit queer for a minute or two. When I came up again they were bandaging the eye. There was water running.

Coulson was saying: 'Never know *what* you're going to find. Halliday warned me in this case that . . .' His voice changed completely and he said: 'Well, old man, it's all over. Wasn't too bad, was it. Feeling better?'

I said: 'Success?'

'All very good so far as the surgical part goes.' Because of the change in his voice I didn't believe him. 'Now we must have rest and quiet for a few days. Peace and patience.'

I said: 'Never told me what sort of football to look at. Soccer or rugger.'

'What? Oh, that.' He chuckled politely. 'Soccer preferably. It's round, you know.'

'Was looking at rugger ball. Hope it won't affect result.'

He said: 'Now back to bed. See he gets absolute

quiet, sister. I'll be round tomorrow or Wednesday, Mr Gordon. That's right. Just a little patience now. We'll have you up and about early next week.'

Then the hours of darkness and doubt. After a while, shut up in the black room of your head, your mind gets like a squirrel, going round and round, treading the familiar ground for the sake of being on the move. Then you've got to stop it, stand four square with yourself, say: This is me, all that ultimately counts; you're cosy, shut up like this, think, reason, get to know yourself, build something to show for it, be rational, sane in the darkness, creative. And your mind stays politely quiet for a few minutes – then as soon as it can it slips back to the treadmill.

The hopeful things. 'Perfectly clear lens, Saunders,' he'd said. 'Better than I'd hoped.' Did that mean much? Not said to me but to the other surgeon. Not for effect, then. Clear lens. Better than hoped. But what had he hoped? What had he been afraid of?

Then his later voice; dry, different. 'Never know *what* you're going to find. Halliday warned me in this case . . .' A dry voice, tired and vaguely flat. Disappointed perhaps. Or faintly angry. Halliday had warned him, but hadn't warned him perhaps of the right dangers. *What* you're going to find. What had he found? A healthy eye or a diseased one?

A few hours after the operation, when the cocaine was wearing off, they gave me more luminal to ease things up, so I didn't get too much pain. It ached most of the time, that was all. Once a day they took the bandages off and put in atropine drops to keep the pupil dilated; and they put in some sort of antiseptic drops at the same time. The shades were always very carefully drawn, but in the second before the drops bleared everything, I knew I could see. I could see the white glimmer of the nurse's cuff and the dark ridge of her shoulder, and daylight filtering in through a few cracks and the dropper moving towards my eye: then blob ... 'Not today, Mr Gordon. Another twenty-four hours perhaps. It depends what Mr Coulson says. You've only been bandaged two days yet,' and so on.

Of course I was excited about that, but past experience, and one or two other blind people I'd talked to in those early days, had taught me that the knife can sometimes bring sight back for a few days but can't keep it. Now and then I still got flashes of light in the other eye, but they didn't count for anything.

Pierre's flat with the light and the fire on and the feel of his sticky hair. The smell of Walter's new American car. The concertina at Villefranche. Charles Bénat's voice, casual, indifferent; yet something in the man like a thin taut wire ... I thought, if I'm still blind, will I still have the heart to go back and grope again? Stay with the Wintertons a month to break the ice. I thought of Alix, things about her that made her different from anyone else, the complex mystery of a personality that 'got across' in spite of my disability. The touch of her hands was not like other people's; they were always warm, quick and sure; the 'roundness' of her voice, like a singer's, only she didn't sing.

I thought too of Rachel, wondered if she ever remembered the times we spent together, if her marriage was a 'success'. I thought of Bénat's advice: 'Come back in a year. On the law of averages...' Rachel had been married too. She and Alix. Everything about them was so different. I'd met Rachel when an officer in the RA, with all the faintly glamorising effect of uniform, of being on leave, of wanting and getting a good time in a short time. When I met Alix it was all different. From one angle it seemed that my friendship with Rachel was the abnormal one – from another, Alix. It depended the way you looked at it.

On the sixth day Coulson came with Halliday. Nurse Rogers was with them but not the matron.

'Good morning, Mr Gordon. Morning. Well, feeling all right today? Think it's about time we had some of these bandages off.'

'High time from my point of view.'

'Yes, I can understand your impatience. Natural enough. Still, it's no good spoiling the ship. I've brought Mr Halliday along.'

'So I gather. Good morning.'

'Good morning. I'm glad to hear that things have gone so well.'

'Have they?' I said. 'So am I.'

Coulson said: 'We've been telling him that for six days but he rather doubts our veracity.'

'Proof of the pudding,' I said.

Nurse Rogers had pulled the shades to, and now she began to unwrap the bandages. I began to sweat.

I could see the light before the last was off, and as that came Halliday was standing at the foot of the bed and a rather stout middle-aged man was peering down at me on the opposite side from Nurse Rogers.

'God Almighty!' I said.

'Proof of the pudding, Mr Gordon,' the middle-aged man said. 'As you see, Halliday, we've been lucky.'

After a minute Halliday grunted and said: 'Pull one of the shades up, nurse.'

Nurse Rogers let in more light. She was a small dark young woman with good teeth. When I could get a chance past the peering heads I saw it was raining.

'God Almighty!' I said.

Halliday was plucking at his lip. 'It's quite surprising. One of the most satisfactory I've seen. If no irritable tendency has developed so far . . . I congratulate you, Coulson. And you, Gordon.'

'A very good patient,' Coulson said. 'A tendency towards scepticism, but we must forgive him that.'

I said: 'I can see better than after that first operation.'

'So you should. There's no inflammation to interfere with the sight.'

I felt like crying into the bed-clothes. I cleared my throat irritably and said: 'How long is it likely to stay like this?'

'You're all right. Don't worry about that. Of course, we'll have to take care of you for a few days yet.'

Somebody'd put some flowers on the dressing-table. They were yellow chrysanthemums and pink Michaelmas daisies, and the vase was green. My hairbrush was on the table, and the letter Nurse Rogers had read me, from Caroline; and a glass of water and a box of some sort and a handkerchief.

I said: 'I can see without my glasses.'

'Yes, the old ones won't be much use to you now,' said Coulson. 'Halliday'll fix you up with a new pair in a day or two. You'll probably feel better to keep on wearing them.'

They talked for about five minutes. It all seemed quite casual to them, just a matter-of-fact part of the day, a matter for sober satisfaction, just as it would have been a matter for sober regret if it had gone the other way. I wanted to shake them out of it, make them realise.

As they turned to go I looked at the clock on the table: it was twenty minutes past eleven; I looked at the chart beside it and saw that my temperature was sub-normal; I looked out again at the bit of greyness which was the October day. The silver rods of rain showed up against the window opposite. I was glad Nurse Rogers went with them to the door; it gave me a chance of trying to look normal again before she came back.

Even then I worried a good bit. All that night and the following day, because the stakes were so high. In the evening when Coulson came in I tackled him about it.

He said: 'We're hiding nothing from you now. I suppose it's natural you should feel like that. But you must understand in an operation of such delicacy it would be inexcusable to claim too much. In your case one had to be specially cautious because of the complications which followed the last operation, d'you see. If that had come again . . .'

'And what possibility is there in the future?'

'A cut that heals satisfactorily in the eye is no more likely to give you trouble than a cut that heals in the body.'

I said: 'I met a man in hospital in Sussex, naval gunnery officer, blind from blast. They operated on one eye – for a detached retina, I think. In a week he could see right enough, but a fortnight after leaving hospital the thing slipped and he was as blind as ever . . .'

He said: 'What a man you are for worry. There's nothing to slip in your eye. I haven't stitched anything on or pinned anything up. You're all of a piece.' He got up. 'Joking apart, have you looked at yourself in the mirror yet?'

'Not closely.'

'Well, you may think the new pupil I've given you is a bit tent-shaped. Don't worry, it'll round off in time.'

'I don't care what shape it is, so long as it works.'

At the door he came back, blew out a breath. I wondered what he was going to say.

'If you feel like it, six months or twelve months, come back and I'll attempt something with that other eye. I believe I could make it function to some extent. Even though you might not get a lot of advantage, it's much healthier to have an eye that isn't a dead loss, and it always helps the good one to see better.'

'Thanks,' I said. 'I'll think about that.'

CHAPTER FOUR

WHEN YOU come out of Dartmoor after a long stretch it may be that you would feel something the way I felt that afternoon twelve days later, standing on the corner of the street watching the traffic lights change colour and the buses grind to a stop and the taxis panting and the crowds.

I remember that day I met Alix, feeling blindness had caught me up at last and that I'd really no place in the world, that I was a ghost of a man, waiting to go. There was an affinity with this day, for I felt a ghost of a man who had just come back. Rip Van Winkle, the returned soldier, the released convict, peering about for a friendly sign, a familiar face. Every now and then my eye would get bleared up, not with the old troubles but with feelings that I couldn't keep in hand. I wanted to cry like a kid.

In spite of all Coulson told me I was still scared. Scared stiff. It was too good to be true. They said the sight was five-sixths of normal; but with glasses I could see practically as well as I'd ever seen, except that it was one-sided and therefore still clumsy. But I'd got used to that way of looking last year and the year before. It was

162

like opening up a black-out curtain and finding the sun there all the time.

. . . It's no good going over all I did and felt those first weeks and months. There's the mental change as well as the physical. Your attitude doesn't adapt itself in a day. In my case I seemed to be harking back not to the few months of semi-seeing at the end of the war but to the pre-army life of six years ago, and the gap was hard to jump.

I did the things one would expect, saw something of Lewis and the office, tried to pick up the threads of a few friendships. But often people had developed their own interests, and I wasn't somehow quite ready yet to meet them half way. I was not properly awake – and still insecure, still groping.

After a while I moved from the hotel, took a flat in Kensington, though it wasn't as good as the old one.

Christmas in Oxford. Aimlessly strolling. Every day I went out, keeping mostly clear of the main streets, through the quiet alleys and closes of the town. I remember one day it snowed, and I walked down Bear Lane and Oriel Street and Merton Street to Magdalen Bridge. The water was a kind of bottle-green, moving as slow as a snake, and the Tudor towers glimmered in it. The trees were all built up into a white architecture of their own; and the snow sky had broken up and there were pools and drippings of green in it as if a thaw had come. Starlings were chattering in the snow, fighting for a crust. I remember a boy on a bicycle came wobbling across the bridge, his wheels making new and finer lines among the ruts. I walked into St John's Quad, where the snow was hardly disturbed and old Magdalen crouched in the quiet. As I went home, through Queen's Lane and New College Lane, the sun set and an afterglow flushed into the sky. It lit up the towers and spires. I felt as if I was seeing something for the very first time.

During that week the tightness inside me began to slacken off at last. I began to feel the change was true, not just another promise which would go wrong like the last.

In the new year I stayed with an aunt in Yorkshire. More walking here, though of a different kind. It seemed for a time as if that was the thing I wanted to do most; not to think much but to give one's body something regular to do while one's mind took a holiday.

It was queer about France. Before the operation there'd been all that urge to go back. Lying under the bandages, I'd thought: if things come right I'll go by the first plane. But when sight came it was different. For one thing there was the risk. This that had come back was worth so much and, by experience, was so chancy, that I was afraid of doing half the usual things, of getting over-tired, of sitting in draughts, of reading too much or jumping or bending or moving suddenly. Life in a bathchair would have been worth accepting if that were the only way of staying whole. Silly, perhaps, but . . . try the alternative for a while.

Then when spring came and a slow reassurance, and the sense of invalidism began to lift, another reluctance grew up. Perhaps it was going to be all right, all the things that I'd wanted so much were more or less permanently back: to be able to read and drive a car and meet people on an ordinary basis. If that were so, then I wanted just those things and no others, normalcy and nothing else. France was the unusual. France was the place where I'd been made a fool of; the very smell of the flowers and the food and the streets would bring back vividly the double frustration.

Oh, there was the pull of Alix – it wasn't the sort of thing one 'got over' – there was the niggling anxiety that by not following it up at once something precious and important was being allowed to slip away, that in a sense I might be letting Alix down somehow; there was the itch to know, the old pugnacious desire not to be beaten; but just at present these feelings all together weren't quite strong enough to shift the balance.

Other things began to relax too. When I finally got down to reading I read a good bit; philosophy, poetry, things there'd been no time for since that year in Paris. I felt faintly ashamed, trying to work out something to fit my view of the universe now things were going well. The time for that, when the really big person would have showed himself, was last year. Instead I'd been bitter and suicidal. I'd developed a terrific inferiority complex which must have stuck out a mile. I'd been egocentric about the whole thing.

I found I could see almost as well without glasses as with, except for long bouts of reading, but I kept them on just the same as a protection. I put in a certain amount of work, but couldn't settle yet to regular attendance at the office. Lewis grumbled sometimes.

In May it seemed a good idea to spend a fortnight fishing in Devonshire. That would set me up for the summer. After that maybe one would settle down to law, in September think out the French business afresh, see if one wanted to face it then.

Going to Devon meant rather more of a pack-up than previous visits to sisters and aunts. I dragged out the larger case, which I had last used in France.

A queer feeling; even the smell of the inside of the case was reminiscent. It struck at me with a sensation of alarm, as if there was danger in it, or had been, and the old gods were calling. A few odds and ends hadn't been taken out. I'm not tidy at the best of times, and blindness doesn't help. There was the torn-off bill of my dinner on the train, a couple of programmes of concerts with the Wintertons, the pair of shoes bought from Alix wrapped up in an old paper. Those gave me a turn. I unwrapped them, looked them over; the smell of the leather seemed to bring back that day. I wondered if I'd been a fool to funk going back, to leave something like that unfinished, a loose end to life.

I put the shoes away and tipped out the other things: bathing trunks, a pair of shorts, a beach towel, threw them on the bed; and began to pack the things needed this time. Alix's shoes might as well go after all, as they wouldn't look out of place in Devonshire. I was going to wrap them in the same newspaper, but having taken it up I stood beside the bed reading it, as I often did now, for the sheer pleasure of being able to read.

It was a copy of the Nice paper I'd taken regularly. In a bottom corner of the back page was a paragraph

166

headed: 'Motoring Tragedy'. The notice began: 'The victim of the car accident reported in our edition of yesterday has been identified as . . .' I'd passed the name and was going on before it came back at me like a blow in the chest.

'. . . has been identified as Pierre François Grognard, the well-known Nice restaurateur. His body was recovered late yesterday afternoon . . .' I glanced up quickly at the date. The day before I left Nice. Of course, I'd wrapped the shoes up to pack them. By then I'd given up bothering Old Larosse to read anything.

'. . . His body was recovered late yesterday afternoon by gendarmerie and ambulance staff from Grenoble. The car was badly smashed, having fallen nearly four hundred feet, and it has not been decided whether any efforts will be made to move it from where it has fallen at the foot of the Gorge du Cheval. The road on which the accident took place is notoriously dangerous, but no fatal accident has occurred there since 1929, when a van fell over barely half a kilometre from the scene of the present tragedy. M. Grognard appears to have been motoring to Grenoble at the time and the wheels of his car skidded on the loose surface.

'A native of Normandy, the deceased man settled in Nice some twelve years ago and opened the first of his luxury restaurants in 1937. During the war he rendered valuable service to the FFI by supplying them with intelligence gained from his waiters who served the German officers in his restaurants. M. Grognard, who was thirty-five, leaves a widow but no children.'

167

CHAPTER FIVE

I WENT to Devon after all, but didn't catch much in the way of fish. When I arrived back I pottered about for a day or two, and then on impulse rang Rachel.

She sounded a bit surprised. 'Yes, Giles, I'd love you to come down. Michael's away unfortunately. What train can you come by?'

I told her, and when I got there in the afternoon she was waiting at the station to meet me. She was as lovely as I remembered her, though perhaps a bit fuller in the face. She linked my arm and led me down the platform.

I said: 'Who's been telling tales?'

'What about?'

'You know what.'

She frowned. 'With not hearing anything of you I got anxious and phoned your office. Perhaps it wasn't my concern any longer, but I felt that way. They told me you'd been away six or seven months in France. Eventually I got on to your cousin and he – told me things weren't coming up to scratch.'

'You haven't telephoned recently?'

'No – I had Susan, and . . .'

'What, another?'

'Only number two. She's three months old. Also I didn't ring again because I didn't know if it was bad taste on my part, seeing what had happened. I thought perhaps your cousin thought so.'

'No, that's just his normal voice.'

We passed the ticket barrier. 'Darling, tell me about yourself,' she said. 'Is it – very bad again?'

I said: 'You see that clock over there?'

'. . . No, afraid I don't . . . Which? You don't mean the one in the tower?'

'The one with the grey seagull sitting on top. It's twenty minutes past three by it. And on the second ledge—'

'Giles, how did you— Your eyesight's as good as mine!'

'Not quite.'

She got the car going and we drove off.

She said: 'Why ever did your cousin tell me . . .'

I explained. We reached the house and went in. I admired Jeremy and Susan, and after a while we had tea. When we were alone again she said:

'What does it feel like, being able to see again after – that?'

'Just what you'd expect, only more so. And not without a tag of responsibility somewhere. Every now and then I feel I ought to build a church or endow hospital beds or give all my money to the poor. Then I do nothing about it and feel very ashamed.'

She got up and brushed together the crumbs Jeremy had dropped. 'I've never got over feeling a bitch about the way everything happened. Is there *any* worse time or way of telling a person than the way I did it?'

'There wasn't any right time or way of telling me that. You performed the rites as decently as they could be done.'

'No ... I don't know. You see, I *had* to then; I couldn't go on pretending. I'm not a bitch by nature; at least I don't think so ...'

'Nor do I. So you couldn't have fairer than that.'

'All the same I've never felt square with myself. And after hearing from your cousin ...'

'Oh, that. That only obscured the issue. In more ways than one.'

She didn't speak for a minute. 'Why've you come down suddenly now, after all this time? Any particular reason?'

'I took it into my head. I thought: I'll go and see Rachel, stir up all the old memories. Feeling that way, I suppose.'

She shook her head doubtfully. 'Are you thinking of getting married?'

'What an extraordinary idea!'

She laughed. 'Just now when you were looking at me I wondered if perhaps you'd – fallen for someone else and felt you had to come and take a look at me to reassure yourself that you'd really got over our affair.'

'Ingenious brain.'

'Yes. Perhaps I'm conceited. Perhaps you got over it long ago.'

'You talk as if it were distemper or the measles. Tell me about yourself. Are you happy?'

'Very. But doesn't that turn the point of the question?'

After a minute I said: 'Anyway I don't think your question's quite a nice one to put to me in the circumstances. Whether I've "got over" our—'

'Oh, that wasn't the question at all!'

I thought, oh, yes, it was, darling Rachel. But it was self-esteem and not love of me that prompted it. Good for Michael.

I said: 'I'm going back to France pretty soon.'

'Business or pleasure?'

'Neither really. I just feel I want to go.'

'For long?'

'I don't know.'

She said: 'What is it, Giles? What's been happening to you there?'

'Why?'

'You sound – different. Tougher, somehow.'

'Tougher?'

'Not physically. But you were always so easy-going. Light-hearted. It's as if the – the roundness has gone.'

I said: 'Your memories of me sound pre-war.'

She got up. 'Well, I suppose they are, aren't they. As good as. I haven't seen much of you since you were wounded.'

'And precious little before that.' I stared with pleasure at her tall figure by the window. 'The dark satanic side didn't have a chance when you were around.'

'Ha!' she said.

'And anyway these last three years haven't been exactly a joy-ride.'

'I know that, darling,' she said quickly. 'No one can complain if the – roundness has gone. Anyway, I like you just as well. Only I shouldn't think you're nearly so easy to manage.'

'Tell me,' I said. 'D'you find loving someone – as you do – a good way to be?'

She looked at me. After a bit, deciding I was serious, she said: 'Yes, Giles; once you've had it, it seems almost the only way to be.'

'I wonder how it works when there's one-way traffic only, I mean when the other person doesn't seem to put a lot of store by you.'

She flushed. 'Are you talking about me or some female you've met in France?'

I said: 'Matter of principle. Hypothetical case only.'

'Then I should think it was pretty unsatisfactory. But there have been cases.'

'D'you think I'm a likely subject?'

She looked at me again. 'No,' she said.

'No. I don't feel it myself.'

She didn't take her eyes off me for a long minute.

'You are in love with somebody else, aren't you?'

I stared back at her.

'I don't know,' I said. 'I've never seen her.'

There was no sense in seeking a job for what might possibly be quite a short stay; yet the tourist allowance wouldn't go anywhere. So that meant an application to the Treasury after all. Halliday turned up trumps, and after about three weeks, impatiently borne, permission to draw on sterling up to a limit of £440 over a period of six months was granted me.

When I left England it was almost a year since coming home.

I took a midday plane, and soon enough we were circling casually round the Nice municipal airport, with the coast stretching beneath us from Rapallo to the Estérels. As we got down you could see a bus crawling like a bug along the Middle Corniche, and the toy harbour of Nice, the deep-blue, land-locked bay of Villefranche – yes Villefranche – and then the gracious curve of the Promenade des Anglais, the edge of the beach and the sea freckled with black dots, the crowded shopping streets, the white villas on the wooded slopes, then we were past and dipping towards the mouth of the Var.

I'd written the Wintertons about events this year, but hadn't told them I was coming out again and had booked at a hotel; one where the view was unfashionable and the food good. I chucked my bag down, saw the advance luggage had come, then went out. I never do feel like unpacking the first day anywhere. Much less so this time.

I walked all over the place, wandering about in a rather aimless mood, not quite believing that at nine o'clock this morning I'd been in Regent Street.

The bougainvillaea was out. That was the first thing that struck me. The royal-purple mass of it hung down over every other villa wall. It seemed to over-ride all the other colour, even the blue and mauve and green of the sea. The roses were still out, and the agaves and some

173

of the fruit trees. The sun was hot but the air fresh and invigorating in a way it wouldn't be in another month or so.

Human nature's a queer thing, and instead of getting a sense of the unhappiness of last year, instead of being beset by all sorts of uncomfortable memories, as expected, I just felt very, very glad to be here. Perhaps it was the air, perhaps my spirits were ripe for the change. After I'd been out for about half an hour I felt ready to go anywhere and do anything. I couldn't understand what had kept me away so long.

It wasn't so much design as chance that took me towards the old town. One had to walk some way. But once there it was only three minutes to Alix's old flat. Rushing one's fences of course.

Strange to go up the cobbled street, see the kids playing about, the women sitting in the doorways, knowing I'd been up this street before and yet not recognising it. The sun made knife-edged shadows. I wasn't sure of the doorway.

Luckily the postman was there and a woman was taking in letters.

'Yes, monsieur?'

'Are you Madame Colloni?'

'I am.'

'Does Mme Delaisse still live here?'

'Oh, it is the blind man, isn't it? You were here last year in the spring.'

It came as quite a surprise to be recognised. *Was* I the blind man?

'Mme Delaisse? No, monsieur. She never came back.

174

She sent for her things about a week after you called, but that was all.'

'Who came for them?'

'For her things? Oh, she wrote – and then a van came. The furniture was nearly all mine.'

'Do you know her new address? Where are her letters forwarded?'

'She never left an address, monsieur. I don't know where she is living now.'

I walked back down the street. The sun beat on the uneven pavement and reflected up. Some washing hung from a first-floor balcony; there was a chair in the street; the people in the doorways watched me with frank easy curiosity. Alix might have been murdered too for all that woman cared. Did one imagine the hint of reticence, the suggestion that further questions would be choked off? The shrugged shoulders and the slanting eyes seemed to throw out responsibility, to want to turn away before the topic was properly done with.

Back slowly to the Avenue de la Victoire. Crowds of holiday-makers with their sun-glasses and beach-wear and gay trousers; cyclists, trams, taxis in a mêlée; the plane trees weren't rustling today. A shoe-shop on the right going up. Dark after the brilliant sun. Over there was where I'd come a crash. No sign of Alix. An assistant moved across.

'I'm enquiring for a Mme Alix Delaisse. She used to work here. Do you know if she still does?'

She brought back the manageress.

'Mme Delaisse left a year ago, monsieur. We don't know her present address.'

'Did she leave to get married?'

'Not to my knowledge. She took a holiday and then wrote saying she was not coming back.'

I chewed my lip. 'She was an unusual type, wasn't she, madame; well educated, superior for this work? Do you know anything of her history?'

'She was a war widow. The war ruined many people's fortunes. She did not confide in me.'

'No,' I said. 'Thank you.'

'And of course,' she added a bit frostily as I was going to turn away, 'this is a shop where only assistants of superior character are employed.'

I hadn't really expected much; it was a question of checking up first in the most obvious ways; the sort of thing one could do in the way of preliminaries, narrowing the field.

But it was all very well to say stop at that. Once the movement was begun . . .

I bought a stick and a pair of sun-glasses and caught a bus for Villefranche.

I felt fine, as if a burden had got lost. It was exciting to be on one of those crowded buses again and to see the road ahead and the sweep of the coast-line, and not to lurch blindly about, never knowing which way the thing was going to lift or turn.

The woman from the flats had been helpful in one way. It hadn't occurred to me until then that last year's disability might be put to some use.

There were two American cruisers anchored off

Villefranche. Flags fluttered at the mast-heads, and picket boats crawled to and fro, splitting the blue linoleum of the bay. But so far as I could see the crews had not yet been given shore leave. The steep little town drowsed in the evening sun.

There was no difficulty here. Eyes half shut, I went over the familiar ground that led to the Café Gambetta. Down the hill towards the quay, second on the left, follow straight along till you come to the steps. I got to the street where the Rue St-Agel should have been, stopped and looked up. Rue Carnot. As before.

Along the Rue Carnot until one should have been opposite the Café Gambetta. There was the Café des Fourmis. As before.

Tapping now and then with the stick, I crossed the road and went in.

It was much as one had imagined it: a bar along the side, half a dozen tables, bead curtains at the other end cutting off the second room. In the second room was the piano.

The card players were not there. A couple of old women haggled over a shopping bag. A whiskery chap in a blue overall was reading the café paper. Two or three other men were about. A tall youth in tight blue trousers and rope-soled shoes leaned over the bar talking to François (or Raoul).

'Monsieur?' There was no doubt now that Raoul recognised me, but I don't think any of the others did. I ordered coffee, sat down at a table and waited. After a bit he sidled out of the bar, wiping his hands on his apron, and disappeared through the bead curtain.

Nothing happened and I tried to go on staring at the shelves of wine bottles. Raoul came back with my coffee.

'D'you remember me?' I said.

'Monsieur?'

'Used to come this way about a year ago. Surely you remember me playing the piano?'

'No, monsieur. I have been away, on my term of service.'

He went off. Then the bead curtains parted and someone looked out. It was annoying not being able to recognise people except by their voices, because it was the sound of their voices they'd naturally withhold from me. This was a man about thirty-five, thick set, with heavy brown hair and a sour expression. Armand Delaisse?

I drank the coffee and ordered a cognac. Then a couple of big men came in talking. They stopped suddenly at a little movement from Raoul and looked my way. They recognised me, exchanged glances and then went through to the inner room. But I also had recognised them. One was Dramont, the other was my 'comrade in arms', Scipion. Both looked startled but neither had made the slightest attempt to come over and greet me.

I raised a finger for Raoul. He came across.

'Is it permitted to go into the next room?'

'No, monsieur.'

'But I always used to. I played the piano.'

'I don't know. It may be permitted some evenings.'

'Does Mme Alix Delaisse ever come here now?'

'I don't know the name.'

'Or M. Pierre Grognard?'

'No, monsieur. I don't know them.'

But somebody did. The boy at the bar had turned quickly and his face was alert and a trifle scared. After a while three men came in and started playing cards. Two of them recognised me and whispered between themselves. But I got up and left. This morning I'd been walking down Regent Street. I still kept telling myself that. It was enough for the first day.

There was a little alley running down between the café and the next house. Half slope and half steps, it fell steeply because the café was built on the hillside and the balcony of the back room looked over the next lowest street to the sea. This meant that the sea side of the building had three stories instead of two, and there was probably a back entrance to the place via this alley.

Next time I thought I'd go down that way.

CHAPTER SIX

JOHN SAID: 'Why didn't you write and let us know you were coming? It's still possible to kill the fatted calf in this country. Kay's away but—'

I said: 'I'm not ungrateful. Believe me. It just happened I got up steam in a hurry.'

'We were full of joy at your letter. My God, I thought last year . . . It shook us both up more than you realise. And you of all people.'

'*Very* nice of you. I'm still busy with the Te deums myself.'

Another shock, to have had so much to do with him last year and yet not properly to have seen him since before the war. All the time I'd pictured him at twenty-one. At thirty-one he was fatter and had lost a lot of hair, and his fresh colour had deepened. Having matured at sixteen he'd picked up a middle-aged look before his time. Yet every now and then the forgotten schoolboy stared out.

'Kay's away, you said?'

'. . . She's in England. Bit of a holiday. She needed it. Can't think why, of course. This climate suits me down to the ground.'

'Some people don't transplant easily.' But is it that, I thought? He's happier this year: the hang-dog sound has gone.

He looked at me and grinned.

'You know, the French outlook appeals to me. We fit in.'

I said: 'There are forty million French outlooks. Which particular one do you find yourself fitting in with?'

He grinned again, but sheepishly. 'That's more in your line of country nowadays – from what you told me last year.'

'Which reminds me of my grievance. At least it's a grievance if your finger is as much on public events as it ought to be.'

I handed him the crumpled newspaper cutting about Grognard. He pretended to read it through while he thought out his line.

'Yes,' he said after a minute. 'I did see it at the time.'

'Then why didn't you write – or still better phone, because I was still in Nice when this came out.'

He took out his pipe and lit it. 'Honestly, old boy, what good would it have done?'

'You might have given me the chance of deciding.'

The match flickered about his face. 'Well, I reasoned differently. I thought, here's a man who's in trouble. He's blind and he's in a foreign country. He's met a woman and lost her, and he feels generally frustrated. He's entangled in something that in any case will bring him no good—'

181

'Ah, that's nearer the truth. The old legation caution coming out.'

'Not entirely. But partly. Why not? Anyway you were just turning your back on the scene. When I saw this paragraph you were due to leave on the following day, tickets bought, seat reserved. If no one else told you, was I going to phone up and stop you, or post it after you to bring you back? In any case, this account of the accident wouldn't have helped you very much.'

'Accident?'

'Well, whatever it was.'

'Can you tell me another thing. Why was this piece tucked away in small print in a corner of the paper?'

'Better go and ask the editor.'

'Well, what else do you know?'

'Grognard was buried in Nice. I went along to the funeral.'

'Was Alix there?'

'I don't think so.'

'You see it mentions his widow in the cutting.'

'Yes. His first wife was there in the usual weeds. The cutting may refer to her if the paper didn't know he'd married again.'

'He may not have married again.'

'What d'you mean? Bénat told you he had.'

'Whose body was it I found three days before the wedding?'

'It could hardly have been his! This was nearly a fortnight later.'

'Don't you think the coincidence a bit steep?'

John shrugged his shoulders moodily. 'What are you going to do about it?'

'Plenty.'

He said: 'You're only sticking your neck out, Giles. Of course I can't advise you now: you've got your sight back – some of it anyway; you're free, white, etc., etc. But it won't be any particular fun if in a week or two I have to tog up for your funeral.'

'I'll keep above ground.'

'There are quicksands about, old boy. Trouble then is you never know when you're going in deep.'

The Carlotta Restaurant was in the Rue Diano Marina, which is just out of Nice. It was all John had said and more. There was a flowered terrace with orange umbrellas, and exotic orange and gold nude figures climbing round the doors and windows. Inside the carpets were green and white, and concealed orange lighting lit up ivory white walls draped in green. The waiters were silent and discreet. I went in at a quiet time, but with the summer season not properly begun this was probably unnecessary. I looked at the menu and thought it was lucky I'd chosen a cheap hotel.

When the meal was half through I beckoned the head waiter. He was a middle-aged dark fellow with the sort of chin that needs shaving at four-hourly intervals.

I said: 'I was very much distressed when I returned to Nice to hear of M. Grognard's death.'

'Ah, you knew him, monsieur? Yes, it was a sad accident.'

'How did it happen?'

'He was motoring to Grenoble from Grasse. Something went wrong with the car, or he skidded, we don't know. The roads through the mountains can be very dangerous.'

'Was he found at once?'

'Oh, no, monsieur. It was more than a week. He had gone on his holidays, you see. The hotel at Grenoble was expecting him, but took no action when he did not turn up. It was not until he was expected home that inquiries were begun.'

'It must have happened at a very inaccessible spot.'

'At the head of the Gorge du Cheval. The worst possible place. They were many hours recovering the body.'

'Was he alone?'

'Yes. Quite alone.'

'Your cuisine here is as good as ever.'

'Thank you, monsieur. We endeavour to maintain a standard.'

'Have the restaurants been sold?'

For the first time he hesitated slightly. 'A limited society has been formed to carry on the restaurants for the benefit of the widow. Can I get you something further?'

I said: 'I didn't know M. Grognard was married. Was it shortly before his death?'

'I think they were separated for some years.'

'He was friendly with a Mme Delaisse. Do you know what happened to her?'

'No, monsieur. I didn't know anything of M. Grognard's private life.'

After that there was nothing to be gained by going to Grasse to examine the register of the Parish Church. Instead I rang up the Villa Lavandou.

'Is M. Bénat in?'

'I do not know. Who is speaking?'

'Oh, I'm sorry,' I said. 'I have forgotten something. I'll ring him later.'

It seemed likely that if Bénat was away the answer would not have been just that. I put on my sun-glasses and took a bus to Cagnes. There I went to the same garage and was lucky enough to find Maurice, who welcomed me like an old friend.

Maurice made the humbug so much easier. He helped me into the seat beside him, telling me to bend my head and mind the step. He took my walking-stick and gave it a reverential place on the back seat. He said did I want a cushion for my back or an extra eyeshade to shield my face from the glare of the sun.

On the way we discussed state lotteries, which he couldn't believe were not run in England on a big scale, the rise of prices since the devaluation of the franc, the national bicycle race that was taking place, and his mother-in-law's sciatica.

Trying not to seem to, I admired the sweeping green valleys we drove through, the snow on the mountains in the distance against the steep sky, the mellow embattled beauty of Vence. After that the road deteriorated as it climbed along the side of the valley.

'You are going to see M. Bénat again?' Maurice said.

'Yes. You know him, I remember your saying.'

'Well, not *know* him, monsieur. Everyone knows of him. He is admired everywhere for his exploits during the war, quite a legend in these parts. It is said he killed several hundred of the Boche. Many people owe their lives to him.'

'And now ... after all that, he is just a lawyer again.'

'Oh, that is only his profession. And even in it he does much for ordinary people – fights for *their* causes, never gives up, carries it right to the top. That is what counts.'

We were silent for a while.

'Hullo,' I said. 'Still repairing the road?'

'Ah. You remember.' He smiled through cigarette smoke, and then raised his eyebrows.

'Yes,' I said quickly. 'At least – I guessed so from the bad surface.' Careful, you fool. No one will be taken in.

We bumped along past some men and a lorry. Maurice said: 'Here they come for a few days and then go away for a month. So they make very little progress. On the main road it's better.'

Just then the villa came in sight, a big low place with cinnamon-coloured walls. After a few minutes we got among the lavender. It really was a sight: two great fields of it on either side of the road, and the long low house with its broad veranda and white steps.

I said: 'I'm not expected, so perhaps you could stop

here. If you'll just give me a hand as far as the steps I can manage from there.'

He did this, and presently I found myself at the door, carefully groping for a bell. There wasn't much attempt at an ordinary garden, just lavender, planted at one time, but now mostly growing wild. There were stables over to the left and beyond that what might have been a pillared swimming-pool. In the distance two women were working in a field of vegetables.

The door came open and a young black-browed man looked me over.

I said: 'I've called to see M. Bénat.'

'By appointment, monsieur?'

'No, but I think he will see me. Gordon is the name.'

'I'll inquire if he's in.'

He shut the door, and I heard his footsteps padding away down the tiled hall. I wondered if gradually my hearing, touch and smell would grow less acute. They hadn't shown much sign of it up to now.

It was just as well, otherwise his voice would have given me a shock coming from behind. But I'd heard those footsteps too.

'Mr Gordon. An unexpected pleasure. How are you?'

I held out my hand and had it shaken.

'Sorry to come on you like this. I happened to be in the district.'

'Of course. This way. I'm working in my office. It's just round the corner.'

He was the only person so far who was much like I'd

imagined him. Slight build, sallow face, long decisive nose, clever prominent bottom lip. He wasn't handsome but you could see that women would be interested.

'Down two steps here, now level across the grass, then through the french windows. Good. You're very clever at finding your way about, Mr Gordon.'

I wondered why I'd been asked in this way instead of through the house. It was an ordinary room he showed me into, a big flat desk, filing cabinets, a few books and papers open. Grutli rose from behind a chair and looked at me.

I said: 'Do you do some of your business up here?'

'I like to be able to.'

'You've got a non-paying client this morning.'

'Who? You? Oh, well, we're part of the same profession, aren't we. The profession of master illusionists. We invent taboos and then get people to consult us on how to evade them.'

'Sometimes,' I said, 'taboos aren't all we invent.'

He didn't pick it up. 'And how is England? Still going bankrupt in an affluent genteel way?'

'No ... I'd say still keeping solvent in a poverty-stricken harassed way.'

'It always amuses me,' he said, 'when people talk of England turning socialist. How can that be when every Englishman is at heart a capitalist? The most that can ever happen is a progressive liberalism of ideas in a community of obstinate conservatives.'

'We're tied to Europe.'

'Ah, and Europe is on the point of disintegration, eh? Quite so. Come here, Grutli, your ear is turned back. I don't like untidy dogs. If you can't control your ears, my little, we must tie them down with ribbon. What brings you back to Nice, Mr Gordon? Not the decay of Europe.'

'No,' I said. 'If it weren't in bad taste one might say the decay of Pierre Grognard.'

At times his face looked dark, as if in shadow. 'Oh, yes, of course. Pierre Grognard. Cigarette?'

'Thanks.'

He said: 'You've heard, of course, that he is dead.'

'I told you so last year.'

'But you were mistaken then. Because he was very much alive when I saw him in Grasse.'

'And also when he got married?'

'I spoke of his *intention* to get married on the Saturday. He obviously changed his mind. That day he must have left for Grenoble.'

'And what happened to Alix Delaisse?'

'She's still about somewhere.' He sighed. 'Oh, yes, you were interested in her. I remember now.'

'I haven't been able to trace her.'

'Perhaps she has married someone else.'

'D'you happen to know which hotel in Grasse Grognard stayed at from the Wednesday to the Saturday before his death?'

'How should I?'

'No. I only wondered if you could help me. I can find out.'

'Surely the subject's a little out of date.'

'It's just getting interesting to me.'

He inhaled and swallowed some smoke, sat very still

watching me. I listened for that faint tick-tick in his breathing.

I said: 'I shall spend a few days making inquiries in Grasse – then go on to Grenoble. There must have been an inquest, and Alix Delaisse would most likely have been called.'

'You feel under some obligation to Grognard's memory?'

'No ... But nobody likes to be fooled. Those were your own words. And I want to find Alix and know the truth.'

'I hope you're successful.' He got up. 'It's time for an aperitif. Even Pierre wouldn't object to our having that, I'm sure. He won't be any colder in ten minutes.'

He rang for drinks and we talked casually while they were brought.

I said: 'When I called last year I'd no idea how widespread your fame was. How does it feel to be so much admired?'

'Not very different from being hated. It gives one a feeling of being in the centre of things.'

'But hero-worship's pretty difficult to take, I should think. What are the antidotes you use?'

He glanced at me. 'Hero-worship, where it exists, comes I suppose from the old religious sense of wanting to bow down to something – it doesn't much matter what. It's like a biological function that's half atrophied.'

'Well ... The Führerprinzip, isn't it? Can you accept that?'

'One acknowledges its existence. One tries to rationalise it.'

I heard a car coming up the valley.

He said: 'The difficulty of course is that the demagogue is seldom adult enough to keep his balance. He lays down his own principles, his own laws, and then doesn't keep them. That's why he never lasts.' He had heard the car. 'Naturally I'm talking in general terms now. The popularity of Charles Bénat isn't likely to give anyone sleepless nights. Another drink?'

I accepted, and watched him pour it out. He began to talk about the occupation. That didn't prevent my hearing the car stop outside, the slam of the door, quick footsteps on the steps. Grutli began to get restive and his tail whacked the floor, but Bénat instead of saying anything just put a restraining hand on the dog's head. I got a queer premonitory twinge in my stomach.

Bénat said: 'How is John Chapel? Haven't seen him for six months or more, and then it was for only a word in the street. I often wonder what whim of fate—'

And then the door came open and Alix stood there.

I knew her at once of course.

When she saw me she went dead white, as if she was going to collapse. What colour I was I don't know, but just for the important seconds Bénat was looking towards the door. One hand on Grutli's head, he had the other to his lips. She looked from me to him, and he made a quick expressive jerk with his head.

'I'm sorry, Sarah,' he said. 'I haven't finished the papers. I'll see you in five minutes.'

Just for a moment I thought she was going to burst out, but she didn't. I took a grip of myself and looked away. It was just in time, because Bénat looked at me.

'These are Venetian wineglasses,' he said. 'You can probably feel the delicate cut of the stem. I found them in a hotel that had been commandeered for Italian officers. Pretty things.'

'Pretty things,' I said.

The door closed behind her.

I said: 'Do I know that person who's just gone out?'

'Sarah? I shouldn't think so. My secretary.'

There was a brief silence. We were both trying to think of something to say.

I finished my drink. 'Touching on Grognard, does anyone know why he was motoring to Grenoble?'

'I certainly do not. But then— Will you excuse me a minute? I think my secretary wanted to see me.'

'Of course.'

He got up and went out. The Great Dane rose and ambled after him, just getting his nose in the door as it swung to and levering it open again.

As soon as I was alone I stood up, listening. Bénat's footsteps went down the passage. I heard him call something.

Hands were uncertain with the shock of seeing her, and head in a whirl, but this opportunity had to be taken, and at once . . .

Round to the desk. There was a good spread of papers on it; some letters, what looked like invoices.

192

Glance over them. Restricted sight made this more dangerous, and I was careful to keep the unshuttered side towards the door. The quiet-walking manservant could be a danger. Grutli had left the door open, but there was nothing to do about it.

Letter from a client in Avignon about a will ... Marriage settlement on one Ambrosine Coste, post-office worker at Cannes ... Judgment given before M. le Procureur-Général in Paris ... Consignments of lavender invoiced. (Coals to Newcastle?) Estimate for repairs to windows ... Consignment of miscellaneous goods for M. Godeau of Roquebrune. Was Bénat a dealer?

Someone was moving about not far away.

A diary? Small black book was shut. No. A list of engagements. Very laconic. 'June 18: D.G., Sospel ... 22: Marcel C. Rue St-Martin ... 23: Dine at 9 with W.W.' (The dog was coming back.) '24: Café Gambetta.'

I moved round the desk and slid into my seat. The door swung wide and Grutli came in. A dozen paces behind was Bénat.

He stopped inside the door and lit a cigarette from the stub of the old.

'I'm sorry, Mr Gordon, I'll have to ask you to excuse me. My secretary has brought me some business that will have to be looked into at once.'

'Of course.' I got up.

His face appeared again out of the smoke. 'We haven't progressed far with your Grognard business, have we? I suggest that we have a meal together one evening next week. We can discuss it further then, eh?'

'Thank you.'

'Good. I'll get Mathieu to help you to your car.'

As I left the room the Great Dane came across and sniffed at my trouser leg.

'Queer,' said Bénat. 'I don't think Grutli likes you.'

CHAPTER SEVEN

I KEPT telling myself that at least she was alive and well, but by the next day I felt rather sick about everything. Up to now there'd always been the hope that she had somehow been prevented from seeing me or writing. Deep down – at least since reading of Pierre's death – there may have been a vague melodramatic expectation that she was locked away somewhere. At least it wasn't quite as third-form as that, but, having known her well enough to fall in love with her, one went on trying to find some explanation which would leave the shreds of self-respect.

Well, there had been no suggestion of coercion this morning. I'd seen her car on the way out, a new high-powered Studebaker. Beautifully dressed – in a cream linen frock with a tight bodice and yards of stuff in the skirt, crimson sandals and a crimson brooch – she'd looked perfectly confident and at home in the second before she saw me. Then her face had fallen, she'd gone pale, and turned and crept out. A real lover's welcome.

Nothing was made better by the effect of the meeting on me. Six weeks ago I had gone down to Portsmouth to see Rachel, and come away knowing I was free. All things considered, it might have been gratifying to feel the same about Alix. But that one short glimpse had had the opposite result.

Only one good thing came out of the confusion: the words Café Gambetta written in his book. The twenty-fourth would be next Monday.

Sunday was spent with the Wintertons. As soon as they knew I was back in France they had telephoned and made a date. I was glad now of somewhere to pass the time and some company to take my mind off things. But I didn't realise how much company.

The command was to arrive in time for drinks before lunch, and Claire met me in one of her usual flowing robes, kissed me like a favourite brother, and told me that as the American cruisers were in they'd invited half a dozen of the senior officers to lunch. Her hair was silver blue with a steely sheen in the bright sun.

She hardly said this before the American navy arrived behind me, and in a minute or two I was shaking hands with Vice-Admiral Carrol and Captain Grabo and half a dozen younger men. The room was in a babel of talk and it went on all through lunch. Walter was in his element, and the seal was set on the afternoon when Vice-Admiral Carrol worked it out that one of his ancestors must have been executed by order of Walter's ancestor, the Governor of Boston. After lunch things might have slacked off a bit, but Claire had had the bright idea of asking about a dozen of the best-looking girls in the neighbourhood to join us in a bathing party. This was a terrific success, and we spent the afternoon on the pebbly but pretty beach, lying under sunshades or swimming; and some of them put on goggles and breathing tubes and tried to spear mullet. I had my first swim for five years.

Tea and drinks were brought down from the house, and we sat on li-los and watched the sun move towards the thousand-foot cliff behind and the shadows of the beach wall creep across the stones. At seven the younger officers left, and I got up to go, but Claire waved her plump fingers disdainfully.

'Of course not, dear Giles. You have no duty to bother about. It's so nice to see you again after all this time. Sit down and have a drink, dear boy; I have a dinner-party all planned for nine.'

It isn't hard to give way when you're enjoying yourself, and I took a seat on the veranda. One sign of a good party is that it doesn't give you time to think. For some hours I'd nearly forgotten Alix, and I watched the colours quickening and changing on the sea and the mellow evening sunlight flushing the wooded promontory of Cap Ferrat. Villefranche was hidden from here. Let it stay so.

Walter was saying in his modest American voice: 'The whole trouble, Admiral, is that Lend-lease ended too soon. It should have gone on for five years after the war. That would have given Europe a chance to get on her feet again; *and* cost us less in the long run.' I lit a cigarette. I thought, no human being's ever satisfied for long; I've been restless since Friday; but put this on record: satisfaction here and now. Just in seeing the smoke curl up and the high cloudless sky going remote with evening, and the bougainvillaea climbing over the veranda wall. Just to be able to see. To hell with Alix.

I remembered saying that once before.

About eight we went in and got tidied up. I caught a glimpse of a dining-table set for fifteen. About half-past eight the guests started arriving.

The first two were French, a M. and Mme Lemaître. I'd heard his name in Nice and knew he was on the Conseil Général and had a hand in a good deal of local administration. A close-cropped man of fifty-odd with a serious unhumorous look, and wearing the ribbon of the Legion of Honour. His wife was a tiny little nonentity, round and soft and wrapped in wool. On their heels were Sir Robert and Lady Funchal, whom Claire had run to earth somewhere in Monte Carlo. Sir Robert had just retired from the Diplomatic Service and was thin and grey with a lot of delicate veins at his temples and the sides of his nose. Lady Funchal was nearly as tall as he was and looked like a neglected monument; all the ruins of great beauty were there.

A gap then, and we were all getting going among ourselves and drinking champagne cocktails when another man drifted in. He was about forty-five, tall, wary and sharp-faced, with thin nostrils. He talked like a Parisian and his name was Deffand. Behind him, but not with him, was a French actress, called Maggie Sorques. 'In Nice all through the war, dear Giles,' Claire cooed in my ear, 'and collaborated with practically *everyone*.' A fat little author called Henri Cassis came just before nine, and then a French naval officer, a

Captain Vigre, who was a prominent Gaullist. The last guests to arrive were Charles Bénat and Alix.

It was the second time in three days I'd had that sort of shock. It begins in the middle and works its way out, to the shoulders, the elbows, the knees, and the joints of the fingers. Then it's gone and everything's moving again.

Alix was wearing a frock of heavy white crepe cut Grecian style with a gold ornament, and the rest of the company suddenly looked drab. Claire sometimes did the introductions casually, but tonight, perhaps knowing Americans like the thing done properly, she was careful to go round.

Both Bénat and Alix had seen me and Alix had changed colour under her make-up; but there was no backing out of the door this time. When they got to me Bénat said:

'Mr Gordon, of course, we've had the pleasure of meeting before.'

After a minute I was holding Alix's hand for the first time for thirteen months.

'Madame Delaisse?' I said. 'Yes, indeed.'

Something in the way Alix looked made Claire raise her post-impressionist eyebrows. I watched them pass on. I'd just changed into ordinary untinted glasses, but didn't yet think they realised I could see. Anyway, it didn't much matter now. I made no movement towards them and we all chatted amiably until half-past nine, when dinner was served.

I got Mme Lemaître on one side of me, which wasn't much fun, and Deffand, the Parisian, on the other, there being not enough women to go round. Alix was put right opposite me. Between Captain Grabo and Sir Robert Funchal. I stared at her and stared at her.

I knew now why I sometimes caught the glint of her eyes in those first near-blind days. She had those rare eyes which attract the light, and whenever she turned her glance there was a glint from their clear whites. Claire had always been crazy about candles – at least ever since she was old enough to care about looking younger – and tonight there were three silver candelabra down the table. The general talk was partly in English in deference to the American guests – which was hard on Mme Lemaître, who didn't know a word of it; but I found that Alix knew more than she admitted. The exception was where Bénat talked in an undertone to Maggie Sorques. I noticed Alix look towards him once or twice. Claire had put Lemaître opposite Bénat, but although they must have known each other they hardly exchanged a word.

Alix kept glancing at me and then glancing away with a puzzled frown. Her skin was very fine with a faint tan, her amber-brown hair thick and with a deep sheen. She had a look of frankness and spirit. I'd thought her very young when we first met, but now she looked all of twenty-four, or whatever it was. I wondered if she'd matured a lot this year.

Half-way through the meal talk at the head of the table came round to the increase of violence everywhere. Sir Robert didn't take it seriously: crime always increased after a war, he said, the wonder was the majority of people were still so law-abiding. In five years things would be back to normal – always provided political revolutions didn't occur. Henri Cassis, the little author, had been listening, and he said in a voice just loud enough to carry up the table:

'Is it true there were two people murdered in Nice last night?'

A quiet voice will sometimes shut conversation down, and this did. Most of us looked at Lemaître, who seemed to be directly in the line of fire.

Lemaître said after a minute: 'In the Old Town. An affair of knives, I understand.'

'What was the cause of it?'

Lemaître shrugged his shoulders.

Admiral Carrol said: 'I read some place that the incidence of crime in the Alpes-Maritimes was higher than for the rest of France. That true, monsieur?'

'The difference is negligible, Monsieur l'Amiral. I would say that any department with a land frontier is slightly more susceptible.'

Lady Funchal said in her tired drawing-room voice: 'I suppose this department – French for only a matter of eighty years – has problems specially its own. And the large commingling of Italian blood – that will make it more liable to affrays. Like Corsica, in fact.'

Lemaître said: 'I see it differently. People have no faith these days, no courage. What symptoms of law-lessness there are are too widespread to be the problem of one department. The cause is not racial but moral.'

'You mean the Communists?'

'Ah, yes, the Communists,' said Captain Vigre, sitting up.

Lemaître chewed for a bit. 'Sir Robert, I think, excluded political unrest. For the moment I was doing the same.'

Walter said: 'Well, what's at the bottom of it all?'

Lemaître shrugged again. 'I'm sure it's not a subject to thrash out at your dinner-table.'

Charles Bénat sighed. 'We talk of courage. But perhaps M. Lemaître hasn't quite the moral courage to call a spade a spade.'

It was the first time he had joined in any general discussion. Lemaître said stiffly: 'That is as M. Bénat is pleased to think.'

Cassis put down his glass. 'I don't see how you can divide the social scene. Political, moral, economic causes: they all inter-relate and overlap. The sources of people's behaviour are always complex when you dig under the surface. It's pleasant to say, this man is a bad citizen because he is a Communist, or because he doesn't go to church or because he hasn't a living wage, but nothing is ever as simple as that.'

'I suppose you'd have us all psycho-analysed,' said Claire, staring interestedly at the tips of her silver-blue finger-nails.

Lady Funchal said: 'I always think of psycho-analysis as a science which explains everything and solves nothing.'

The conversation was a bit ragged and, except for the spark between Bénat and Lemaître, didn't seem to be getting anywhere. Lady Funchal had a way of flattening things out. Next to me the Parisian Deffand breathed hard through his long, thin nose.

'I have no objection to speaking plainly,' said Lemaître suddenly, as if he had made up his mind about something. 'The cause is moral – or social if you will. Its origins no doubt are as wide as M. Cassis insists. But much I lay at the door of the young men of M. Cassis's profession . . .'

'At mine, monsieur?'

'Well . . . the young writers, the intellectuals, the students, the men who think for their generation, who set the example – men often prominent in the best sense during the war. They were the leaders then, fighting the invader, risking death and torture. Those who died were rightly honoured as heroes. But some of those who lived – where are they now? Many are betraying their country as eagerly as they defended it!'

Bénat said something to Maggie Sorques which made her giggle. There was a minute's pause. Lemaître was getting heated. I think, from her expression, Claire thought of changing the subject, but didn't get it out in time. Alix unexpectedly was ahead of her.

'That's one side of the picture, Monsieur Lemaître.'

'And what is the other side, please, madame?'

She glanced at Bénat with her clear, cool eyes. 'Being a woman, I don't know it all. But one can see a little – try to understand. When a soldier comes back home from a war he has to change all his habits – just overnight. Yesterday he was a hero to kill other men. Today he would be a criminal. That is hard for a time, but there are many other changes to bring his mind back to peaceful ways. So often he comes back and there is no trouble ... The man who has been in a resistance is different. He doesn't come back; he stays just in the same place, and life goes on in the same way around him. His nerves have been at a greater stretch than the soldier, because for him there are no rest times, no leaves – and often for weeks he has worked alone, out of touch with his friends, not knowing if they are dead or have betrayed him. Well, he is in civil life already so he cannot come back to it – but all the laws of his land which it has been good to break are now suddenly no longer good to break. Everything is upside down. It isn't killing; it is the little things. Yesterday it was clever to travel without a ticket, to hoard food, to tear up the tramlines, to print false notes, to lie, to cheat, to steal. Today it is wrong. And not only have all the good laws come back but all the bad ones and the petty ones as well. Instead of the new world that he wanted to see he finds the old one thrust back on him with all its shabbiness, its frustrations, its betrayals ...' She stopped and looked again rather appealingly at Bénat. 'I cannot finish. You go on, Charles.'

Captain Vigre said: 'Yes. Bénat is still a name to conjure with. Twice captured, seven identity cards, decorated by de Gaulle. Let us hear you speak for your contemporaries, monsieur.'

Bénat moistened his lips with the tip of his tongue. 'This isn't the time for speeches. I shouldn't want to be thought of as the Führer of the dinner table.'

There was a laugh.

'No,' said Walter in his gentle drawl. 'We'd like to

hear what you feel. If you go on too long we can always cry quits.'

'I shall not go on too long because I have nothing to go on about,' said Bénat. 'What is M. Lemaître complaining of? He talks of betrayal, but that's a big word. He casts up the shadow of a lion, but I think it's only a mouse.'

'I'm complaining,' said Lemaître, 'of just what Mme Delaisse has spoken of. The revolt has continued. And I differ from her because I'm sure that with any faith or understanding it need not have continued at all. The intellectuals of M. Bénat's generation – seven out of ten of them – are working against France. Many have become Communists, I know. Their aim is the overthrow of liberty as generations of Frenchmen have come to know it. As for the de Gaullists, they claim a better intention, but I wonder what the end would be—'

'That,' said Vigre, 'is not the—'

'But tonight I'm speaking specially of a third group. They are the men who are anti-social for shoddy personal ends. They became outlaws under Darnand and Pétain. They remain outlaws under the Fourth Republic. The highly organised black market, the immense illegal currency deals, the smuggling of gold, the manufacture of absinthe, the violence and intimidation where it occurs: these are all the work of educated and intelligent men. One can tell by a sort of conceptual stamp ... Such men would be of untold value in any legitimate sphere.'

'Well said!' muttered Deffand.

'As it is, they are striking at the heart and stability of the country. And some of them, as I say, men with the most *admirable* of war records. They risked everything for France – now they are lining their pockets and living in luxury without caring what the cost will be.'

This time I heard what Bénat whispered to the actress. 'I thought *I* was supposed to be making the speech.'

'And so you shall,' said Lemaître, also hearing. 'But at least you can't say now that my complaint is unspecified.'

Another course was served. But there was no chance of the talk being diverted. Everyone was waiting for Bénat.

He dabbed his mouth with his table napkin. Alix was looking upset, and one could tell the argument touched her closely. I didn't like the way she looked at Bénat.

Bénat said: 'I haven't been briefed for the defence of my generation, so I can follow no instructions. Anyway, I'm entirely an individualist and couldn't pretend to speak for them.' He looked at Admiral Carrol with narrowed eyes. 'Always supposing there is any truth at all in M. Lemaître's accusations, which I of course question, I am going to shift the responsibility elsewhere. First, I'd say that what M. Lemaître mistakes for the failure of a generation is really the symptoms of a graver complaint. In fact, the most fatal of all diseases: old age. Europe has been civilised for centuries; senile dementia is now setting in. People try to disguise it; but the heirs are already quarrelling over the deathbed. America, however blatant and noisy – pardon me – has drawn from its parent most of Europe's one-time faith in human progress. Russia – a half-brother, for its mother was Asiatic – believes in the civilisation of the ant. They are irreconcilable and argumentative. Would you blame our generation for slipping away from the noise and smell of the sick room?'

Captain Vigre tried to say something, but Bénat went on.

'No doubt you blame those who accept the Marxist mystique. But why should you blame the few who have abandoned themselves with courage to the doctrine of despair? Simply because it makes them less satisfactory citizens in a world where an acceptance of citizenship means exploitation? How very good this Veuve Cliquot is, Mr Winterton. I've not often tasted better.'

'Thanks,' said Walter.

Deffand beside me broke his long silence. 'I'm a plain man, not an intellectual,' but he didn't say it apologetically. 'If you'll pardon me, all this seems to be a pretentious way of dressing up what's really only an evasion of common loyalty and common responsibility.'

Bénat's contemptuous bottom lip dragged a bit at one side. 'Let's be unpretentious then. Loyalty to whom?'

'To France!' said Lemaître. 'To one's fellow citizens. To democracy.'

'What loyalty do I owe to my fellow citizens? Supposing *I* wished to go in for a life of crime – which is not likely since I have as much money as I want – what would deter me? Dear, dear. Loyalty to the shabby politicians in Paris, who change governments once a week and spend their lives in political trickery and manoeuvre? Loyalty to the stupid peasantry or to the greedy property owners who now employ me in their legal troubles? Loyalty to those who escaped to England and stayed there all through the war making speeches? Loyalty to those who endured the occupation by first making a fortune out of the Germans and then doubled it catering for the Americans? Loyalty to the new rich or to the old poor? Loyalty to my old comrades in the resistance who have suffered the common disillusion? Ah, yes, perhaps. And how better to show it than by keeping one illusion alive? To me – as to some of them – there is only one God, Charles Bénat, world without end, amen.'

He smiled and put the wineglass to his lips again. 'The voice is Jacob's voice, but the hands are the hands of Esau. How much easier we all find it to talk than to act. Now it's Lemaître's move.'

'I have nothing more to say.'

Captain Grabo said: 'I can see the way M. Bénat feels, and he's put the case for the renegade, but it'll only be a question of time before these men are rounded up – just as they were in the States. Prohibition created an artificial social order, just as in a different way foreign occupation did here. Breaking the law was in fashion. When the artificial condition was removed it went out of fashion, and most of the gangsters went with it.'

Lemaître said: 'I think you will find that a strong new line is going to be taken over here. These men will be put down with a firm hand. Proof, we know, is hard to get, but—'

'Is there any truth,' Cassis said, 'in the rumour that a man from the Paris Sûreté is already at work in this area?'

Lemaître picked up his fork, scraped round his plate sombrely.

'I don't know,' he said.

I'd been watching the expressions on Alix's face. It came as a bitter pill to realise she was in love with Charles Bénat.

After dinner I saw her alone at the other end of the room, and moved round to speak to her. She didn't look towards me, but I could tell by some change in her attitude that she knew I was on the way.

I said: 'It's thirteen months since you telephoned. The taxi service in this town is bad.'

She didn't look up. 'Is your eyesight better, Giles? How much can you see?' At close quarters the 'round-ness' of her voice was deeply reminiscent.

'Enough to tell when the game isn't straight, I think.'

She flushed. 'I'm very sorry about last year. It must have seemed strange to you.'

'Strange isn't an overstatement.'

'Why have you come back?'

'I wanted to see you again. To see you for the first time.'

'It won't do any good.'

'So I noticed this evening.'

'What do you mean?'

'I came back, too, because of Pierre. Last year I found

him with a wound in his head, and it puzzles me how he got into a car afterwards and drove a hundred-odd miles into the mountains.'

She said in a cool undertone: 'Pierre had an accident in his car. That was all.'

'I suppose you did phone me from his flat that evening?'

There was a little burst of laughter behind us. Bénat was having fun with Cassis and Maggie Sorques.

'Oh, what's the use of talking about it?' Alix said. 'I don't want to talk about it. Pierre was nothing to you.'

'No,' I said, 'but you were.'

'I *wasn't*.'

'D'you remember the last day we spent together at Monte Carlo, and then home, where Pierre was waiting on the stairs?'

'I must have been crazy.'

'Agreeably so.'

She half turned as if wanting to get away. 'It was some midsummer madness. I was – sorry for you. Well, I'm not sorry for you any longer.'

'I'm glad of that. We can start on a different basis.'

She smoothed out a crease in her frock – a gesture that began gracefully enough, but ended with a disquieted flick. 'There's no question of starting again, Giles. I want to make it quite clear.'

'Nothing at all is clear at the moment.'

'Will you please go away. Go back to England. If you think I care anything for you, you're wrong. Please understand that.'

'Are you afraid of what I'll find out?'

'There's nothing to find out. Nothing you can find out. Pierre fell over a cliff, and was killed. He has been buried twelve months. D'you think anything you can do or say . . .'

'Why did you phone me that night?'

'I have regretted it ever since!'

'Well, that's something to go on.'

'It's *nothing* to go on. I've – regretted ever meeting you. It made you unhappy and – it was no use to me. It was a foolish interlude, without a future. Now it's over, has been a long time. I've got my own life to live – in my own way. Please leave me alone!'

Lady Funchal was drifting towards us. She seemed to have her eye on me. I said: 'Back in England I was laid up for a time – used to imagine meeting you, but it wasn't a bit like this. Is it you or I who have the grievance?'

She looked up through her lashes but didn't say anything.

I said: 'I've not often been good at telling myself fairy stories, but this was one I got away with. It helped a lot at the time. I knew you might be married to Pierre – if I was mistaken and he was alive; Bénat told me you'd married him – but I used to try and imagine it the other way. I used to think, the rest may be dross but that's pure gold – somehow; it must be. The thing I wanted sight for more than anything was to see you. Well, in a way, that's *quite* a success . . . But one thing's missing. I used to imagine a rather different sort of welcome. I seem to have been building castles in the wrong part of Spain.'

She said: 'Please leave me alone.'

The party went on until about two o'clock in the morning. We played chemmy, and I stayed till the end because I wanted to know where the Wintertons had met Bénat and Alix.

When the last guest had gone Claire said: 'Of course you must stay the night, Giles. We wouldn't *think* of your going home now! We still have a pair of your pyjamas and your old room's ready.'

I made various protests which as usual were swept aside. When Claire had got her way Walter said:

'Let's see, where *did* we meet the Bénats? It was at that evening affair at the Negresco, wasn't it? Last December, some sort of an evening celebrating the heroes of the Resistance. He was quite the lion of the evening. Made a witty speech, I remember.

'Then we saw them a second time at the Casino in Monte. She's a pretty creature, isn't she? Where had you met them before, dear boy?'

I said too casually: 'Oh, last year they were about Nice. In those days she was friendly with a man called Pierre Grognard.'

Claire moved her eyebrows into a cautious frown. 'By the way, Walter, conversation got rather dreary at dinner tonight. Arguments are such fun if no one takes them seriously. Lemaître might have been in his *cour d'assises*.'

I said: 'Who was the fellow sitting next to me, Deffand? He only opened his mouth twice.'

'We don't know,' Walter said. 'Lemaître introduced him. He's down from Paris for a month or two. Claire swears he's the man from the Sûreté.'

CHAPTER EIGHT

WHEN I got to Villefranche about five on the Monday I found it *en fête*. The crews from the American warships were ashore and the little inscrutable town was full of young sailors. Nearly all of them looked as if they'd just been turned out by some immense dry-cleaning store, as if they'd all been steamed and polished and brushed until no blemish was left. A single stain in a hundred duck suits would have stood out a mile. The town was fuller than usual of locals, girls and others who had come in to see the fun – or share it. The quay was as busy as any main street on a Saturday night, and much more interesting. Dark youths in turbans peddled oriental jewellery, old women sold scents, jeeps sputtered over the flagstones, cafés hung out banners of greeting, officers strolled about on their long non-European legs.

About eight a French military band appeared in honour of the visitors and played a number of marches with magnificent *élan* underneath the Hotel Welcome. Then a dance was started outside the Pavilion. I had passed the Café des Fourmis twice earlier on, but as dusk began to fall I climbed up again and made my way through the narrow alleys of the town.

Up here were the less immaculate of the visitors. A piano tinkled in a shabby bistro and a sailor danced with an Algerian girl. Their shadows swelled and shrank on the rough stone wall. Two older sailors, half drunk, argued interminably in the middle of the street with a naval policeman, while half a dozen ragged children gaped. A glare of light showed five ratings in another café flirting with some girls of the town.

There was a good deal of noise and music at the Café des Fourmis, but most of the noise was being made by the usual patrons. Four sober American lads sat self-consciously at a table by the door. I didn't go in but went across to the bistro on the other side. The official difference between a bistro and a café is that in a bistro you're supposed to stand at the bar for your drink. But this place, like many, had one table, and I found that from it you could look into the Café des Fourmis. I ordered a cognac and prepared to wait and see if anything happened.

Nothing did happen for half an hour, except that a few people entered and a few came out. Three more Americans went in and sat at another table without speaking to the four who were already there. A van drove up and some bales were brought up the alley and loaded into it. On the side of the van was 'Bonnet et Cie. Du pain bien boulangé. Rue des Martyrs, Nice.' I didn't take much notice of it until a reflection of light caught the face of the driver and I saw it was Scipion. I got up from the table and moved to the bar to pay, then strolled outside. The van had just started its engine. I heard Scipion say to a big man standing by the side: 'Back in an hour, maybe.'

The van drove off. The big man slouched into the café. The street was quiet again. I walked to the end and back. It was a quiet night but cool for the end of June. Down on the quay the music was fast and cheerful; the picket boats were busy like phosphorescent insects; and, a little withdrawn, the two cruisers glittered in the dark blue silence of the bay. I went back to the alley, and, seeing there was no one about, turned down.

It was dark between the high walls, and the narrow way was cobbled, with big uneven stones. But blindness teaches some things, and I didn't stumble or make a noise. At the bottom was a bit of a garden about twelve feet square with a low wall round it, and within the garden down some steps were two doors leading into the Café des Fourmis. One was ajar and a slit of light came through. The other was shut. I'd never heard a dog but it was something to look out for. Otherwise there didn't seem a lot of risk. I tried the gate and it opened easily.

There was a palm tree in the middle and a few vegetables growing; at the end were grape vines. Not an inch of space was wasted. The garden was about four feet above the level of the doors, and from half-way across it you could see into the room that was lighted. It was a store-room and wine cellar. There was no one in it. A couple of mosquitoes danced around the unshaded electric bulb. Then a man and an old woman came down. The man was a stranger, but I recognised the voice of Mère Roget. She was smaller and older than I thought.

She said: 'They should have sent two vans. My God, what organisation. By the time they come back it will be midnight.'

'No,' said the man. 'It's only half an hour's run each way. And if it is too public we'll send them back and they can come tomorrow.'

Mère Roget picked up an armful of bottles. 'I don't like it. We have had the stuff a week. Get rid of it, I say. What are the Americans drinking?'

'Not much. They are not the right type.'

They went back up the stairs.

Silence fell. Down in the next street two voices were singing:

> 'It ain't kinda fair on Maudie,
> Who's faded round the edges
> An' a haybag too . . .'

Some of the right type for Mère Roget.

Down the steps and up to the first door. I tried the latch, but the door would not open. On to the next door. It was plain that the cellar was empty. Wooden steps led up to the kitchen above, but some sort of a door had been shut at the top because the voices from up there were muffled. In the left-hand wall of the cellar was another door, leading into the second cellar whose outer door I'd tried.

Weigh up the risks. If the communicating door was

open it wouldn't be difficult to slip through the lighted cellar to the other. What gain? A knowledge perhaps of the goods Mère Roget didn't like to store.

One does things on impulse sometimes and without the best of reasons. It didn't seem so rash at the time.

Open the door eight inches more; inside, the smell of wine and straw and old stone; shut the door the same amount. Six steps across the flagged floor. The middle door was shut. Lift the latch. It's open. Very dark. Go in and pull the door to behind you, then quietly lift the latch and shut out the last light. Well, that much done.

Same smell in here. I felt for the switch and found it, but this seemed too risky just at present. A match. Four scrapes before it flickered. Square cellar. Wine bottles by the dozen poking their heads out at me. Bales of the sort I'd seen loaded; boxes; big square cardboard containers sealed along the tops with brown paper.

The match went out.

I thought of my lighter and fished that out. The flame was smoky but one wasn't always burning one's finger. I went across to the bales. They were heavy and fairly hard. The one I looked at was stamped 'G. Ravallo, Napoli'. I got out my penknife and slid it along the seam of the bale. These things are never as easy to open as you hope, and by the time I'd made a sizeable gash it didn't look such a good idea. Outside I could hear the two Americans going on with their song.

> 'It ain't kinda fair
> In this one-horse town
> On a high-class dame like Maudie . . .'

218

I pulled back the wrappings and found some sort of grey wool, tugged it out and found it was a pair of socks. That was a bit of a surprise. Then I turned them up and saw them stamped 'Made in USA'.

Someone started coming down the steps. I slid down behind the bale and waited.

It didn't seem to be Mère Roget this time. Two men were talking, and there was the rattle of bottles again. I hoped the wine they wanted was in the first cellar. They were arguing about something, but I couldn't get the hang of it.

. . . After an age they went up again, and I re-lit the lighter. There were about twenty such bales as the one I'd opened. I went over to one of the cardboard containers and used the penknife again. The top of the thing was full of corrugated cardboard and shavings, but underneath were packets of cigarettes in clusters of five twenties held together with gummed paper; it didn't seem worth adding up how many there might be in each container.

Time to go. The object of coming here was served. I stuffed a couple of packets of twenty into my pockets, and the socks into my breast pocket. I'd had enough last year of telling stories without evidence. I blew out the light and picked up my stick. All quiet outside. Heavy feet were moving overhead, and the piano had begun again. Not this time with Blind Giles and his Provençal songs. I opened the door into the other cellar and saw a man standing by the steps looking at me.

He was a big man, nearly as tall as myself and much heavier. He'd evidently been watching for me to come out because he had a knife in his hand. We looked at each other and his jaw dropped. There was one thing to do.

I poked about with my stick and said: 'Is anyone there? I don't know where the devil I am. I've gone wrong somewhere.'

He licked his lips and fingered the knife blade with his thumb. Then abruptly he reached up and thumped on the door above. I began to grope towards the outer door.

'Stop!' he said. It was my one-time friend the fisherman.

I turned eagerly. 'Roquefort! And I have been looking for you everywhere! After all this time. Where are you?'

I changed my direction but still contrived to get a bit nearer the door.

'Stop,' he said again. 'What are you doing down here, monsieur?'

I said: 'They kept telling me this wasn't the Café Gambetta, and I know it is, so I tried to find my way in by a back entrance.'

He thumped again. This time there was an immediate answer, and he moved aside as Mère Roget and the other man came down.

Mère Roget said: 'What . . .' and then stopped as she saw me.

'He was down here,' said Roquefort. 'In the other cellar. I heard him moving when I came down.'

The other man began to sidle round towards the door.

I said: 'Who's there? Roquefort! Why is everyone so unfriendly?' Another step.

NIGHT WITHOUT STARS

'Don't move,' said Mère Roget. 'How have you got in here?'

'Mère Roget!' I said. 'I saw Alix yesterday and was asking how you were. I'm glad I've found you all at last.'

The other man stopped moving when the old woman jerked her thumb at him. I could see she was weighing it all up. She didn't know what to make of it, and didn't want bloodshed. It all meant more danger from the police.

'My name is not Mère Roget,' she said. 'That was a little joke we had, monsieur. Then the joke was over and we didn't want you here any more so we did not admit you. If you want to know all about it, go and ask Alix.'

'I did ask Alix, and she told me the same thing. And Roquefort and his butterflies. Was that all part of the joke?'

She said to him in an undertone: 'Go and see if anything has been touched.'

I knew then that this bluff wasn't going to last much longer. I watched Roquefort move towards the middle door.

'And Scipion,' I said. 'And the others. What a curious display of bad taste! Do you often get fun out of people's infirmities?'

Nobody answered. Roquefort went in and switched on the light.

'Anyway,' I said. 'I'm not going to push in where I'm not wanted.'

I turned and went out through the door slamming it

221

behind me. Then I made across the path in great strides as the man tried to open it again behind me. Passing the second door I heard Roquefort drawing back the bolt. For once I slipped in the dark, but got out into the alley with probably a couple of yards' lead. The gate banged, might hold them a moment, but two more men loomed up suddenly on my blind side and I knew I was done. One of them clutched my arm and I was just going to do something about it when he said:

'What's the hurry, pal? Just hit the turn into the straight?'

The other put his arm heavily round my shoulders and breathed rye whisky.

'*Pardon, monsieur,*' he said. '*Avez-vous un . . . Est-ce-que vous avez un . . .* What'n hell's the French for match, Joe?'

'*Allumette,*' I said, rather short of wind. 'And I've got one here if you'd like it.'

The first man went off into a crow of laughter.

'He's English, Herbie. Just when you were getting warmed up, too.'

Herbie waved a dignified hand. '*Merci, monsieur. Je vous remercie pour le louer de votre allumette. Le soir est beau, n'est ce pas? Voulez vous joindre nous dans un – un boisson?*'

I said: 'Were you the two who were singing just now?'

'Yeah,' said Joe. 'Like to hear us? Herbie: Feller here wants to hear us.'

I said: 'Let's wait till we get to the top of this alley.'

CHAPTER NINE

IN THE hotel next morning in the light of day it looked different, but at the time I felt lucky to get away. I didn't waste any more time than I could help with Herbie and Joe, and was glad to be out of the town.

It was plain from now on that I'd do well to keep clear of Villefranche. Nobody there loved me any more, and they might not be willing to waste opportunities arguing next time. I smoked one of the cigarettes, and it seemed good Virginian tobacco. But when I looked the socks over I found I was wrong about one thing. They weren't grey, they were khaki.

By the afternoon post a letter came from Charles Bénat.

'DEAR GILES GORDON,
    'We didn't have an opportunity for private conversation at the Wintertons' last night, but I see that you will require more in the way of satisfaction than I have so far been prepared to give you. You, I think, owe something in way of explanation, too. I shall be in Marseilles until Friday, but if you will care to come to dinner that evening perhaps we can

talk this thing over in a friendly spirit and come to
an understanding. If you can let me know, I will
send a car down to your hotel to pick you up about
seven.

> 'Yours sincerely,
> 'CHARLES BÉNAT.'

So friendly a note was a surprise. I wondered if he'd
heard of last night's adventures when he wrote.

I spent the afternoon writing; it seemed a common
precaution. About six the telephone rang. It was the
porter.

'A Mme Delaisse to see you, monsieur.'

Something missed a beat. 'Where? In the hotel?'

'Yes, monsieur. At the desk.'

I said: 'I'll come straight down – no, will you ask her
please to come up.'

'Very well, monsieur.'

I stood and looked about the room, swept up the
papers I'd been writing, shoved them into a drawer on
top of collars and socks, put my jacket on. I'd time to
straighten my tie before the knock came at the door.

When she came in her expression was rather taut. I
wondered where that little teasing self-deprecating
laugh had gone. It wasn't just I who had changed.

She stood with her back to me for a minute while I
shut the door. She was wearing a scarlet frock with a
white collar.

I said: 'Whatever you've come for it's good to see
you.'

She said: 'How soon can you leave Nice?'

I walked over to the window and pulled up the Venetian blind, for the sun had left the front of the hotel.

'Sit here. It's cool and airy and we can talk.'

She came slowly over. 'Giles, I am not playing. You had better leave Nice at once.'

I looked at her sitting on the chair, went on looking. 'Why?'

'You should know that. Why did you go round to the café last night?'

'Temperamental impulse. Do they feel annoyed?'

'They phoned this morning. I didn't tell Charles before he left for Marseilles.'

'Thanks for the breathing space. So I've got till Friday?'

She looked quickly at me. 'How do you know?'

I told her about the invitation. 'It's too much to resist a promise of an explanation, don't you think? After all this time?'

She began to fumble in her handbag, but I got out my cigarette-case and offered her one. As she took it I said: 'Recommended. Special Villefranche brand.'

She looked at the cigarette. 'You must be crazy, Giles. You must be mad. You've recovered some of your sight. Why didn't you go somewhere and enjoy yourself? What good is all this prying and interference going to do you?'

I stopped with the lighter not yet burning. 'D'you really need that explaining?'

'Then what . . .?'

'I don't care what black-market business Charles and

your Villefranche friends are running. I don't even care who killed Pierre Grognard. He's in his grave and can stay there. It's nothing to me. Don't you realise that?'

She looked at me. Then she flushed as she'd done at the Wintertons' place.

'. . . If you care for me you'll not interfere with my friends.'

'Oh, rot; rubbish; nonsense. What else can I do? Why don't you tell me what there is to tell? I'm no Puritan. There's a black market in England as well as in France. I don't think much of it, but I shouldn't rush to the police at the first sign. I like murder a lot less, but it's not my job to bring every criminal in. Grognard's death worried me a good bit because I found his body. Is that unnatural?'

'Part of it isn't my story to tell—'

'All right then! I came for an explanation, which it isn't unreasonable to expect. I wanted an explanation, but if you can't or won't give it me, then let's drop it. Drop it for good and all. Grognard's buried and Villefranche forgotten. But what I'm not prepared to forget is *you*. I want to see you, talk to you, have your friendship – at least for a little while, just to make sure. You say last time, last year you were sorry for me and that was why . . . Well, I don't believe it! You say it was all a mistake. That may be. But it was your mistake, not mine. And I want a reasonable chance of being convinced that it was even yours . . .'

I lit the lighter, a bit out of breath, but she seemed to have lost her cigarette or something, so I lit my own.

She said in a different voice: 'I think I can tell you about Villefranche. That first day, when it was wet, I knew I shouldn't really take you to the café; but in a way I wanted to. You were – likeable, and on impulse I wanted them to meet you. Their real selves, you know, are the people you met when I was with you, not the people of last night ... Well, when I took you that first time, just to be on the safe side I told you the names we'd used during the war – still use sometimes – so that no one knew who people or places were. When we went in that first time I asked for Mère Roget. It was a cue to them to use these other names which during the war had become almost as familiar to them as their own. The only one who kept his real name was my brother-in-law, Armand, because he was away, a prisoner, and didn't have any other. It was not really intended to deceive you, but to reassure them. It was intended as a defence against their criticism. If they said, you shouldn't have brought him here, I could say, but he knows nothing, not even your real names ...'

'Good,' I said. 'That lets out Villefranche.'

'I wish it did. But now with your interference last night it's no longer for you to say when this shall be dropped. Do you think you'd wish to drop it if you were in their position? Their existence now depends on your good-will. And why should they think you have any good-will for them at all? Perhaps nothing will be done until Friday, but you should leave by this evening's train.'

'And if I stay?'

'Your life will not be safe.'

There was a pause. I looked out of the window. 'That your car?'

'Yes.'

'It's the model they call the sideways Studebaker, because you can't tell whether it's coming or going.'

'Perhaps.'

'I think that's the nearest thing we've got so far to the design of the future.'

'I haven't come here to discuss cars.'

'No,' I said, 'but it's a long way from a shoe-shop and an apartment in the Old Town to driving an expensive American car and wearing the clothes you wear now.'

She said: 'I've come here to warn you. I can't do more.'

'Why bother even to do that?'

She shrugged slightly and was silent.

'Old times' sake?' I inquired.

'If you like.'

I said: 'You've changed, Alix. God knows what's done it, but you're only half the same person. You wouldn't have come over from the shoe-shop, have tried to help me this year.'

'Stop being – interested in me then, and go.'

'I'm not interested in you, I love you . . .'

There was a pause after that. Three or four people were round her car, staring at it.

I said: 'Believe me, I'd get some satisfaction out of leaving this town for good, but it wouldn't solve anything for me. So just for a little while I'm not going.'

She looked up at me. 'You're a sticker, aren't you?'

I tried to smile at her. 'Obstinate streak.'

She said: 'You'll soon forget me. You're romantic and think yourself into loving me. There are plenty of other women in the world who will fall for that story – and enjoy it. You're quite young, nice-looking, have some money, I suppose. It shouldn't be hard.'

I watched her but didn't speak.

She said after a minute: 'You think you love me. I don't want that sort of love. If you married me you'd soon want a change. One gets tired of the same diet, week in, week out. Well, I don't want to begin.'

I walked across the room and back. 'What *are* you afraid of?'

'Afraid of? Nothing.'

'Yes, you are. I've only just realised it, realised it isn't quite what I thought.'

She stretched out the toe of her scarlet shoe, stared at it. 'Always such imagination.'

'Painful lack, I should think, not to have seen that much before.'

'No, no, be honest. It's not fair to keep thinking up new excuses for staying.'

I sat down opposite her. 'Listen, Alix. You've been to the wrong school—'

'Yes,' she said, looking up, pushing back her hair. 'I've been to the wrong school. It's the school of experience, where people have to face facts and not dream silly dreams—'

I said: 'No, that's the school of Charles Bénat.'

She said: 'Leave Charles out of this . . .'

229

WINSTON GRAHAM

'How can we if he's so deep in? You're living with him, in love with him apparently. No doubt he's a brave man and a clever one – still has the glamour of the Resistance. He's got a following, people admire him. But believe me, he's plain poison. Already you've imbibed half of his sham philosophy—'

'No,' she said, and got up. 'Stop, Giles, you needn't say any more. I only came here to warn you – to ask you to leave Nice. Will you do that?'

I glared at her. 'Like hell I will.'

Her lips were trembling, but I think it was anger. She was as furious with me as I was with her.

I said: 'I know Bénat's attitude to women. Well, that's his look-out. What he looks for he'll find, and good luck to him. But I could kill him for applying those standards to you.'

'He hasn't applied those standards to me!' she said. 'My God, must you *always* think in terms of sex? Aren't there any other ideas in your head?'

'There might be if you were honest with me just for a change.'

'I've told you no lies this afternoon, Giles. Charles is my brother.'

CHAPTER TEN

I wrote to Bénat.

> 'Dear Charles Bénat,
>
> 'Thank you for your invitation to dinner on Friday evening. I shall be glad to accept. Don't, however, bother to send down for me; I can arrange transport.
>
> > 'Yours sincerely,
> > 'Giles Gordon.'

On Wednesday morning I went round to see John. He was busy, and I didn't stay more than a few minutes.

'Listen, Johnny; I've an envelope here I want you to keep for me. If you don't hear anything from me on Saturday morning will you pass it in to the police?'

He stared at me. 'That won't be much comfort to you if I have to, will it? Frankly old boy, are you one step nearer finding out what happened to Pierre Grognard?'

'I'm not sure. Did you know that Alix Delaisse was Charles Bénat's sister?'

'Good God, no! You've traced her, then?'

'Yes, she's living at the Villa Lavandou.'

John said: 'Come to think of it, they're not really unlike. I only saw her properly once. But what was she doing in a shoe-shop?'

'Have you heard of a man called Deffand?'

'Ye-es . . .'

'Have you heard there's going to be a serious attempt to clean up the black market?'

'Yes. Periodically they make these threats, but nothing much ever comes of them. Trouble is that the people who are trying to put it down probably buy nearly all their own things that way. The rot's gone too deep.'

I took out the socks. 'Have you seen this sort of thing before?'

'Um? Where did you get them?'

'Oh, knocking about. What would they be worth in a shop?'

'Dear me, old boy, I'm not a draper. Three or four hundred francs perhaps. What did they cost you?'

'They've cost me nothing – yet.'

'I note the qualification.'

I said: 'Johnny, where would I go to hire a car for a few weeks – to drive myself?'

'There's the De la Rue Garage just round the corner from here. Say I've sent you. In any case they'll probably charge you the earth.'

'I've a feeling my allowance will last me as long as I want to stay.'

He looked up. 'Thinking of going home? Good. Best news I've heard. Well . . . you know what I mean.'

'Don't write me off yet. Anything can happen in a fortnight.'

Johnny chewed his pen. 'Who told you they were brother and sister?'

'She did herself.'

'D'you think it's true? I mean, she hasn't always been the most truthful of—'

'The resemblance is there, as you say – in the build and colouring, and still more in the way of speaking. I should have recognised that.'

'Did she say why she was living as she was when you first met her?'

'She said she'd quarrelled with him.'

'I wonder if Grognard knew they were related.'

'I hope to find that out on Friday.'

I went to the De la Rue Garage and arranged about a car. Not that I was going to use it on Friday, but I wanted to be able to have one on tap if needed. I phoned Maurice in Cagnes, and arranged for him to pick me up at the hotel on Friday. To take a chauffeur to the Villa Lavandou seemed a reasonable insurance against harm.

Later that day, coming out of the bank, I saw Scipion on the other pavement. I'd been conscious once or twice of being overlooked. Not knowing how much I could see, they were probably less cautious than they might have been.

Some of the Villefranche people could be intimidating if they turned nasty, but Scipion was not one of them. When he saw me coming he turned his back, but I touched him on the shoulder.

'Join me in a Pernod. It's a long time since we had one together.'

'I don't know you, monsieur,' he said stolidly.

'Oh, yes, you do. And you can't watch me better than by sitting at the same table.'

He said: 'I don't know you, monsieur.'

'Well, have it your own way. Share a drink with a perfect stranger.'

'I've no wish to do that, thank you.' But I took his arm in a friendly way, and led him into a café. It was difficult for him to refuse without making a scene, so he sat there uncomfortably and sipped his Pernod. I tried to get him talking, and after a bit he began to thaw. Whatever his name really was he couldn't resist the old soldier appeal. Then I asked him about his ulcer. It hadn't been too good but he wouldn't see a doctor again. Seeing a doctor meant admitting something to himself. I told him he was a fool and he looked at me with anxious bloodshot eyes and argued it out. Suddenly he blinked and shook himself.

'I should not be sitting here. You are too friendly, too winning.'

'In a war we'd kill each other without the least ill-will. We can surely share a drink in the same spirit.'

He said: 'It would be hard to explain to the others.'

'I won't tell them.'

'You pretended to be blind, didn't you?'

'No pretence to begin with.'

'Then how did you know I was – Scipion?'

'I recognised your voice when you came into the café last week.'

'What is your object in all this?'

'I wanted to find Mme Delaisse again. I've done that, so you can keep your café.'

'You are – not very safe, monsieur.'

'The danger will subside when Charles Bénat comes back.'

He said in surprise: 'You know him?'

'Yes. I'm dining with him on Friday evening at his villa.' He stared at me and blinked quickly.

'What is the name of his villa?'

'Lavandou. This will be my third visit.'

'Where is it?'

'In the hills beyond Vence.'

'You have some arrangement with him?'

'I've no arrangement with him, but I'm going to talk it all over with him. I certainly shan't go to the police before Friday night, so you can call off your dogs till then.'

He said: 'I wish I could believe you.'

'Phone up Mme Delaisse and see. I talked the whole thing out with her yesterday.'

He got up. 'I must go now.'

'Finish your drink.'

'Thank you, no. I must go and report.'

I watched him move away among the tables. The meeting had been worth forcing because it might prevent any hasty action before Friday. They might telephone Charles Bénat in Marseilles, but the chances were they'd hold off until after my visit to the Villa

235

Lavandou. I knew Alix would back me up if they consulted her.

Anyway I was safe enough as long as I kept about in public places.

I got up to the Villa Lavandou at eight o'clock on the Friday.

It was a thundery evening, with heavy clouds coming in from the mountains. I thought of 'Up through the darkness, while ravening clouds, the burial clouds, in black masses spreading, lower sullen and fast athwart and down the sky.' Big spots were splashing on the bonnet of the car as we drove through the fields of lavender; over the sea the sky was still clear like a taut green flag.

Maurice had wanted to go back and come for me again at midnight, but I persuaded him to stay. Charles Bénat was waiting for me when I was shown in, and came across and shook hands. He shook hands the way he talked, grasped the subject briefly and then dropped it away from him. Grutli rose from the splendid hearth-rug and gave a low growl.

Bénat said: 'Good of you to come.' His glance flickered over me. 'Let me get you a drink. Alix will be down in a few minutes.'

I was pleased to hear it. 'This time I can admire your room,' I said.

The whole thing was in good taste, but rather extravagant, the ceiling being white with cinnamon tracing; and there were cinnamon satin draperies and a good lot of delicate wrought-iron work.

He said: 'I've already apologised for it once, but it amused me at the time. Let me see, you like gin, don't you. And French, was it? I think we shall have thunder this evening.' He came back with the glass. 'And how's the black market?'

I stared down at Grutli who was sniffing at my chair. 'I've some socks at home I should have worn tonight, but they didn't match. Khaki's a difficult colour.'

'Khaki market, d'you think?'

'My own guess is that they're surplus army stock, sold in bulk in Italy by someone who'd no business to have them – shipped here illegally from Naples, and sold at about four times what they fetched in Italy. Of course it's only a guess.'

'A good guess. But they'd be dyed before they were sold. It helps distribution.'

I met his gaze. 'Yes?'

'Yes,' he said. 'Cigarette?'

I took one.

'Chesterfields,' he said. 'Bought illegally and sold on the black market at two hundred per cent profit. Ah, here comes Alix. I believe you've been seeing something of her in my absence.'

'A bit.' I got up.

She looked lovelier every time I met her, but perhaps that was my delusion. Anyway she'd never greeted me yet with a smile in her eyes. Tonight she looked uncomfortable but at least not unfriendly.

'And here too,' said Bénat, 'comes the rain. Lucky you arrived in time; it's always disagreeable driving in these downpours.'

We went in to dinner with the rain roaring on the roof. As we sat down there was a crash of thunder and Alix looked round quickly. The manservant pulled the curtains across.

Bénat said: 'D'you remember that evening at home, Alix, when the *curé* came to dinner and the chimney of the house next door was struck by lightning?'

Alix pulled in her skirt as she sat down, stared with grave cool eyes at the table. 'And the bricks fell on our roof and Henri dropped the plates. Father Verré was terrified.'

'Not without reason. He suspected it was a visitation from God.' Bénat indicated my seat. 'A greedy old satyr, Verré. Debauched half the girls in the village.'

'I thought you lived in Dijon,' I said to Alix.

'Just outside. But of course you know that ... My father was a country doctor.'

'Who died in a ditch in a drunken stupor at the age of fifty-four. You'll take the oysters, Gordon? They're not black market, so your nonconformist digestion will not be taxed.'

I said: 'My digestion's strictly undenominational.'

She moved in her chair. 'Why do you say that about Father, Charles? It *completely* misrepresents him ...'

Charles looked at me with a slight lift of his eyebrows. 'Quite true. But it's the only thing I ever admired my father for, and I like to remember him by it. It was the only big-minded gesture he ever made.'

She said abruptly: 'This must be boring you, Giles.'

'Not at all.'

She toyed with her fork for a minute. 'Well, in fairness it can't be left there.'

'Don't spoil the story.'

'When I was nine,' she said, 'my mother went off with another man, went to live in Paris. It was a – great shock to my father – naturally ... when he realised it was true he went into Dijon and got drunk. It was the first time he'd ever been drunk in his life, and on the way home he – fell and died from exposure. It was—'

Charles said: 'The only thing which spoils the memory is that the whole thing was plainly unintentional.'

I didn't say anything. I looked at Alix's long-fingered hands with the fork in them, at the cameo on her breast; it was an old one; I watched it rise and fall.

'And your mother?' I said to Charles.

'My mother was an intelligent woman who found herself at nineteen tied by arrangement to a dull little man of forty. The only grievance I have against her is that she bore and bred us before going off to live a life suitable to her gifts.'

'How would you wish to have been born and bred?' I asked.

Bénat looked at me. The question interested him. 'I think I should like to have been the first experimental ovum split and reared in a test tube. One might have stood a chance of growing up without so many of the usual complexes.'

'I doubt it. You'd have been a mass of clinical frustrations.'

Alix murmured: 'The clinical perhaps as well as the cynical.' There was a bubble of amusement in her voice.

Bénat looked slightly irritated, but he didn't reply. 'I haven't to give you a description of the dishes that come in, have I, Gordon? It would be embarrassing explaining the *bouillabaisse*.'

'Thanks. I can see very well.'

'As you could on your last visit.'

'Yes . . . I didn't know you so well then.'

'And last year?'

I told them. They listened closely. I couldn't read Bénat at all. He was both polite and off-hand, so that when you seemed about to see behind his courtesy he had turned his mind away and lost interest in you. In his own odd way there was something faintly regal about him. He wasn't putting on a show of not being interested in what I'd found at Villefranche; he really didn't care.

We were about half through dinner before he said: 'I suppose you want me to tell you something about Pierre Grognard.'

'If it's agreeable to you.'

'Hardly agreeable . . . But I've considered it all round. On certain conditions I should be willing to tell you what I know.'

'The conditions?'

'Some you may find distasteful.'

I looked at Alix. 'Well?'

He said: '(A) that you tell no one else what we tell

you. (B) that you stop making tiresome inquiries. (C) that you leave Alix alone.'

A nasty little sting in that, coming suddenly at the end. I was still looking at her, but she kept her eyes away.

'By (A) I suppose you mean, not tell the police?'

'Among others. Yes.'

'Is it Alix's wish that the third condition is put in?'

After a minute she said: 'It was Charles's idea to tell you the truth – Charles makes his own conditions.'

'But do you want me to accept them?'

She met my eyes for a half second over the top of her wine glass. 'Yes . . .'

I didn't say any more while the next course was served. Since the first meeting with her a week ago I'd tried to believe she was unfriendly because of what I might discover. Now I could cheerfully have got up from the table and gone.

Charles said: 'Well, Giles?'

I said: '(A) I agree to. Fair enough. (B) goes without saying. I'm bored with them as it is. (C) is . . .' Stop again and think a minute. '(C) goes a bit far. I can't tie myself so closely without knowing what you're going to tell me. If I'm satisfied at the end that Alix doesn't want to see me, I'll drop out quickly enough without invitation.'

Bénat sighed. 'Disagreeable, bargaining with a guest. That's one thing we never did with Pierre.'

She put her hands down on the table suddenly. 'I don't think I can go through with this, Charles.'

'Oh, Giles *must* have his curiosity satisfied! What do

you say? Is it to be left to his decision whether he shall go on pestering you or not?'

'My pestering so far,' I said acidly, 'has consisted of one uninvited visit up here.'

'Yes,' he said casually, 'but it won't be confined to that, will it, unless we take some precautions? Tenacity is a sign of the bulldog breed. Let me fill your glass.'

I said: 'D'you insult all your guests so charmingly?'

'Only those who are intelligent enough to understand and conceited enough to care.'

Alix said: 'Oh, what's the use of this, Charles? If you intend to tell Giles about Pierre, then tell him. You can't make conditions.'

'Would you rather I made threats?'

'No, of course not.'

'Then I make conditions.'

'I accept the first two,' I said. 'The third I think must wait.'

He broke a piece of biscuit and gave it to Grutli. 'Oh, well, perhaps that's for Alix to consider. I leave it to her. Shall we go into the other room?'

CHAPTER ELEVEN

HE SAID: 'Am I the only one to take cognac? Really all the other wines only set the right note for this.'

His thin sallow face had no flush on it as I felt there was on mine; I glanced at Alix, who was standing by the window, one hand on Grutli's shoulder. The rain had stopped; its drumming had been with us nearly all through dinner; now the piled clouds were turning and splitting one over the other so that soon the sky would show.

I said: 'Is your mother still alive?'

Alix half turned but looked away again, waiting for Charles to take it up.

'She's in Barcelona at the moment. She got mixed up with some Colonel who had to leave the country when the Germans retreated. She must be forty-nine by now. Getting stout, I expect. She had a few years of freedom before she let this sex business clog her life again.'

Alix said: 'You were going to tell Giles about Pierre. I married Jacques Delaisse in 1944. That's how you should begin. Two months later he was captured and hanged.'

'He won't understand anything if you tell him that way.'

'Then tell him your own way, but get it over. I think that will cure him of his ambitions to associate with us.'

Bénat said: 'Nonsense. There's a glamour about murder. Especially to those who've led sheltered lives.'

I said: 'So it was murder.'

'If you accept the conventional definition.'

'Which of course you don't.'

For once I caught his gaze. He smiled perfunctorily.

'As a matter of principle, no.'

'Do you for loyalty – or any of those things?'

'Well, loyalty is only another name for enlightened self-interest, isn't it?'

'I wonder that you're willing to trust my self-interest.'

'It's an experiment.'

'Rather an expensive one for you if it doesn't come off.'

'Oh,' he said. 'You have no proof. And it would be expensive for you too.'

We stared at each other. 'Go on, then.'

'I'm afraid it will take a little time. I must first explain that during the war I controlled this district for the CADF, which worked in liaison with the Forces Françaises de l'Intérieur. Among the two hundred men and women under me were both Pierre Grognard and Jacques Delaisse. I believe they were close friends, but their work for the Resistance was quite different. Pierre was used for contacts and intelligence, Jacques was an active saboteur. Pierre I knew slightly, Jacques not at all. If you're unfamiliar with the way the underground movement worked that may seem strange, but in fact of all the people under me I only knew twenty-eight by name. Knowledge was danger, instruction was by contact, the movement interlocked, but everyone's knowledge stopped short at the first, second or third link beyond himself – usually the first. It was the only sure way of cutting one's losses . . . My sister began carrying messages when she was eighteen. Sometime after that I heard she was going to marry Jacques . . . I couldn't give my consent to the wedding or be present at it because at the time I was living with a goldsmith in Toulon under the name of Flaubert. I made some inquiries about Jacques from a friend who knew him and was told that he was handsome, agreeably reckless, and enthusiastic in his work for the movement. That was all I knew, but my own feeling was that a man like Delaisse could hardly have the character or the breeding for Alix . . .'

I tried to tell from the silhouette of Alix's head against the window how much she resented this, but she didn't stir.

'However, in April of that year, 1944, I was arrested in Antibes – and this time identified. A disagreeable experience.' He got up and went to the table. 'I didn't suggest a Benedictine. Would you like that?'

After hesitating a second I said I would.

'They didn't give you Benedictine at the Villa Mont Fleur. But they had other means of loosening the tongue. They burned my feet chiefly; that's why I limp. If—'

'Don't say any more about that, Charles.'

'Well, it's an experience not without its own peculiar

adventure. There's a point at which pain can do no more – and then you become superior to God and the devil. You're *free* ... Most interesting. Well, I stood it for three days and then feigned madness. A dangerous trick, because at that point there's only a single thin fence of reason between pretence and reality ... On the fifth day I escaped. Two days later Pierre Grognard was arrested and six others. A fortnight after that Jacques Delaisse went and three more. A sweep of our best men.'

It had been going dark in the room. He switched on a couple of table lamps, and they brought all the colour back: the cinnamon satin curtains, the lace-like shadows of wrought iron, Alix's hair and skin.

'I think those days and weeks my last ideals were squeezed out. Thinking I was going to die, I forgot my more enlightened views and it seemed worthwhile to be keeping faith with the men under me. Then I escaped, and most of the men were arrested just the same. I might have told the Germans all I knew and saved myself the heroics. Anticlimaxes can be very salutary.'

He put the drink beside me. As he bent I noticed there were tiny beads of sweat round the roots of his hair. It was the first time I'd seen him so close. His eyelids were very thin, almost transparent. For all his appearance of suavity and balance, there was something here that I wasn't so sure about.

'Of the eleven men arrested five were taken to Cannes for questioning. Two died there and three survived. Jacques Delaisse and two others were hanged in Nice. Grognard was taken to a concentration camp near

Toulon where he was kept until released by the Allied landings. Is my telling brief enough for you, Alix?'

'Yes . . .'

'The arrests had been very smart – a little too smart. We all felt there had been a deliberate leak. For a time we were all under suspicion, but in the end, by elimination, we came to think of Grognard. He had no witness to his movements – and when he came back he was much better off. He had made money out of the Germans legitimately – we did not begrudge him that – but confidential reports showed him a man of wealth . . . There were other little things.

'It was hard to believe the worst. He'd been one of our earliest and most active members. He'd lost his father in the first war and was known to have Communist sympathies. He had proof of his captivity in Toulon. The thing was impossible. Then early last year he began to pay attentions to Alix.'

The great dog shook himself till his collar fairly rattled, came across and put his head on his master's lap. Charles's hand slid over the creased, shiny skin. A hand shaped like Alix's but sinuous instead of smooth.

'Will you go on, Alix?'

'No. You.'

'We – Alix and I – had had our differences of opinion – over her marriage, and some other things, and when peace came she chose to live her own life and earn her own living. She didn't care very much for Pierre; but I felt – and the relatives of those who had been betrayed felt the same – that it was up to her to encourage him for a while to see what came of it. There's nothing like

247

infatuation for unlocking a man's tongue. We didn't, of course, need evidence to satisfy a court of law – only to satisfy ourselves. It was at this stage that Alix took pity on a blind man, and so made things difficult for us all.'

I said: 'And incidentally saved the blind man.'

'Quite incidentally. I expect if you know her at all you'll realise that she's a woman given to these sudden impulses ... Tiresome conflict between inclination and duty. Then after some weeks she was silly enough to take you back to her apartment and Pierre surprised you on the stairs. This naturally made things very strained between them. He'd been jealous of you, but now felt himself deceived as well. They might have quarrelled finally, but she was conscience-stricken, felt she had let us down. So she made it up with him, even though his terms had changed. Now you must tell the next part, Alix.'

'I can't.'

'Oh, yes, you can.'

She turned slowly from the window, sat on the arm of a chair, put her hands round her knee.

'Oh, God! ... Well, then ... I can't tell it like Charles, detached, amused. Perhaps I have a sense of humour that doesn't work in this. After that meeting on the stairs I was very upset. In those days it seemed to matter ... Both my friendship with you and my loyalty to – them. I thought, somehow, in a few days, I can find something out; then be done with it all. I hated it. When I saw him next time his attitude was ... if you, why not him? He proposed we should go off for a fortnight, be

married while we were away. I knew he didn't mean
that, but I agreed. I was sure, once we were alone
together . . . in that way. Once or twice he'd begin to
say things, and had to pull up short . . . While this was
going on Charles was away, but I went to Villefranche,
told them. I wrote a note for Charles that he'd get when
he came home. The arrangement was to spend a few
days in Grasse first – then go on to Grenoble, and
perhaps Paris. The evening before we left Pierre took
me out to dinner; then he asked me back to his flat. I
didn't usually go, but in the circumstances didn't like to
say no. When we got there he began to make love to
me. I found when it came to that I . . .' She got up. 'It's
hot in here, Charles. Can I open a window?'

'I'll do it for you.'

He opened them, but a wind came into the room and
began to blow the curtains wide. She said in a low voice
that seemed a part of the new noise of the cool air and
flapping curtains:

'That's how it is sometimes. You undertake something without facing up to it. Then it comes and . . . I
tried to pretend that night – but the feeling was too
strong. He stopped at last – upset of course . . . With a
man like Pierre it had always been hard to keep him at
a distance. It had meant – pretending to a special
loyalty, and getting him to accept that estimate. Now
he began to taunt me – about you and . . . to sneer. I
kept calm over that and because I was calm he grew
more angry. He began about other things, trying to
smear – unforgivable things as I thought then . . . I lost

my temper too ... We quarrelled wildly. And then suddenly it all stopped. In his anger, in his need to hurt me ...'

She paused, pushed backed her hair, said carefully: 'He did what we'd been waiting for all the time. He said he'd seen someone in a place in Hyères – and it happened I knew that other person had not been near that place until a fortnight after Pierre had been "arrested"... You see, if Pierre was taken on the 30th April he couldn't have been free in Hyères on the 11th May.

'The quarrel stopped too suddenly. He started to apologise for his anger as if he meant it, and all the time I could see he was turning this over in his mind – getting nearer the truth every minute. The way I'd been that night showed I didn't love him and never had: he worked back from that. I knew when he realised the truth because the sweat came out on his face.'

She straightened her back, let her hands fall. 'Then he asked me if I was still willing to go away with him. I had to say I was. Then he said would I come with him tonight, drive up to Grasse, sit and watch the sunrise in the mountains, have breakfast at a wayside *auberge*? I knew then that he wasn't going to let me out of his sight. I knew when I went up into the mountains he would kill me. It was at the back of his eyes, like pain, like – like a new *sort* of lust ...

'I tried to make excuses, but it wouldn't do. He was so frightened that if the worst came he was ready to kill me there in his flat. So I said I'd go. We were both pretending and half knew the other was, but were afraid to let the pretence fall. There's – an awful chasm between the last thought and the first act ... I said I must go and pack a few clothes; but he said we could send for anything I wanted and he'd buy me things in Grasse tomorrow. Then I said I couldn't possibly go without at least telephoning Mme Colloni – otherwise she'd get alarmed and call the police.'

Charles Bénat shut the windows and went across to the bureau behind me.

She said: 'I suppose it was panic, that call to you. But there was no one else. If I phoned a Villefranche number he would know at once that I was not getting my apartment. My only hope was that you'd realise there was something wrong and begin to ask questions which I could answer yes or no – as you did. When you offered to come round I thought that might save me. I only had to delay long enough in the flat and Pierre would be helpless ... But I made one mistake. He wasn't very far from the phone and heard it was a man's voice at the other end.

'Of course, even then I tried to put him off. I said I'd got on to Mme Colloni's husband – I tried any sort of excuse that came into my head. But excuses were no use any more ...'

She stopped.

I heard Bénat come up. He put a black spanner into my hand. It was eight inches long.

'That's what I killed him with,' he said.

I looked at the spanner. Grutli, interested, came over

251

and sniffed at it, his great head nearly level with my shoulder. Alix reached for the cigarettes and lit one; I saw her face twitch. I handed the spanner back.

'Exhibit A.'

'I've killed three men with that,' he said. 'An accidental choice in the first place, but it happens to be weighted right, and fits the pocket. Of course the other two were Germans.'

'And they hardly count, do they.'

'In some things you have the right ideas.' He went back and put the spanner away.

I said: 'And how did you contrive to kill Grognard?'

'I came back from Lyons in the afternoon to find Alix's note waiting on my desk. She told me briefly what she'd decided to do. All the rest of the afternoon I tried to work but could not. So eventually I faced up to the fact that I was not willing to let my sister go with this man merely to clear up who had betrayed a dozen saboteurs. The act itself of course is unimportant, but I didn't look on it with favour in the circumstances. It was like rewarding a cheat with the first prize ... And it was' – he hesitated, his lip drooping – 'it was unsatisfactory for reasons of prestige. Alix spoke just now of coming to the brink of a thing before realising all that it means. Perhaps for once that happened to me. Our attitude seemed irrational. Revenge is as useless as regret.'

'I agree with you there.'

His face was curiously in the shadow again. 'It's true, isn't it, that only the present is valid. A cut finger today is more important than yesterday's martyr. Well, I decided to put a stop to this particular – cut finger. I drove down and went to Alix's apartment. Mme Colloni said she had gone out with Grognard. I phoned one or two restaurants and discovered they were at the Luxembourg. They were just leaving when I got there, so it interested me to follow them. They went to his flat. I drew up outside and waited, hoping she would come out alone. Unless it was unavoidable I did not want him to know anything. After about twenty minutes, when I was trying to think up some excuse for calling, I saw a shadow on the curtain, and a hand pull the curtain roughly aside and then itself seem to be pulled away. It was a woman's hand. The curtains fell back, but I went up at once and rang. I rang twice and knocked before Pierre came. He opened the door a few inches and was obviously shocked at the sight of me. After a minute while we kept up the courtesies he tried to shut the door. I forced my way in. Alix's bag was on the settee. I went through to the bedroom. She was lying on the floor. I turned back as Pierre reached the bureau in the corner where he kept his revolver.'

Alix stubbed out her cigarette and got up. 'That's enough, Charles. The details . . .'

Bénat said: 'After I'd hit him I put my hand over his mouth and supported him a few paces to the settee: that is always the way, not to let them cry out, not to let them fall. Then I went in to Alix. After three or four minutes she began to come round. Then the door-bell rang.'

'Yes,' I said. 'Very inconvenient.'

'Alix told me what she had done and we hoped you

would go away. It wasn't until I helped her back into the living-room that I saw the outer door had been left ajar. We got into the kitchen just before you began to push the door open. My own preference would have been to use the spanner again, if more mildly, but Alix said no.'

'Very considerate of her.'

Alix gave me a long steady look.

'We went down by the back stairs,' Bénat said, 'and waited outside in my car, which was on the other side of the road, hoping that you would find nothing. As time passed we wondered if you had also left by the back stairs. I left Alix in the car and rang Villefranche. Then I rang Pierre's flat and you answered. When I got back you were just coming out. Throw me a cigarette, will you, Alix.'

I said: 'I wonder if it ever occurred to you that you might have put the murder on me?'

'It did. But there might have been flaws I knew nothing of. And again Alix would have nothing to do with it. I have the stick you left in the flat, but I suppose you don't use one now.'

'Not except when intending to deceive.'

'I'm sure the opportunities for that must be decreasing.'

'That first time I came to see you,' I said. 'Was Alix here?'

'No. I sent her to Dijon. She was – very much shaken up. When all this was begun we knew there would be some risk to her, but it had hardly occurred to us that things would happen as they did. We had thought of her being able to report to us, and then dropping out and taking no further part in anything we did to Grognard. There would have been no question of her disappearing from the town – an act which obviously might cause comment. But as you had been dragged in there was no alternative to her going. She could not continue in her flat or at the shoe-shop if you were likely to come round asking questions.'

I said: 'How forbearing you've been not to use your *Totschlager* on me.'

Bénat inclined his head. 'Glad you appreciate it.'

'Several people have been predicting an early funeral.'

Bénat said: 'What people?'

'Oh . . . John Chapel among others.'

'What does he know of this?'

'Not more than he knew twelve months ago.'

There was silence.

'Well,' said Bénat casually, losing interest again. 'Now you know the truth. Honour is satisfied. Is there anything more we can do for you?'

'. . . I can understand your not wasting too many sleepless nights over Pierre.'

'I've wasted none,' said Bénat. 'And the conditions?'

While they had been talking I'd been watching them both, trying hard to understand things that went a good lot deeper than the killing of Pierre Grognard.

'Oh, the conditions . . . Well, I've a proposal to make.'

They both looked at me.

I said: 'This has all been very friendly – except the

last condition. For people of such good taste it strikes rather a wrong note, don't you think? Robs the evening of its – warmth.'

'What do you suggest?'

'That you extend your trust a little further. What do you do with yourself when Charles is away, Alix?'

'Oh . . . the usual things.'

'Well, I suggest that – for the sake of last year – you agree to spend three or four days with me, doing the sort of things we did then. Perhaps it would be a bore to you, but it would be a gesture to end on. That done, I'll leave Nice and not bother either of you any more.'

Alix got up.

Eventually Bénat said: 'Are you a poker player, Giles?'

'Yes.'

'I thought so.'

Alix said: 'I don't think it will help anyone if I agree to meet you.'

'It will help me.'

'Is that important?'

'I think so.'

'He means,' said Bénat, 'that he still hopes to make you love him. Failing that, he will go back to the fogs with a beautiful memory.'

'I don't want to revive anything of those days,' she said. 'I'm trying to forget them.'

'You'll have the rest of your life to do that.'

Bénat yawned. 'Why don't you go to bed with him, Alix? Then he could return home satisfied.'

'No,' I said. 'Profoundly dissatisfied.'

She looked at me queerly through her lashes.

'Grutli,' Bénat said, rubbing the dog's ear, 'we are a patient and an understanding family, but this foreign gentleman requires all our patience and forbearance. We have confessed murder to satisfy him, and thrown in a little illegal trafficking to make a full load. We have bared our hearts and offered our bodies, but he rejects them and asks for our souls. What would you say to that?'

The Great Dane barked gruffly.

'Exactly. We would say that he is asking for the impossible, like the little dog baying at the moon. Or worse, for the moon does exist. The gentleman is out of date; he hasn't read the right books; he is sublimating his sex instinct and giving it a halo. Very disgusting. Perhaps after all the spanner would have been more valuable.'

'All right,' said Alix, who was still looking at me. 'If you want me to meet you, I will for a few days. It won't do any good, but I'll do it. I don't dislike you; I've nothing against you now. You don't mind, do you, Charles?'

'Nowadays,' said Charles, his lip drooping again, 'the fashionable word is not soul but Ego. A rose by any other name – at least it has the advantage of depriving the religious-minded of a useful lever. But be careful, Alix, that this ardent Englishman doesn't re-convert you. Also in turning your mind back to superstition, be sure that he doesn't protestingly seduce you after all. It comes better that way, and one doesn't need a cassock to be expert at the game.'

I said to Alix: 'You'll do that?'

'Yes . . . If you want me to.'

'Can I see you tomorrow?'

She shrugged slightly, embarrassed. 'As you please.'

'I'll keep to the contract. One week.'

'One week. All right.'

'I'll phone you in the morning.'

I glanced at Charles, and he looked down quickly at his glass.

'I suppose you've no objection?'

'Would you take notice of it if I had?'

'No,' I said. 'After all, you've had her for a year.'

There was a sudden short silence.

'As you graciously put it,' Bénat said.

I realised as soon as I'd spoken that that was not the remark of a poker-player.

We were back in Cagnes by soon after midnight. The sky was limpid, and the last clouds crouched over the sea. It seemed ages since Maurice had driven up under the shadow of the storm.

The precautions I'd taken looked a bit juvenile: letter deposited with John, a chauffeur asked to wait. Bénat's cool, logical, civilised brain had blown foolish suspicions away. His way of telling his story had put it all on a nice commonsense level. The German occupation, the betrayals, the killing of Pierre, were all 'thrown away' as a sort of intellectual amusement. One didn't imagine it as the violent truth.

That was clear enough to reason. Everything was fine.

But one's reason doesn't fill up the whole picture. Instincts get a share. It was pretty evident he was telling the truth about Grognard; no one could doubt that. This was something deeper that was troubling me.

I came away feeling for some obscure cause that there was a tremendous antagonism growing up between us. And I drove back to Nice with the uneasy suggestion in my mind for the first time that my life was really in danger.

CHAPTER TWELVE

'So I'll not need my black tie this week,' John said. 'Here's the letter. I suppose you wouldn't like me to read it before you destroy it?'

'I'll not destroy it. It's going to the bank, with certain additions.'

'And where did you go last night that you needed to do all that cloak-and-dagger stuff?'

'Only out to dinner with a friend.'

'Lady?'

I made a non-committal noise.

John took out his pipe and began to fill it. 'And Pierre Grognard?'

'That's satisfactorily cleared up. More so than I'd reason to hope. He brought the accident on himself.'

'Um? Sworn to secrecy or something?'

'Yes. My feelings – in this – are with the person who told me.'

John lit his pipe. In between gasps he said:

'I'd like to know sometime. Remember and tell me when we meet in England.'

'I'm not likely to forget.'

'By the way, d'you recollect mentioning a man called Deffand? Met him yesterday.'

'Yes?'

'Yes. He *is* the man from the Sûreté.'

'Ah.'

'Rather a new type. Somebody means business sending him down. If he gets proper support he may do a lot. You should meet him.'

'I have. At the Wintertons'.'

'Don't know how the devil those people get to know everybody. Look, I'm going to lunch in half an hour. Join me if you like.'

'Thanks very much,' I said. 'But I have a date.'

He looked slowly up, appraisingly. 'With the girl you were with last night? Or is it rude to ask?'

'Yes to both questions,' I said. 'With Alix.'

She was waiting as arranged at the corner of the Place Masséna.

It was very hot, and she was hatless and bare-legged, in white sandals and a white, full-skirted silk frock. I came up beside her and stood looking at her for a minute, taking in the shape of her nostrils and the fair hair down in front of her ears and the single faint line along her forehead made when she raised her eyebrows; the dark level, pencilled but not distorted, line of her eyebrows and a small mole at the nape of her neck and the thickness of her hair at the parting.

Then she turned and saw me, and the sudden glint of recognition didn't seem wholly hostile.

261

'Have you been there long?' she asked.

'Not long. It was pleasant while it lasted.'

As if to divert attention she said: 'I really don't know what good this is going to do. After you left I was sorry about this arrangement.'

'Let's have an aperitif.'

I led her up the Avenue de la Victoire and we walked in silence for a few minutes. The street looked different for having her beside me.

I said: 'D'you mind if we try this shabby little place?'

We went into the café opposite her shoe-shop, where we had first met. The table we'd had was empty and I went across to it. The same waiter came over and I ordered the same drinks. Her face was polite but expressionless.

She said: 'What are you going to do when you go back to England?'

'Try to become a lawyer again. Like Charles.'

'Charles is – everything,' she said.

'So I've noticed. Naturally I won't attempt everything. In England it doesn't always pay.'

'Lucky England,' she said coolly.

'Have you ever been?'

'No.'

'It would have its drawbacks to a Niçoise. But the sun is seen from time to time.'

'I'm not a Niçoise.'

There was a brief silence while we sipped our drinks. I said politely: 'Do you like your new life?'

She looked up. 'My new life?'

'Well, there must be a difference. Did you bring your car down this morning?'

'Yes. I parked it.'

'I have a car, too, though modest. I thought it would be useful for going about.'

She stared out at the passing people. 'When I came over that morning I didn't think it would amount to all this.'

'No ... One suffers the penalty of being kind. You interfered that day and perhaps saved me from – dramatising my grievance. Now I'd like to repay the debt by saving you from yourself – as Charles would say.'

'I don't want saving from myself, thank you very much.'

'Nor at the time,' I said, 'did I specially want saving from suicide.'

'I'm sorry. I'll know better next time.'

It was queer, all the noises were the same; the thin rattle of the trams, a woman arguing about lottery tickets at the next table, a man selling newspapers. To-day it was hotter, that was almost the only difference.

I said: 'What made you change?'

'What do you mean?'

'After Pierre was killed, what made you go in with your brother?'

'Wasn't it the natural thing to do? Besides ...'

'Besides what?'

'Oh, nothing.'

'Besides what?'

She made a little gesture. 'Who wouldn't? Why be a shop assistant at a few thousand francs a week when everything's there for the taking?'

'No conditions attached?'

'What do they matter? That's part of the fun. I help sometimes; the risks are small but there's excitement. Life's too short to sit in a corner all day learning the rules.'

'Don't be sure the risks are so small,' I said. 'You remember Deffand at the Wintertons'?'

'Oh, the Sûreté man. He's clever, they say; but you can't swim in a bog. In a few weeks he'll be recalled and someone else sent down. It does not worry us.'

'So you like your new life?'

'Of course.'

'Why did you jib at it at first then? Why did I find you in the shoe-shop to begin?'

'I don't think it was part of our agreement that I should sit and be cross-examined.'

I smiled. 'All right. Let's go and lunch at Biffi's. You don't mind, do you?'

We lunched at Biffi's, at the same table, and the same waiters served us.

She said: 'It's so strange you can see. I keep feeling I must help, tell you things . . . It's uncanny.'

'Be careful of that. Mother instinct. It can lead to all sorts of disturbing complications.'

'I don't think there's any danger now.'

264

I helped her to wine. 'I wonder, has Charles *any* illusions?'

'Why should he have? It's safer to be clear-sighted.'

'I don't know . . . Personally I like my illusions. The universe is pretty terrifying; and so's the world – getting more so every year. People talk about the law of the jungle, but the jungle is a haven of peace and mercy compared with Europe this last fifteen years. It seems to me that the only things that can now make life and one's common humanity bearable are just those little graces, the spiritual adventures – call 'em what you like – which altogether weigh practically nothing in any material scale. Why shouldn't one believe in God and Santa Claus and the Moonlight Sonata if one chooses to? Perhaps it's sad to be the victim of sentimentality, but is it sadder than to be the victim of one's own disillusion?'

She said: 'We in Europe are the victims of the time. Isn't that it? Everyone learns from experience, and we have learned that the only way to survive is to see clearly, to believe in nothing but what we personally know, to accept nobody on trust, to work for ourselves alone and to take pleasure where we find it.'

'Conviction's grown on you in the last year.'

'Perhaps.'

'When I met you we'd a lot in common. We were both off balance because of the war. Since then, thank God, I've lost my grudge; but yours has completely changed. Resentment's one thing; rebellion shows spirit. But disillusion isn't spirit. It's death.'

'As I said,' she answered coolly, 'we've nothing whatever in common now. That's why there is no point in these meetings.'

'Alix, I could shake you.'

'That was not in the agreement either.'

'Well, be careful you don't goad me too far.'

The waiter brought the fruit.

She said suddenly: 'I don't think you can say Charles trusts no one. Last night he told you the whole story of Pierre Grognard. What greater trust could anyone put in your honour?'

'I thought it a generous gesture. But – is it trust if you add a threat? And I wonder sometimes whether there isn't a certain relief, even a certain satisfaction to one's vanity in – in—'

'You're most unfair to him,' she said. 'He's been generous to you all along. D'you think it would have been difficult for him to have had you put away? Instead he's treated you with every courtesy, entertained you, explained everything as it happened, put himself—'

I said: 'I'm glad loyalty isn't one of the virtues you've entirely thrown overboard.'

'You don't like Charles, do you?'

'I like him. But I'm sorry for him.'

'Sorry!'

I met her indignant look. 'Yes. I think he's a man with a brilliant past and no future.'

'What do you know about it?'

'Absolutely nothing at all. It's only one of these feelings one gets.'

She didn't speak.

I said: 'In a way he's symptomatic. As you are, Alix. You remember at the Wintertons' he talked about Europe being sick. Well, he's right. And he's one of the signs of the sickness. If the symptoms multiply the patient will die. If the patient recovers, the symptoms will disappear. What shall we do this afternoon?'

'What you please.'

'We didn't meet that first afternoon, so the field is open. It's hot, shall we bathe?'

'As you please.'

'Have you a costume?'

'In the car.'

'Can I get it?'

'No. I'll walk down with you.'

We sat on the beach under a large blue-fringed umbrella, and the heat shimmered all round us on the stones. For a time we hardly talked at all. She wore a two-piece white bathing costume.

She was sitting with her hands about her knees; and after a bit she glanced at me and saw me looking at her.

I said: 'Do you mind?'

'What?'

'Admiration. Or does it offend the new rules?'

She said: 'I should hardly have thought you wanted to admire a running sore on the face of Europe.'

'Oh, I didn't specify the disease.'

'Well, most symptoms are disagreeable.'

'Seriously. Before I lost my sight I took it for granted, like breathing, hearing, taste. I don't suppose I shall ever do quite that again. And I suppose it's natural to be more susceptible now to shape and colour – quicker to see beauty in any form – aesthetically appreciative, if that word's allowed. For instance, the glitter of light on a fish's scales – or the different shades of blue in the sea at this moment – or the silky sheen on a woman's back – or the way—'

She said: 'I think you're making it up. You were always interested in those things.'

'Interested, but not so conscious of them. Anyway, what would you rather I took note of: the khaki shadings on a black-market sock?'

She turned her face away. 'I wish you were not so silly.'

'It might be a saving grace. At least you'd never need to extend your hero-worship to me.'

She looked at me quickly, the laughter dying from her eyes. 'What do you mean?'

'I don't know ... But I'm used to groping in the dark.' (And sometimes by chance the gropings found an unexpected mark.) 'Do you swim?' I asked, anxious now to change the subject.

'Of course.'

'Let's go out to the raft, shall we?'

'All right.'

When we got in the water I said: 'I'll race you.'

'All right.'

She swam like an eel, with hardly any splash and was at the raft yards ahead of me.

'You see,' she said breathlessly, her eyes glinting.

'I see.'

It's difficult to be unfriendly on a raft with the sea water drying quickly on you under a blazing sun. I felt I was making good progress, though it wasn't fundamental progress. It all might slip away in a second.

When we got back to the shore I suggested we should take a pédalo. This curious Mediterranean invention, in which two people lie back on a double-sized deck-chair fixed on buoyant metal floats and propel themselves precariously across the sea by means of pedals fixed to tiny paddle wheels, is a profoundly silly-looking but very pleasant way of spending an hour. I expected her to refuse, but she agreed after a short hesitation and we climbed in and were pushed off by the man in charge.

We went round for about ten minutes almost without speaking, but somehow I could tell that some of her defences were lowered. That was why I kept quiet. I steered well out to sea, and after a bit we both stopped paddling, and the craft rocked gently up and down on the swell.

It was terrifically hot, but invigorating because of being so close to the sea.

She said after a long time: 'Why are you so hard on us, Giles?'

'*Hard?* I don't know what you mean.'

'Why d'you despise our way of life? We can't help what we are. Circumstances made us. Perhaps it's good to have illusions if you can cling to them; we've had them torn away.'

'What Charles is hardly concerns me. What you are concerns me enormously.'

'You mustn't let it.'

'You've lost the one person who could have made all the difference. I know . . . And there's no way back for you the way there has been for me . . . Don't think I'm questioning that. But what puzzles me is that all that had happened when we met *before*.'

She said: 'Last year you thought I was loving; this year I'm not. Isn't that all?'

'No . . . I don't think it is quite.'

'So all our explanations to you last night were so much wasted breath? You're still completely unsatisfied.'

'I'm grateful for your confidences – I said so. You cleared up last year's mystery. This year's mystery remains.'

'Oh, nonsense! There is no other mystery at all. You imagine it!'

'We're going round in circles,' I said.

She raised her head. 'Are we? Oh . . . you mean in argument.'

'I do indeed. If you can call this argument.'

There was a fairly long silence, but it wasn't quite such a peaceful one.

I said: 'You complain that I'm hard in my judgments and despise your way of life, when all the time you've given me the impression that you despise mine.'

'So I do,' she said sharply, as if reminded of it. 'So I do.'

For the life of me I couldn't hold my tongue.

'That sounds like the Gospel according to Charles. Book Three, Chapter One.'

'You hate Charles,' she said. 'You think I can't think

for myself. That's utterly wrong! He never pressed me in the least to go back to live with him. If I wanted to I should leave him today. But I don't want to! I love and admire him—'

'I can see that.'

'We reason alike, we feel alike. We've the same *sort* of brains. I can be a great help to him. I'm proud to help him.'

'Isn't pride one of the weaknesses of the new philosophy?'

'Oh, you're so smug!' she said, sitting up and rocking the thing. 'I hate you – with your self-satisfied judgments, your – your so careful sanity, your middle-of-the-road righteousness. I don't think I can stand any more of it!'

'Are you sure I'm the smug one? Or is it you and Charles? I don't know. But look at it this way. Two men belong to more or less the same generation. When one of them grows up he sees a statement which says – which says, well, for instance, "Blessed are the meek, for they shall inherit the earth." It sounds nonsense to him, but he thinks the man who said it may just possibly have been wiser than he is. The other fellow reads the same sort of thing. Because it sounds nonsense he's convinced it is nonsense, because he believes that no one wiser than himself has ever lived. Which of those two would you say was self-satisfied?'

She said: 'I can't answer all your arguments. Why don't you go and say them to Charles? He will soon be able to answer them – and destroy them!'

'Sheltering behind the big guns . . .'

'I *cannot* endure your insults!' she said angrily. 'You're unbearable!'

She got up and the floating deck-chair dipped violently.

'Sit down!' I said. 'You'll have us out!'

Instead she balanced for a moment and then dived into the sea. The contraption, released of her weight, leaped up into the air at the front and I toppled over into the sea the other way.

I came up gasping, having swallowed about a quart of water. The pédalo, of course, had righted itself. I still had a horror of getting my face under water, and this made me so furious that I left the pédalo there and struck out after her.

We were a good way from the shore, and by the time we were half-way there she had drawn well ahead. But from then on I began to overhaul her. About twenty yards from the beach I drew level.

I swam alongside for a minute. 'Disagreeable temper.'

She looked at me as if I were a complete stranger and changed her course to make for the beach at a tangent.

She had spurted again, but again I overtook her. This time I grabbed her ankle and pulled her down.

She came up spluttering and looking rather white.

'Don't, Giles . . . I'm . . . nearly done.'

'Say, please.'

'Leave me alone . . . Let me go.'

She had wriggled free.

'Say, please.'

She looked at me as if to say, I'll drown first.

We were nearly home. I caught her arm, though this time only the threat was there.

'Please . . .' she said.

When our feet touched the stones she stumbled and nearly fell, but I took her elbow and we got out of the water together. I was dreadfully out of condition for this sort of thing. The young Italianate beach attendant burst upon us.

'My God, monsieur, this will cost you a pretty penny if the pédalo is lost! They are not to be used as diving-buoys. I will have your name and address! My God, this is a formidable liberty. It will cost you—'

When I got my breath I said: 'I'll come out with you in a canoe and get it in a moment.'

I saw Alix back to her umbrella and then we went out and retrieved the pedalo. It took a time because the thing had drifted westwards, and then of course I had to chug back alone.

When I arrived back at the umbrella she had gone.

CHAPTER THIRTEEN

I DIDN'T see her again that day. When I thought it over it didn't seem to me that I had come out of the first meeting very well. It was a bit silly to squander one's opportunities on argument and then get into a temper because one got one's eye wet.

Next morning she rang me. I'd been half expecting it.

'Giles? Oh . . . this is Alix . . . I've decided not to see you again.'

'Oh? Why?'

'I thought yesterday would have made it clear.'

'I understood you'd promised to meet me for a week.'

'I promised to try. Obviously no good will come of it.'

'Good for whom?'

'For either of us.'

'I don't think you can judge for me.'

'Well, I'm not willing to risk being drowned.'

'I was under the impression you began the drowning episode.'

'You see, it's useless. We should begin to quarrel

274

again as soon as we meet. Besides, I'm not willing to go on. I'm tired of being insulted, thank you.'

I said: 'Quite frankly I'm rather ashamed about yesterday. Whoever started it, it was unpardonable of me to take the liberties I did. I'm extremely sorry if I upset you.'

'Oh,' she said, and sounded a bit nonplussed. 'Well, it wasn't all . . .' and stopped.

There was a long pause. I thought she'd rung off.

'Hullo!'

'Hullo,' she said.

'I'd like to put a proposition to you – that we go out today and that you should call the tune – decide where we go, what we shall talk of. On my side I promise to change the subject when anything displeases you. Does that seem fair? And if we quarrel today that ends it.'

There was another pause.

'Why not let it end here?' she said.

'I should like to try once more.'

There was another pause. I could hear Grutli barking.

She said: 'Today is Sunday. I didn't promise to meet you every day . . . I'll meet you tomorrow – on those terms.'

I thought swiftly. 'All right. And thank you for your forbearance.'

She said something, but I couldn't tell what it was, and rang off.

*

In spite of what I'd said to Alix I was getting used to sight again. If the body is adaptable in disablement, so it is in taking recovery for granted. Already there were hours, almost half days when I forgot having been that way: the present preoccupation of course helped. It seemed monstrously ungrateful to let the smaller things become important again.

I spent Sunday alone and didn't go far. The next day I met Alix as arranged and kept scrupulously to the bargain. I had to. These were high stakes. We drove to Cannes for lunch and had dinner at St Raphael, played baccarat at the Casino there and returned to Nice about twelve. I wanted to go with her to the Villa Lavandou, but she said she was safe on her own. We made arrangements to meet on the Wednesday.

This second day together went fairly well. She had evidently decided to ignore the enormities of Saturday. We talked quite a bit in something of the old friendly strain of last year. Sometimes we laughed and joked in the old way, and we kept away from controversy most of the time. Yet the whole impression of this day was that I'd not made as much progress as on the first. She was keeping me quietly at a distance.

A cleft stick. These were the only terms on which she would see me. Yet only by tackling the issues . . . And time was getting short. A meeting on the Wednesday, then perhaps another on the Friday, and she would consider her promise discharged. No condition had been attached to the promise that we should spend the time arguing first principles. She was giving me her company.

And all the time I was getting in deeper water. There was no question about that.

On the Tuesday morning someone called to see me at the hotel. I was in the lounge at the time writing a letter desultorily on my knee, and I didn't quite get what the concierge said. I saw Deffand's tall figure in the doorway and rose to meet him.

By himself, away from the glitter of the Wintertons' candle-lit dining-room, he was more impressive. He looked like a schoolmaster with his narrow scholarly nose, but he wasn't the sort of schoolmaster one would have wanted for tender children. His close-set eyes acknowledged me with a gleam of politeness, and then went quickly round the room, summing up the imitation Louis Quinze furniture, the three elderly French women chattering together on the veranda.

'Monsieur Gordon? We met at the Wintertons' you'll remember. I hope you'll excuse the informality of the call.'

I asked him to sit down.

He said: 'We're quite private here? I'm not keeping you from any appointment? Good. It's a small matter I came to see you on. Would you care to see my credentials?'

I looked over the leather-bound *carte d'identité* with the photograph, the police embossment, the grease marks.

'Really,' I said. 'I'd no idea.'

He breathed down his nose. 'You must be one of the few people in Nice, then. It's hard to keep a secret in a small community, monsieur; and although Nice is the third city of France, it has the elementary make-up of a country town. It was the same when your Scotland Yard inspector came to inquire about the illegal currency transactions. At least I have kept my name out of the papers.'

I said: 'Can I help you in some way?'

'That's what I hope.'

I offered him a cigarette, and he took it with yellow-stained fingers, put it between his lips, rolled it across slowly to one corner of his mouth.

'I understand, Monsieur Gordon, that you've had some interesting experiences in Villefranche.'

This was rather a shock. I cursed John. It seemed impossible that anyone else ... 'Oh, last year. I was very short-sighted at the time. There was some confusion over the name of the streets. But it was all cleared up eventually.'

He looked at me. 'This year?'

'What d'you mean?'

'I mean, was it cleared up this year?'

'. . . Yes. Naturally when one can see properly . . .'

'Naturally. You found the street you were looking for?'

'Yes.'

'And the café?'

'Yes.'

'What was its name?'

I hesitated. 'Would that be of interest?'

'It could be.'

'The Café Gambetta.'

278

'I don't know the name. Where is it?'

'In the Rue St-Agel.'

'Where does that lie?'

'Not far from the quay. You go up from the Pavilion and turn right.'

'I see.' Deffand breathed thin spirals of smoke from his nose. 'Villefranche has recently been the centre of certain black-market activities – unfortunately. Also there have been shipments of gold over the Italian frontier. We suspect that the consignments start from there. I wonder if, in your movements about Villefranche, you have seen anything to rouse your suspicions?'

I lit my cigarette. The old ladies were chattering away.

'I'm afraid I can't help you.'

'Nothing at all?'

'I only wish I could.'

Deffand leaned back. He had the air of a man who has met with and quietly overcome a million setbacks.

'An interesting discussion we had the other night at the Wintertons'. You know them well?'

'They're old friends.'

'It was the first time I'd met them. I was invited through the courtesy of M. Lemaître.'

'Oh, yes,' I said politely.

'Do you know the Bénats well?'

'I've met him half a dozen times.'

'Wasn't it you I saw in Cannes yesterday with Mme Delaisse?'

'. . . It was.'

He blew another couple of spirals. 'I confess I thought their attitude a little unbecoming last Sunday.'

'Surely they were only putting the other side of the picture.'

'Surely. But I think M. Lemaître had them well beaten.'

'Of course.'

There was silence for a while.

'Unhappily in law-breaking,' he said, 'there is no middle course.'

'I'm inclined to agree.'

'Who is not for the law is against the law. One cannot have the best of both worlds.'

'It would be folly to expect it.'

'Certainly. Did you know that some of Mme Delaisse's relatives live in Villefranche?'

'She told me so. Relatives by marriage, I think she said.'

'Have you met any of them?'

'. . . Yes. I believe I did once. A brother-in-law – Armand, was it – and an uncle. But of course I was blind at the time.'

'Did you ever meet her mother-in-law, Jeanne-Marie Friedel?'

'No-o. I don't think so.'

'Her second husband was an Austrian Jew who shot himself when France collapsed. It is said that she organised the escape of more than a hundred young Frenchmen to England during the war.'

'Very good.'

'Yes. Very good. But one wonders what she is organising now.'

'Perhaps she has retired to pass her old age in peace.'

His eyes met mine. 'Women like that never retire, monsieur. They are born to active conspiracy. Tell me, are you likely to be seeing Mme Delaisse again?'

'Yes. Tomorrow.'

'I should like your undertaking that you will say nothing of this call.'

'I give it you.'

He got up. 'You're staying in France a few weeks more?'

'It's rather indefinite. Probably only a week or two.'

'I'm sorry you don't feel willing to help me in my task.'

'Not unwilling. Unable.'

'Ah,' he said. 'Divided loyalties. Dangerous, as I've pointed out. British nationality, at times so valuable, is at others a snare. One feels a little withdrawn, aloof, and so becomes more deeply entangled than one realises.'

We walked to the door.

'If at any time you feel you want to talk things over you will find me at M. Lemaître's house, or care of any police station.'

'Thank you,' I said, and watched him go.

CHAPTER FOURTEEN

I HAD to force the pace on Wednesday. Either way I stood to lose, so it was better to go down making a fight of it.

It may be at that time that I gave the impression of being an obstinate and persistent man to more people than Charles Bénat. If so there was another cause beyond the obvious one. The feeling I'd mentioned to Rachel had never been shaken off: it was a confused conviction that because of getting my sight back I 'owed' something to life. I'd never got properly straight with myself over it; and now this feeling had perversely associated itself with Alix. Of course, I wanted her for herself; but the moral issue had wormed its way in and wouldn't be got rid of. I felt I *had* to help her, somehow.

Possibly Charles's cynical comments weren't far off the mark; I don't know. I remember when I saw her walking across the square to me on the Wednesday all these things seemed to come up together.

She said with a smile: 'Hullo. Am I late? I had to make a couple of calls for Charles on the way.'

'No,' I said with difficulty. 'It's all right. I got the boat.'

'Good. There's quite a breeze, though. Do you ever feel sea-sick?'

'Practically never.'

We began to walk down to the old quay. It had been agreed that we should spend part of the day sailing and fishing and I'd hired a cutter, though this time with an outboard motor.

As we got in she said: 'I hope it doesn't rain.'

'Not much likelihood, is there?'

'Well, we can't put in to Villefranche this time.'

'I'd not be popular?'

'They don't understand your lofty motives.'

'I had no lofty motives,' I said, 'except to find you.'

'It would be difficult to explain that.'

The sea was a bit choppy out of the harbour because a strongish south-easterly breeze was blowing. But it was hot.

'I liked most of them,' I said. 'It's a pity we had to quarrel.'

'. . . I think they liked you.'

'Roquefort . . . and Scipion, and Uncle Henri, and Mère Roget – whatever their real names were.'

She didn't speak.

I said: 'Is Mère Roget's name Jeanne-Marie Friedel?'

That made her look up. 'Why do you ask?'

'Idle curiosity.'

'Who told you? You're not – going on . . .'

'No.' I was tempted to warn her again about Deffand, but didn't like to break my undertaking. To some extent he'd been right: I was trying to run with the hare and hunt with the hounds. It didn't do.

While talking of Villefranche there had been something in her voice. 'D'you go there often now?' I asked.

'I've not been near since last July.'

'That's rather surprising.'

'My life has changed since then.'

'Anyway I'm glad you don't go.'

'Why?'

'Well, they run the risky end of these jobs you're doing. There'd be no fun in being there if the place were raided.'

'Oh . . . there's not much risk of that.' Nevertheless she was thoughtful for a minute or two and glanced at me.

I said: 'Do they dislike your having gone to live with Charles?'

'I've never consulted them.'

This seemed to lead to a blank wall, and I didn't want to start trouble so soon. We got well out into the bay and then put out lines to see if there were any fish about. The breeze was blowing her hair back from her face, making her look like a stranger. She'd got blue linen trousers and a blue jumper on. The trousers had a red stripe down the side and she wore a red belt. We'd divided the fishing lines; two were to be mine and two hers, to see who caught the most. For a long time there wasn't a suggestion of a bite. Then I caught two tiny fish, so we tried another and westward tack.

She said: 'I haven't been fishing since that day a year ago.'

'I used to come out with my father when I was a kid. We had three or four holidays here.'

'Lucky . . . I've never had a holiday here – not that sort. When we lived in Dijon we used to go to an aunt who had a farm near Arles; that was our holiday every year. I hadn't really seen the sea until I was sixteen.'

'I suppose you were in Charles's company a good bit in those days.'

'I don't remember a lot before father – died. That seems to belong to a life almost before I was born. I remember when it happened . . . Charles seemed to grow up overnight. He was only fourteen. After I went to the convent I used to see him every holiday. Then we were inseparable. It was strange for me, you know, to come from a convent where everything was founded on discipline and devotion, into the company of Charles who even then was all for indiscipline and irreverence.'

I said: 'I came back to this coast to try to recapture the old feelings; but it's a dead quest from the start. It's not the place that's changed, but you in the years between. Didn't you feel that when you went home to Dijon?'

She rolled up her sleeve and dipped her fingers into the rippling green water; her arm over the side looked like marble, reflected the glimmer of the sea.

'I had plenty of other things to think about.'

'Did you stay long?'

'About four months.'

'Four *months*?'

She withdrew her hand, let the water drip delicately from her fingers. 'I was ill. I had a nervous breakdown.'

'Oh! . . . I'd no idea. I'm sorry.'

'I . . . stayed with my aunt – father's sister. It took time.'

'. . . Did Pierre hurt you before Charles came?'

'Only my throat. It was all right in a week.'

'I got the feeling that you didn't love Pierre, but I was a long way from guessing the reason. At least Jacques's death was avenged . . .'

'What? Oh . . .' She half-laughed. 'Yes . . .'

I was startled at the laugh.

I said: 'But perhaps you look on revenge the way Charles does, as an act of justice. In this case I think I should myself.'

'I don't look on it in any way any more.'

It was not very promising to be choked off for the second time in half an hour. I had a feeling of having come towards the same forbidden ground from another angle.

'Sometimes surely you must think of that time still, your friendships, your life with Jacques, the kindly bits as well as the unhappy ones.'

She said: 'Will you change the subject, Giles, please? I don't want to talk about it.'

'Right enough. You choose.'

'Tell me about your life. What your father and mother were like, about England and the things you have done and want to do.'

I tried to fill the gap as she wanted it filling, but I wasn't thinking too hard about what I said. The things she'd spoken of or left unsaid went round and round. And to begin I think she was the same. My words had wakened something in her and it wasn't easy to lay it all to sleep again. Her face puckered into a frown once or twice and she seemed glad when I had another couple of bites and hauled in two modest mackerel.

Then there was another bigger one, and she said, with a sudden change of mood: 'You're having all the luck. The boat will be loaded down your side and I shall not have even a crab.'

'You can have this baby sole to put the ballast right.'

'No, thank you. I can buy much better than these when I get home. I shall buy twenty kilos and take them back as the fish I've caught.'

'In the Studebaker?'

'No. You can drive me home tonight. Then your car will stink of fish and you'll not want me any more.'

Ahead of us seagulls were fighting over something, and Alix moved to the bows of the cutter to see if she could see what it was. As soon as she turned her back I hauled in her nearest line and hooked one of my mackerel on to the end, then slid it back into the water.

'It's a piece of shark's fin or something,' she said, bright-eyed. 'Not an appetising morsel. You see, there's no rationing in the seagull world. They leave it to common sense and then the strongest gets the biggest share.'

'Stop moralising and come and take your line. There's something on it at last.'

She clambered back in haste and gleefully pulled the line in.

'A mackerel! My luck has turned. Not a very big

fellow but it's a start! You unhook him, will you, Giles. That's the nasty part of fishing.'

I dutifully unhooked it and dropped it in her basket. She bent over it, blinked as hair blew across her eyes.

'He doesn't seem very lively. Didn't all yours kick and wriggle? He's not really moving at all.'

'Sometimes they swallow the hook differently.'

'Do they?' She bent and touched the fish gingerly with one finger. 'Why, he's nearly stiff!'

'What?' I leaned over from the tiller. 'No, it's only the same as mine.'

'Yes, but yours have been in the basket for five or ten minutes . . .' She stopped and looked up at me accusingly. 'It *is* one of yours!'

We passed close by the quarrelling seagulls but she paid no attention to them. She crouched on her heels, looking up at me with a slight frown.

'Did you do that to tease me or please me?'

'The first if you found out, the second if you didn't.'

There was a long silence.

She said: 'I think perhaps I know now why I liked you last year. Because sometimes you are a little like a – a savant and sometimes you are a little like a schoolboy, and sometimes you are just an ordinary man like other men; and I never know one minute from the next which I have to contend with.'

'I don't know where you get the savant from, but if all that's meant to be kind, thank you.'

'It's not meant to be kind. It is just – meant.'

I laughed. 'Well, let's get on with the fishing.'

We got on with the fishing. We had run across the south-east wind towards Cannes, but we turned the cutter face on to the breeze and just kept enough way on to prevent drifting. We ate some sandwiches.

She said: 'What sort of fish do you eat in England?'

'Never touch fish. Only roast beef and Yorkshire pudding.'

She looked at me.

'And boiled cabbage,' I said.

'That's interesting about boiled cabbage. I know it is a good joke, but also it's true because my father said when he visited England as a student he was given nothing else! Why is that?'

'It's puzzled the deepest thinkers. The English, of course, don't turn their whole imagination on food.'

She said: 'I used to think the English were lacking in imagination, but now I know that's not so.'

'Another sandwich?'

'No, thank you.'

'A pear?'

'No, thank you.'

'Don't let me interrupt you,' I said, 'this is a most interesting conversation.'

She smiled slightly. 'Have I been paying you compliments?'

'That was my impression.'

'Instead of heaping insults on you. Poor Giles.'

'Lucky Giles!'

'Why lucky?'

'I can *see* . . . And I'm out in a boat with you, and

289

we've caught eight fish and the sun's shining, and there's still seven hours of daylight.'

'And I,' she said, 'am now going to be sick.'

'Lie down,' I said, 'put your head on this cushion. It may pass off.'

'Go away,' she said. 'I don't want you to see me being sick.'

'Dear Alix,' I said. '*That* doesn't matter. It isn't going—'

'. . . Dear Alix?'

'Oh, yes, you are whether you like it or not. I'm seven years older than you, and—'

'Giles! Go away!'

I went away. After five minutes she said: 'Well, I have not been sick, if that's any consolation.'

'Better?'

'Not much. Are we going in?'

'As fast as our engine will take us.'

After a few more minutes she sat up, with one hand to her head. 'My God, what a horrible feeling.'

'Don't move about. You're better down there.'

She lay and watched me. I sat whistling faintly into the breeze and glanced at her now and then. Her colour was coming back.

She said: 'What a fool!'

'Nonsense. Lots of people would have been prostrate hours ago.'

She was quiet for a bit longer and then she said: 'I think, Giles, the woman you eventually marry – when you've got over me – will have a great sense of – of support, of balance, of security. Perhaps balance most of all.'

'Very useful in a rough sea.'

'No. I mean it. For the balance is in you. If she gets bumptious, arrogant, cynical, you will – pull her down. But if she makes a fool of herself, feels silly and humiliated, you will – help to restore her self-esteem. You would be a steadying factor, a point of stability . . .'

'You don't know how flattered I am. A pity the one woman who recognises these virtues doesn't want to make use of them.'

'Oh, I . . .' She shrugged. 'I am no use to you.'

'Wouldn't you let me judge?'

'I think we come of an alien race, a different time. It's nothing to do with the miles or the years. It is out of the question, of course, for other reasons, but even if it were not, we could never have made a success of it. Our outlook, our instincts are different; we have no common ground to build on at all. Are we nearer the shore?'

'A good bit. I don't like your reasoning, but I'm grateful you're being reasonable. Is it the seasickness?'

'I don't know.'

'D'you think if I kept you out here till dark you'd go on getting ever gentler and kinder and more self-critical?'

'I should scream at you like a fishmonger.'

'Why,' I said, 'is our coming together quite out of the question? What are the other reasons?'

'One is – that I don't love you.'

291

'Is there someone else?'

'There's no one else. Now you're the Giles I don't like, who asks tiresome questions that show he's no different from other men – with sex on the brain, eternally questing, never satisfied with any explanation that doesn't include it.'

'I should have thought that more a characteristic of women.'

'Not this woman.'

'There's one last tiresome question I should like to ask; but I don't want it to split the Entente.'

'How far are we from home now?'

'About ten minutes.'

She made a grimace. 'If it's the last question, ask it and then leave me in peace.'

I said: 'That last night with Pierre: what else happened between you and him – that you haven't told me – before Charles came?'

Her clear eyes for a second were started out of their brooding.

'What makes you think something did?'

'It's just the way things look to me.'

She said after a minute: 'I'll tell you tonight.'

CHAPTER FIFTEEN

WE WENT to the little restaurant we'd visited several times last year, an ill-lit place in one of the narrow streets of the old town. There was a bistro downstairs, and you stumbled past the telephone up some uncarpeted wooden steps to a low black-beamed room with a lot of ornamental brasses on the walls and fine linen on the tables and an old grey-haired waiter who'd lost an arm at Verdun. It made a sort of fellow feeling between us. He served everything with one arm and I'd never known him drop a thing.

As usual at this time we had the place to ourselves. Alix had changed into the cream linen frock with the wide skirt and the scarlet brooch.

I said: 'I like that a lot.'

She smiled but didn't speak. The smile wasn't nearly so detached as it had once been.

I said: 'You look young and innocent and very charming in it.'

'Whereas in fact I am none of those things.'

'Oh, yes, you are. Didn't you know? Young obviously. And, in a queer way, very innocent, though it doesn't please you to think so.'

'It would please me perhaps if it were true. But it isn't true.'

I said: 'The odd thing is that you think of me as a sentimentalist, a dreamer, a romantic, the one who sees life through a rosy haze. Whereas in fact you and Charles are the true romantics. The only trouble is that your romanticism has got pushed off its rockers and has turned upside down. The cynic doesn't see life as it really is: he sees it through a rosy haze that's turned yellow on him. No one can be a cynic unless he's been a romantic first.'

She laughed. 'I like to listen to your arguments. I don't believe in them, but they're nice to listen to. Go on.'

I watched her teeth. 'No, you go on. You tell me what you think.'

She was quiet for a bit, the laughter slowly dying from her face, the warmth going out.

She said: 'D'you think we expect too much from life? Is that it?'

'Perhaps we're all born expecting too much. It's a question of how we get around to the disappointment. What did you expect, Alix? What did you grow up wanting? What particularly have you missed?'

She said slowly: 'I wonder – if I tell you the little more there is to tell of what happened on that night – I wonder if you'll see it as something small and not important; or whether you'll see it as something big. You're detached. I'm too close – or I was too close. It seemed to take the roots out of my life. The doctors told me it was silly to feel the way I did. I wouldn't

have told them, but Charles told them. They sympath-
ised, they said, but it wasn't right to feel like that. It
was always happening in this life. Disillusion, you
know. The romanticism that has gone wrong; isn't that
what you called it? Anyway, I'm having no more to do
with it. A burnt child dreads the fire. I'm holding out
no more hostages to fortune.'

The old man took away the remains of the langouste,
brought fresh warm plates, polished them on a napkin,
put them before us. Then he came back with the veal in
a silver dish, apportioned it between us, scooped out
savoury-smelling gravy and added mushrooms and tiny
chopped carrots.

When he had gone she said: 'To tell you while I'm
eating shows how far I've now recovered. Twelve
months ago I hardly ate at all. How silly. I can tell it
you quite simply. That night when Pierre saw how I
really felt towards him he wanted to hurt me any way
he could. When he saw that taunting me about you had
no effect he began about Jacques ... He'd been
Jacques's closest friend, I told you that. You know how
I loved Jacques; the memory of the six weeks of married
life with him was like something nobody could touch.
They'd hanged him, but they could never destroy him
for me ... And then Pierre did so ...

'At first I didn't believe a word he said, thought he
was inventing it. It came like a knife in the back. I
couldn't think, couldn't understand. But he began to
give details, details no one but Jacques and I could ever
have known. He said Jacques had been persistently
unfaithful all through those six weeks. You know, I told

you, he was away off and on during those weeks on sabotage work. Pierre said Jacques had been with one woman after another, in Nice, in Juan, even in Ville-franche. Like a dog, going with any bitch . . . Pierre said he'd heard Jacques talking about me with two women in a café, making them scream with laughter, telling them about me and my inexperience, what I'd said to him and what he'd replied, telling them how I adored him, and why. And more – much more . . .'

Alix abruptly put her knife and fork down and lowered her head. Then after a minute she looked up again and smiled briefly with eyes gone very dark.

I said: 'For God's sake.' I moved to get up. 'Listen, darling, please . . .'

She said quietly: 'Feeling paternal again? I'm all right.'

I wasn't feeling that way, but I made no further move, afraid of any gesture she might think was claiming too much. I said: 'You were quite right. It's better buried. Let it lie.'

She pushed her hair back with her fingers. 'Perhaps you can guess how I felt when I began to believe what he said. While I was there with Pierre the worst didn't come. Just then I still carried on like someone who makes the motions of ordinary life without feeling anything. My brain went on, pretending to him, trying to save myself, scheming to call you instead of my apartment, determined that whatever happened to me Pierre shouldn't escape. It wasn't till afterwards, until I came round after he'd tried to strangle me – even later than that: it wasn't really till the next day that the worst happened. There was a sort of great blackness here.' She touched her middle. 'It was as if something had gone, and there was an empty desert. I didn't care if I lived or died. In fact I wanted to die, just to be rid of the bitterness and the pain.'

I didn't say anything. She went on: 'After a while, after some weeks it began to change. The need to die was gone, but there was never any more need to feel anything again. Not only was it bitter, it was cheap. All life was cheap and useless: empty puppets, all worthless, jigging on strings. It didn't matter whether Pierre was dead or alive. I'd gone to all that trouble to find out who had betrayed Jacques; but in the end it didn't matter, there was nothing to punish, nothing to betray. The others who'd gone; they were like Jacques; no doubt of it; there wasn't anything left to believe in any more.'

The waiter came in and said: 'Is there something not to your liking, 'sieur-m'dame? The veal, perhaps?'

When we'd reassured him and he'd gone we made a pretence of getting on with the meal.

She said wearily: 'It was about Jacques that he gave himself away. He was so anxious to destroy that he lost his caution. He said he'd seen Jacques in Hyères with a certain woman. As it happened, though I didn't know what Jacques did with his time, I always knew where he was because one of my jobs was to bring him instructions. And I know he hadn't been anything like as far away as Hyères – not from our marriage until the 10th or 11th of May. He went there then, but that was twelve days after Pierre was "arrested".'

I said: 'I'm very sorry – and ashamed of my insistence.'

'No. You'd a right to know. And perhaps your theories are right. I was born expecting too much. Well now – I expect nothing. That's all over – for good.'

There was a longish silence.

I said slowly: 'D'you think you'll be content to live for ever in a vacuum?'

'. . . Not a vacuum. But one can get along with other things.'

'Such as living well, dressing extravagantly, gambling as the mood takes you, and helping in occasional black-market enterprises?'

'Yes, if you like.'

I shook my head. 'It won't do.'

'What?'

'Plenty of people can get along like that, but not you. It won't do, Alix. You're deluding yourself now just as badly as when you thought Jacques a saint. Instead of overrating him you're underrating yourself.'

'Oh, no, I'm not.'

'Oh, yes, you are, my darling. May I call you that?'

'No.'

'Well, it doesn't alter anything. You can't change yourself *inside* to order. The person you're doing your best to be – in self-defence – couldn't ever have gone through what you've gone through. She'd have shrugged her shoulders . . . carried on living just the same.'

She said rather gently: 'But, Giles, don't you see, it's *because* I went through such a time that I'm determined never to go through it again. I'm not waiting about to be trampled on any more. I'm not going to depend upon another person for my happiness.'

I smiled back at her. 'You're making certain of not being let down.'

'Yes.'

'There's no one now who can let you down except yourself.'

'That's it.'

'But *aren't* you rather letting yourself down by thinking as you do?'

'I don't think so.'

'God knows, I've no right to preach. But it looks to me to be a question of courage.'

She coloured slightly. '*I* think it needs courage to live to yourself alone.'

'Or funk dressed up as courage. Real courage, surely, is in doing something about it, not in running away.'

'Like the goat butting against the wall. He won't learn.'

I said: 'What a big advance we've made since last Saturday.'

'Have we?'

'I think so. We sit and argue like friends instead of playing ricochets in the water.'

She smiled again. 'All right,' she said. 'I admit that.'

After dinner we walked up towards Mont Boron, as we'd done once before. It was a beautiful night; not yet quite dark in the west but the short twilight was going. The profile of the land was blurred against the steely

haze of the sea and the sky. I'd suggested Mont Boron.
It was calculated perhaps, but there was simply no other
way. We might get one more meeting, and at that, after
a break and seeing Charles again, her defences might
have gone up double height. At present she was curiously soft – as if the telling of her trouble had got rid of
some of the hurt inside her.

We went out on the path where we'd been that other
night, and watched the lights of Nice winking and bright-
ening below and all over the distant wooded hillside.

I said: 'Tonight you haven't to tell me what you can
see.'

'No . . .' She stopped and looked over the wall. 'Have
I ever told you how glad I am about that?'

'I'm glad you're glad. I only wish I could have made
something of the rest.'

'Don't think of me as someone who's injured,' she
said. 'I don't feel it. I feel fine – except when it all
bubbles up again as it has done now. But otherwise I
enjoy myself – enormously. Why shouldn't I be fine?
I've everything I want. When you go home don't think
of me as a poor stunted creature shut off from the
Kingdom of Heaven, or something of the sort. Think of
me dancing and singing outside the Gates.'

I said: 'I shall think of you among the Dryads. May I
make a last request too?'

'Of course.'

'When I go home don't think of me as sitting *inside*
the Gates of Heaven reading a lecture to the poor souls
shut out.'

She laughed. It was her old laugh really back this time. 'I know you're not like that.'

'Perhaps I've come near sounding as if I believed it. That's your fault for rousing a contentious spirit.'

We went on further, and then I said: 'Stop here.'

'Why?'

'This was where we stopped before.'

'So it was. I don't know how you can tell.'

'Well, I can. But there's no music. Last time we had music.'

'Yes. I remember, a rumba.'

'And an Italian tenor singing about being in prison and not able to escape.'

'You said something – no, I said something about my mind being hilly and you quoted . . .'

'"The vigorous mind has mountains to climb and valleys to repose in".'

'That's it.'

'You were pleased about it.'

'Why?'

'Because someone else thought the way you did, I suppose.'

'Was it Hazlitt or – or . . .'

'Emerson? I never looked it up.'

She said after a minute: 'And the frogs were croaking.'

We listened together. They were there but further away than before.

'It was somewhere about here that the thing was settled so far as I was concerned.'

She looked at me. I could see she couldn't refrain from saying: 'Was it? Why?'

'Don't know. I think it followed the close-up, didn't it?'

She moved her head slightly, the light catching her eyes. 'Yes . . . That was a little obvious. I'm sorry.'

'It was the first time,' I said, 'that I really got any idea . . . D'you remember I put my fingers on your face like this . . .'

She shrank back against the wall. 'Oh, no. There's no need tonight. You can see perfectly well.'

'And then somehow the rest followed.'

She said: 'Look, Giles, this is a very nice walk and I like you; but I don't want to go that way again.'

'Was it an unpleasant way?'

She shrugged slightly. 'That is not in our bargain.'

I leaned back against the wall. 'Being strictly rational and unsentimental – what's your objection?'

'. . . That I don't want – any of that.'

'Not any part of the way?'

'Not any part. Besides – if you feel as you say you do . . .'

I said: 'It's all over and done with as far as you're concerned. That's admitted. So there's no risk to you in it. Nor have you any fidelity to anyone, as you had last year. The thing's a passing pleasure – or a passing event at least – with no after-thoughts. Isn't it your way of thinking we should take the sensations as they come – make what there is to be made of them – then shrug and pass on?'

After she turned from the wall. 'I'm not scared of

your kisses, Giles, if that's what you're . . . You can kiss me if you want to – if it's going to do any good. You've been very persistent – and kind. But don't think you've *talked* me into it. Your reasoning isn't really very good this time.'

I drew her a little out of the light of the lamp and looked at her. She looked beyond me.

I said: 'Yes, it's in very poor taste and I'm *ashamed* of it. I'm damned ashamed of half the things I've said to you these last few days – *and* my persistence and what you call my kindness. But I'm not ashamed of loving you and never will be. Look at me, you devil!'

She looked at me. 'Alix!' I said in a whisper. 'Wake up! Alix! Can you hear me?'

She smiled slightly. 'I think it's you that's afraid.'

'Yes,' I said, close to her. 'We're both afraid, if it comes to that. I need courage just as much as you. It's not the courage to do what I'm doing now – that's surface stuff. It's the courage to *know*. And there's only you can give it me. No one else – *anywhere . . .*' I kissed her.

After about half a minute she tried to get her mouth away, but it didn't work. Then she didn't resist any more.

I just couldn't believe it. There were footsteps somewhere near and I let her go. But somehow at the last minute my hand touched hers and I grasped it. She let it stay. I couldn't believe that either. The bones in her hand seemed small, childish. I heard her breathing beside me. Something had swelled in my throat, was thumping there.

Four men were coming past, laughing and joking. They were working men, shirts open at brown muscular throats.

She leaned against me. She was trembling, and I wasn't much better.

I said in English: 'Darling Alix. Darling Alix.'

Her hand tightened on mine for a second. She said: 'Oh, God, I'm lost again. Don't let me go.'

CHAPTER SIXTEEN

I SUPPOSE I should have taken that literally. I suppose I shouldn't have let her out of my sight any more at all. It would have been the natural precaution of a strong-minded person. Then none of the rest would have happened.

But in a reasonable world it would have seemed an unreasonable act.

We didn't break up that night until after midnight. We sat in a café and talked – as if we hadn't talked enough these last few days. But it was talk with a difference.

She seemed dazed by what had happened, still unsure of herself, and afraid. She kept looking at me, sometimes with her eyes narrowed, trying to understand.

We talked about all the things that so far had never conceivably been discussed. She was worried about Charles. I was, too, but didn't say so. She said she would have to tell him herself. He was due back to-morrow morning. She would go home tonight and tell him, try to explain when they met tomorrow. Then later I could come up and we would talk everything over. I agreed. At the time there didn't seem

305

much else to do. As I say, we were still in a reasonable world.

I stood for a couple of minutes beside the futuristic Studebaker while she sat with her hands on the cream-coloured wheel.

She said: 'I don't know, I suppose I've been deceiving myself, thinking that I had no feeling ... It was there from last year but ... Giles, even now I'm not *sure*. Which is the real me, the one who came out this morning – or the one you're sending home tonight?'

'They're both part of the same. You're all of a piece; there's nothing irrational about it.'

She said: 'It's no good; I'm *not* the wife for you. In an English village I should be scared of the people, and they'd be scared of me.'

'You underrate your own toughness – and theirs.'

She smiled. 'I shall never, never underrate yours. All through you've had the most ... courage and patience and – and forbearance. I should never have believed—'

'No,' I said. 'Keep off the hero-worship. Anyway, there's no excuse for it. Everything's been done from the most selfish of motives. Alix – I don't like to see you go.'

She put her hand on mine. 'I'll phone you tomorrow as soon as I've seen Charles.'

'You promise – whatever you feel like in the morning.'

'I promise, Giles.'

So I let her go.

*

When I got back to my hotel I felt drunk. Excitement and triumph. I walked round and round the bedroom like a caged tiger. I felt like shouting and singing, and only a consideration for the traveller in silks and linens in the next room kept the situation in hand. In the end I couldn't stick it any longer and went out again, walked through the empty streets for nearly an hour. I felt as if I should never be tired again.

I made plans and changed them ten times; I talked to Bénat, lectured Johnny, explained to Cousin Lewis, bought a house, introduced Alix, spent Clara's legacy, drove Alix about England; there was practically nothing I didn't do in that hour.

Back at the hotel again at last, I undressed and got into bed, but it was no good putting out the light. I sat there and chain-smoked until four. Then at last the light off and sleep for a couple of hours.

Awake at six, and, in one of those queer half-sleepy moods that yet seem to see further than most, I began to think things out.

It all seemed so much clearer now. I thought: the young girl, warm-hearted, exceptionally intelligent, highly strung, adoring her mother. When she's nine that changes, mother leaves them, goes off with another man. Higher the admiration the greater the fall. Father dies as result. Probably at that age thought of her mother in another man's arms would seem intolerable, disgusting. The first scar, long since healed over and apparently recovered from. Then ten years later marries a man and comes to love him very deeply. He's hanged by Germans. A great bereavement, sustained by a

307

memory. Idolises memory of Jacques. Two or three years later she learns he was a common rake of a particularly nasty kind, a liar and a cheat. Scar number two, still festering.

Yet psychologist would say first much more important. Hadn't it left its mark on Charles, too?

Strange issue for a country doctor in Dijon, these two. But the mother . . .

I turned over. Not easy for me. Last year, *before* explosion of Jacques legend, I'd noticed in Alix, something . . . Not all attributable to Jacques tragedy. Nor was everything in her this year the outcome of Pierre's disclosures. It was the result of them, built on something older. You couldn't call it a sense of guilt where sex was concerned – that was too strong; rather a shying away, a *hint* of distaste – and only noticeable now and then. Back to nine, that dated back to nine. Yet she'd loved Jacques naturally, with all warmth of her nature. This thing only a quirk which normal love and happiness would straighten out. I could give her that. *Would* give her that. I'd tackle it – with all the patience of my own love. Six o'clock blues. Not afraid.

Always provided I got a chance. She'd promised last night – this morning? She'd tell Charles. Natural she wanted to explain it herself. Once I got her away . . .

If I could get her away. What about Charles? Where did he come in? Almost everywhere.

By this time I was wide awake.

For some time I'd been pretty sure there was a sort of sex relationship between Alix and Charles, and equally convinced it was not physical sex. Because it

was devoid of physical complications, Alix had come to
look up to him as the one stable and uncontaminated
thing in her world, realistic, astringent, cynical. He
wouldn't let her down as her mother had done and
couldn't in the way Jacques had done. Whether she
admitted it or not, she was still seeking illusion. And he
accepted it.

Accepted it because he wanted her and needed her.
Had done practically all his life. You can't be a man if
no one accepts you as a man. Alix had accepted him as
a man at fourteen. In a queer more adult way she still
fulfilled the same function.

They'd quarrelled when she married Jacques. Not
because he knew Jacques for a profligate, for he hadn't
known. They'd quarrelled because he couldn't stomach
someone taking his place as the most important influence in her life. For the first time he had been pushed
out.

Would he be any more willing now?

I sat up and looked for a cigarette. My mouth was
dry already from smoking too much.

I remembered the glances he'd given me after dinner
at the Villa Lavandou, the uneasy idea I'd come away
with, that when the evening began he looked on me as
a nuisance to be put up with, but by the end of the
evening he hated me. I realised now that he didn't mind
my curiosity about Pierre, my interference at Villefranche. They were part of a danger he'd been in so
long that he was used to it. Anyway it was a danger like
a drug – it stimulated and refreshed. Without it life was
dull and pedestrian. My persistence amused him. It

wasn't until I turned my persistence back to Alix that his view changed. I'd found a weak spot. Perhaps with his keen sensibilities, his special insight into his sister's moods, he'd realised more than either she or I did at the time, that there was some weakening in her taking up of the challenge.

Well, even so, it wasn't anything to get worried about. No doubt he'd use all his persuasion to make Alix change her mind. But I didn't think she would. There might be all sorts of conflicts still inside her – Charles's love and influence could hardly be over-reckoned – but she wasn't weak. She'd keep her word.

And if she kept her word there was nothing more he could do. He couldn't stop her marrying me if she wanted to. God help me, I was worrying over nothing. I lay back in bed and tried to think of all the pleasant fancies I'd had last night.

But the chill wind wouldn't be shut out. It blew round all the nice little day-dreams, turning them back to front and making them look like spectres instead. The greater happiness they promised the longer shadows they threw.

At seven I got up, had a bath and shaved, sat on my balcony watching the morning sun gilding the streets and sucking the vapour out of the night clouds. I had an early breakfast on the balcony, drinking cup after cup of coffee while the sun crept round, warming my feet, showing up the dust on the balcony rail. Charles wouldn't be back till ten at the earliest. Then an hour to talk it all out. Quarter to eight now. Three hours at the very least.

The maid dropped the papers into my letter box and a couple of letters with them. One was the hotel bill, the other was Cousin Lewis telling me that old Hampden had had a stroke and was likely to be an invalid for the rest of his life. There'd have to be some rearrangement of the firm now, said the letter. There was far too much work and responsibility for one principal; I ought to think over my position very seriously; did I feel well enough to put a term to my holiday and settle in as a full partner, or was I prepared to see a new man brought in from outside?

Have patience, Cousin Lewis, I'm on my way. Two, three, four or five days: just as long as it takes Alix to get ready.

Oh, Lord, is it really going to come off? Does she love me or have I hypnotised her into thinking so? I don't believe that, I'm almost sure not; but if I have then by God I'll go on hypnotising her for the rest of her life. For the first time I began to have some understanding with men who had chucked away everything for a woman – the sort of classic love stories that make the dullest films. I knew now what they felt like anyway.

I hadn't patience to do more than glance at the headlines of the news. Everything was in a mess as usual. I couldn't help it. My personal crisis loomed like Mount Everest. At nine-thirty I decided to go and collect the car from the De la Rue Garage, and stuffed the papers and letters in my pocket. But at the street door I stopped and went back. If by some mischance Alix decided to ring up early I wasn't going to miss it. It was a bit like waiting for a call from her after the murder. Somewhere was the uncomfortable suspicion that she might disappear again.

At ten-thirty I smoked my last cigarette, but now my nerve was gone and I didn't go out for more. Now it might come any time. But it didn't come.

Watch the clock round to eleven-fifteen. A great temptation to ring her up, but silly to get in a panic for a quarter of an hour. Mustn't look as if I didn't trust her. Probably Charles was late getting home. If he drove up from Toulon he might not get there before lunch. Or something had delayed him.

At eleven-thirty I phoned down for some cigarettes and checked that no call had come for me. There hadn't been one. The porter brought the cigarettes. They were a particularly poisonous brand, but I don't think it would have made much difference if they'd been brown paper.

At a quarter to twelve the phone tried to ring, but I had it off before it properly got going.

'Is that you, Giles?'

'Yes, is that—' I stopped.

'This is Claire, darling. How nice of you to answer so promptly.'

I said: 'Oh, hullo.'

'How are you? We haven't seen *anything* of you for nearly a fortnight. It's neglectful, dear boy. Have you been enjoying yourself so much?'

I said: 'I'm frightfully sorry, Claire. I wouldn't call it enjoying myself altogether . . .'

'Anything we could help you in?'

'Well . . . no, I don't think so. It's kind of you to offer. How's Walter?'

'Rather hurt about his new car. It's got a gadget missing or something. We were wondering if you'd like to come on Sunday again. Nothing grand this time. Just ourselves and a few family friends.'

'It's *very* nice of you. I don't think I can manage this Sunday. Next perhaps. Could I ring you in a day or two?'

'Do. Of course.' She went on and on. I knew Claire. Normally a reasonable talker, the sight of a telephone did things to her so that she never knew how to end a conversation and ring off. This morning it took me ten minutes by the clock to get away without offending her deeply. The second she'd gone I picked up the phone again and asked the hotel operator to get me the number of the Villa Lavandou.

I thought, what's wrong: it's midday now.

The bell went.

'Hullo.'

'You're through.'

'Villa Lavandou?'

'Yes, monsieur.' It was the manservant.

'Monsieur Gordon here. I want to speak to Mme Delaisse.'

'I'm sorry, monsieur, Mme Delaisse is out.'

'Out? Can you tell me where she's gone?'

'No, monsieur. She went out half an hour ago. But we're expecting her for lunch.'

'Oh . . . I see. Is M. Bénat back?'

'Yes, monsieur. I don't know if he is in the house at the moment. D'you wish to speak to him?'

313

'No. It doesn't matter, thank you.'

I rang off. Perhaps she was coming down to see me; that seemed the most likely thing. But they were expecting her back to lunch. I hadn't wanted to speak to Bénat until I heard from her. Wait. Have patience. Take a cigarette, just for a change; or write a cheque for your hotel bill. Wait. They also serve.

She might be here any minute. 'Don't let me go,' she'd said. I should have held her to that, made her spend the night at some place in Nice, kept a close hold on her. The change was too sudden. She'd slipped back. Perhaps if I saw her again she'd look at me blankly, like a stranger, deny last night had ever happened. What the devil was I so jumpy for? In a minute she'd be here. Then I'd have to pretend confidence, as if I'd never doubted at all.

The telephone rang.

CHAPTER SEVENTEEN

'HULLO,' I said.

'Giles Gordon?' said a man's voice.

'Yes.'

'This is Charles. Charles Bénat.'

'Yes. I thought so.'

'Alix asked me to ring you. We've had a long talk this morning. She explained what happened last night.'

'Oh, yes.' My throat was dry.

'Frankly my first reactions weren't very favourable.'

'I'm not awfully surprised.'

'On principle I've nothing against you, Gordon. But I think the whole thing's been rather rushed, and I'm not satisfied she's as much in love with you as she thinks.'

'Isn't that really for her to decide?'

'Ultimately, yes. But it's my duty to stop her plunging into another unfortunate marriage like the last. If you'd heard her talking about you even as recently as Monday you wouldn't have thought her likely to make you a suitable wife.'

A drop of extra poison. 'I'm willing to take the risk.'

'No doubt. The point is whether I'm willing to let

you take it. Of course she's her own mistress, but I can raise certain obstacles. I'd like to talk the whole thing over with you.'

'Gladly.'

'You realise, I suppose, that she's not very – stable.'

'I realise she hasn't grown up in a stable world.'

'It's more than that. One doesn't like to say it, but . . . sudden impulses which sway her first this way and then that. It makes her difficult to rely on from one day to the next. You must have realised that yourself. Last year she almost admitted her love for you, this year she hated you. Now . . . well . . .'

I began to get hot. 'Are you trying to tell me she's not in her right mind?'

'Don't be silly. You're not trying to understand. I want to talk this over in a quiet way.'

'Then we should meet.'

'I was going to suggest it. Preferably all three of us. What are you doing today?'

'Nothing.'

'Then, let me see, I've an appointment at . . . can you come up to the Villa Lavandou late this afternoon – say about six?'

'I can.'

'Very well, we'll talk it over then . . .'

I said: 'Before you ring off I'd like a word with Alix.'

'She's not here. She asked me to ring for her.'

'All the same I'd like to speak to her.'

'My dear man, she's gone off somewhere in a huff. You'll see her, I promise you, when you come up. We'll have it all out then.'

So with that I had to make do.

I went out and had an early lunch, thought of looking up John, but in the end decided against it. This was no day for the social call.

Charles's objections were quite natural. In fact they were less vehement than I'd expected. He objected, but in reasonable terms, and might yet possibly be won over. There was nothing in what he said I could jib at. Like a reasonable man he proposed a discussion between the three of us. I had nothing to fear from discussion. Then what was there to fear?

After lunch I took out the car. It was a smallish Peugeot of uncertain vintage. The engine was in quite good condition, but had a disagreeable habit of dying on you as soon as you declutched, and no amount of adjustment of the carburettor would cure it.

I drove along the Promenade des Anglais and chain-smoked and watched people bathing, but didn't feel in the mood for it myself. A man came past with the afternoon editions, and I bought a paper and glanced through it idly. There was nothing new and I dropped it on the seat, then sharply picked it up again as a small paragraph caught my eye.

It ran: 'Villefranche Raid.'

'A well-known café in Villefranche was raided in the early hours of this morning by the police, acting on the instructions of the Service de Sûreté. Several arrests were made including, it is understood, one woman, who was a prominent member of the Resistance movement during the Occupation. Charges will be preferred against the arrested persons for illegal traffic in gold.'

There followed some stuff about the new drive which was being made against the black market, but I'd read enough. So some of my Villefranche friends were in trouble after all. It was a shock. Disturbing today of all days. In spite of Charles's self-confidence, Deffand had been able to make a move. I wished now I'd dropped a rather more obvious hint to Alix about it.

This raid had been last night – perhaps in progress while I was talking to Alix. Would Charles and Alix know? Obviously. But his self-confidence evidently remained. There'd been no hint of anxiety in his voice, and he was prepared to spend this evening arguing a domestic matter with Alix and me.

The development both complicated my case and made it more urgent. If Deffand was on the kill it was all the more important to get Alix away, however sure of himself Charles might be. Possibly all the strings were cut between the Café des Fourmis and the Villa Lavandou, but I didn't trust Deffand's long thin nose.

By now it was getting too hot in the car, so I drove back to the hotel, had a shower, put on clean clothes and brewed a cup of tea. One never really appreciates tea except on the Continent where it's hard to get. At four-thirty I was off.

On the way to Cagnes the car began to wander about the road, so I got out and found the off front tyre nearly flat. It just took me to a garage, and I stopped and had the wheel changed. I was ahead of time, so let them repair the tyre before going on. The garage was just in

Cagnes, and I bought another paper to see if there was any later news, but it was the same paragraph about Villefranche. I was uneasy and could have wished it to happen any time but now.

The tyre was mended and stuck in the boot. I got going again.

From Cagnes, gently climbing the green wooded slopes towards Vence. It was twenty-five minutes to six now, so I should be almost dead on time.

Through Vence and branching off from the main road. The hair-pin bends didn't seem so bad when you could see where you were going. Whatever happened I was no longer an invalid, a cripple, jogging along beside a French driver like a useless sack. That was what counted. Keep a sense of proportion.

Now the narrow bit, now another bend, now a slight drop in the road for a change. Across the other side of the valley among a bunch of trees were the chimneys and roofs of the Villa Lavandou. This bit of the road was nearly as bad as ever. They'd started repairing it and done about half and then left it.

But they hadn't altogether left it. As I got round the corner of the bluff I found about six workmen just giving up working and throwing a few things into a lorry.

The lorry was on the inside of the road and he wasn't as far in as he might have been, so I hooted and a man got into the lorry and drew it back a bit. Four of the others leaned on their spades to watch while a fifth, in blue trousers and a dirty singlet, beckoned me languidly on.

I thought the chap in the lorry might have been a bit more obliging because he'd only gone in a foot, while he could easily have backed a couple of dozen yards to a wider part. Anyway he lit the stub of a cigarette and sat waiting for me, so I went. I'd probably a good foot to spare but it felt about an inch and a half, with not being too sure of distance.

I got abreast of the lorry all right and could see my way clear, when I happened to glance at the lorry, which was on the blind side. For a second I thought I'd stalled my engine, but realised that in fact the lorry had started to back and was keeping level with me. My eyes flicked forward and I saw the back of the lorry was going to touch my wing.

I braked and yelled. The wooden side of the lorry grated, jarred, pushed. My car shivered. I pressed the horn, yelled again; a great jolt; my front wheel had slipped. I grabbed the door, thrust it open, couldn't get out for lorry. Jolt. Back wheel. The sky was turning, cliffs moving away. Lorry left behind. Get out of door. The door faced the sky as I got out and the car fell away and I fell with it.

As it happened the drop beside the road was not a precipice but a slope covered with grassy stuff and trailing weeds. I stepped out of the car as it fell, just too late to catch at the broken parapet of the road and so slid down this slope clutching wildly at grass and weeds – which would not stop me, but made the rate of the slide pretty slow. Ahead the car rolled and crashed and then disappeared into silence. I, too, fell over the edge of something, and there was a horrifying instant before I landed in a hazel bush which ended the fall. Then came the last crash of the car a long way down.

After that for a bit there was no more noise except for the crying of a frightened bird.

CHAPTER EIGHTEEN

WE'LL MEET this afternoon at six, Bénat said, discuss the matter then. Alix will be there as well. Perfectly reasonable. Nothing one could object to. All the time instinct hanging out the flags. Ignore instinct. Behave as a civilised person in a civilised society. After all, Pierre might have been killed, but Pierre was a despicable traitor. He got what was coming. Not an English gentleman. Not Giles Gordon, whose only error was an outsize curiosity and a tendency to overrate his own charm.

Little Alix must be protected from her own sentimentality. She'd made a fool of herself over Jacques Delaisse in spite of her brother's objections. Wouldn't do to let it happen again. Alix was Charles's girl. Little Alix had always been there in the past, ever since memory began. Alix was a part of himself, a separate and at times exasperating person, yet tied by some post-natal cord – necessary to him and complementary. Little Alix must go to Dijon again while she got over her new infatuation.

Johnny had been right. Playing with fire. He might have needed his black tie after all. Might still . . . .

In a rage I tried to get out of the hazel bush – and looked down about two hundred feet on to grey-green tree tops.

The shock of being so near the edge made me draw back. There was something glinting a good way down: a window perhaps, or a door that had been smashed out. I thought, well, the carburettor won't be a trouble on that car any more.

I didn't seem to be hurt. When I looked round I began to see how lucky I'd been. Just here the cliff was in a series of limestone buttresses, one below the other, a slope and then a drop, a slope and then a drop. I'd come gently down the first slope, come over the first drop, which was small, and there stuck. It was a good job because this next slope was steeper than the last and much barer. Only under the protection of the cliff, where the soil could lodge, was there this thick growth of weeds and small bushes. I thought, perhaps there's something in the idea of luck averaging out. Four years ago, when the shell burst, the full blast had caught me, while the two nearer men got away with it . . .

I'd lost my glasses. Thirsty and a bit dizzy, I looked round. The slope above ended about twelve or fifteen feet up, and the ragged edge overhung. I'd only fallen that far. Once on that slope, it might not be difficult to make the road, which was out of sight from here – careful handholds and footholds, testing the green stuff and the grass, inch by inch. But how to make a beginning? This was the shallowest point. Twenty yards on, the buttress ended abruptly, the other way it ran down, making the proportion of cliff to slope greater before it also petered out.

I carefully got up, and my head lurched. Something the matter with my eye? No, that seemed all right, thank God. Bump on the back of my head. Didn't remember that. On hands and knees again, I looked down, and the view made me feel pretty sick. There was no going down *this* slope – except the quick way. The bottom of the gorge was green enough, and between the trees was a stream and some goats grazing. Sun was brilliant in the valley, but this side was in the shade. Ten minutes after six. My watch was still ticking.

I lit a cigarette and was a bit surprised to find I could hardly hold the lighter steady.

Work it out. One couldn't climb *up*, unless one was a fly or twelve feet tall just to begin. Going further round the buttress was impossible: one could only go back, following the bend in the cliff that the road followed. A hundred yards back the road made a sharp turn inward, where the cliff formation was V-shaped; and the road followed the inside of the V. It was a deep indentation in the side of the gorge. I began to make towards this round the foot of the first buttress, keeping well in to the wall and scrambling through the low-growing shrubs and stuff towards the corner. It was downhill and the cliff above me grew in size; still, it was movement, progress of a sort.

I got into the wind and the cigarette began to sweal away at one side, so I chucked it down. There was a waterfall somewhere near: the hiss of it had grown louder as I came round. Here the buttress came to an end and the rest was more or less precipice; but it wasn't absolutely straight up and there were a good many ridges and clefts in the rock, one in particular being a sort of volcanic fissure starting practically in the corner and running at an angle across the cliff face to the bushes below the road.

I was still furious – it didn't make much sense, but that's the way I was – and it took me all my time not to try climbing the thing right away. I just had the sense to sit down and take a rest before making any definite move.

Think it out. Down below was the floor of the valley. No houses, no smoke, no road, no railway line. Only the goats. Did the farmer come to milk them? If he did, would he hear any shouts? Very unlikely. The stream added to the noise. The road then? But who would come past but half a dozen cars a day driving along in a cloud of dust? Sensible thing was to stay here one day, or two, or even three, until the search began or the car was found. An ordeal, but safety at the end of it. Safe enough here in the meantime to think over the whole miserable business at leisure.

That fissure was a break in the cliff like a split in a tree. For the most part it looked about four feet wide at the mouth, but here and there it was probably a good deal less. The angle wasn't at all bad, a bit steeper than forty-five degrees, and really only a very short distance to go – the road looked quite close. Not the sort of climb you would choose to make perhaps, but quite a reasonable one provided you kept your mind on the climb and not on the drop. A very different matter from any wild-cat idea of getting up the cliff face. The alternative was to sit and wait. I wasn't in the mood for waiting. It seemed a justifiable risk.

Any experienced climber would have made short work of it. I remember thinking I was lucky to have shoes with rubber soles. I remember thinking, when I get to the top . . . In fifteen minutes I shall be back on the road again . . .

The way up to the root of the cleft was by a few small bushes and comfortable footholds. It was hot in spite of the wind. When I got to the cleft I was panting. I hastily pulled myself into it, because this was right over the precipice, and there was that hint of dizziness in my head which came from the first fall.

In this semi-shelter it was better, though not as comfortable as I'd expected. The fissure didn't slope the right way at the mouth. One could so easily slip out. I began to work slowly up it, with back and hands and knees like an old-time chimney sweep.

There was a good deal of faded green stuff at the edges and some etiolated plant life in its depths. At some seasons it might act as an additional escape for the water draining from the road and the cliffs. At about half-way I stopped to rest. Well over the precipice now. Sweat on face and hands. Wouldn't do. Rest a bit. I leaned back, wriggled out of my coat, took wallet, cigarettes, lighter, passport and pocketknife, put them in other pockets; and then threw the coat away. It went off into the wind, swirling and twirling down like an autumn leaf, and I watched it all the way getting smaller and smaller, till it disappeared out of sight far down. Seeing that made the sweat worse.

There was nothing to worry about so long as I kept cool.

CHAPTER NINETEEN

I LIT another cigarette, to make myself rest.

To take my mind off the drop I tried to think about Alix again. I don't know what the fall had done, but just then I seemed to see with a furious clarity things that had never been clear before. I saw that Alix's hostility when I came back from England had had instinct, and even common sense, at its back as well as fright. The ruling force in her life was Charles and always would be. It had been hopeless from the start to try to break that down. For a few minutes last night I'd succeeded, but she'd slid back as soon as she saw him today. There would never be any permanent cleavage between them; it was like the affinity between twins; I remembered the difference in her attitude to me that night after we'd surprised him in the café at Ville-franche. It had been there unknown to me all the time last year like an underground cable. It always would be there. No way of breaking it.

Only three cigarettes left, but I threw this one away half smoked and began to climb again. It couldn't be a great way now. My fingers and hands were sore and scratched.

The heat of the sun made the air shimmer across the other side of the valley where the slope looked gentler. It was on that side further along that the Villa Lavandou was built – so as to get all the evening sun.

How Alix's hero-worship of Jacques must have piqued Charles. Queer he had not told her the truth if, after the war, he got to know about Jacques himself. Perhaps a dead hero was useful in keeping live ones away. Perhaps I should never know, and in this new bitterness it didn't much seem to matter.

I slipped.

It was only a matter of an inch or two, because I was in a very narrow bit of the fissure, but the shock brought the sweat out again. The rocks held me firmly and there was no danger at all of falling. I groped about with my foot and found the place again and pushed up. Nothing moved. I was fixed a bit awkwardly with my chest wedged between the rocks and not a very good chance of a firm foothold below. I tried to wriggle round and get a hand against something to push outwards, but didn't seem able to get the right sort of leverage.

Rest a minute. Now, let the air out, right out, tense muscles and heave. My foot slipped again. Stop, take three breaths, or half breaths, tense muscles, and *again* . . . no movement. My shirt seemed to stick to the rock. Twist a bit, a fractional shift. Was it for better or worse? Another effort. Keep it up. No air yet. Another shift. My foot slipped once more, and I clawed with finger-nails to stop any sliding back. Lungs expanded, a full breath of air at last.

Foothold again. Now claw away from the insupportable

329

weight; fingers on a new grip, testing, pulling. I was free
... The rest of the fissure was climbed in a hurry, and
after a minute I was getting my breath at the top where
it split into five or six cracks and was covered over by a
steep pile of loose stones and rubble tipped down from
the road.

Nearly done now. Except for that one nasty moment
it hadn't been at all bad. I fished out the cigarettes
again. I felt rather sick. The noise of the water was
much nearer now. It was probably falling somewhere in
the inner angle of the V, which was crossed by a road
bridge.

This was where all the rubbish and all the fallen
stones from the road above had evidently been tipped
for years – and in course of time the thing had become
a small moving mountain of rubble. Any time more was
tipped on it it would slither and slide down the side of
the slope, and so much would go over the precipice into
the valley. When I got out of the fissure my scramblings
had sent a great shower of stones and rubble over the
edge, and so much more had come rumbling down to
take its place. I was sitting on the edge of this slope,
and any attempt to climb it would be hopeless. But just
round the corner, a little further into the angle of the V,
one could get out of range of the tip, and from here the
bushes would make the last lap easy.

With safety so near there was no holding back. I
slipped and slid along the edge of the rubble, and more
stones went rattling over the edge and vanished, as if
they'd disappeared, not fallen.

There was just one bit left. Between me and where

the bushes grew was a little bulge of rock shaped not unlike the upturned keel of a boat. It marked the end of the rubble, was several feet across, and stuck out rather. It meant leaning face forward on it and stretching across to the firm ground on the other side. It was only an awkward stretch of four or five feet, made a bit chancy because the rock bulged out. Anyway, it was a safe enough foothold, just clear of the loose stuff.

I slid to the edge as far as I could and got my left toe fixed firmly into a good solid ridge of rock just clear of the rubble. Then I slowly leaned out over the projecting bit till my weight was fairly distributed. I put my right arm over, hugging the rock, and slid my right leg across to find the ground at the other side.

I groped and found nothing but smooth rock. Nothing at all. Because of my one-sided eyesight I'd misjudged the distance.

I was making some sort of a noise. I heard it almost without realising where it came from, a sort of groan of protest that having got so near safety I was cheated right at the end. It seemed bitterly unfair.

I was only just keeping my balance and began to feel dizzy. The rock seemed to be thrusting me away from the cliff, as if it were in fact an upturned boat I was clutching as it pushed out into the air. I lacked the initiative to draw back or power to cling on. But because my weight just kept me there I didn't fall.

I began to think about the fall. I deliberately hadn't looked down so I wasn't sure what was underneath. But from the way the stones had fallen it was likely to be a sheer drop. There'd be some seconds of knowing before the ground came up *slap* like a hand and obliterated you. Or perhaps you'd fall across a tree and break your spine. Or you might bound from rock to rock hammered at every touch, until a limp rag of a dead man rolled in a bundle down the last gentle slope to the stream.

In light-headedness and frustration I began to toy with the idea of giving myself the inconsiderable push that would start it all. Just a tiny spasm of the muscles, a lifting of the head and shoulders, or a shifting of the left leg.

It seemed to be quite another part of me which at the same time was thinking that when I did get to safety I should dream about this, having nightmares, for the rest of my life. As soon as I shut my eyes I should be back in this place, the wind flapping and pushing at me, over the fall. I should close my eyes as I was doing now, and the cliff and the sky would slowly swirl round so that I was leaning on a slippery rock in space, turning over and over like my coat, like a leaf, already falling, no feeling but the pain in my leg, falling . . .

Pain in the leg, that was real enough. Open my eyes; finger-nails clutching at the rock; left leg aching. All the muscles quivering, threatening cramp. This was the only support, nearly gone. The cliffs and the sky steadied up. This was real enough; I was on the cliff face, no escape. Couldn't move to tomorrow and look back and think: it was terrible but it's over. It wasn't over. There was no tomorrow – yet.

With a great effort I drew myself back, pushed myself back; crouched against the sloping rubble, trembling, fighting the dizziness and the panic. No way up. No way back – not down that fissure again. Shouting would never be heard here through the noise of the water. Queer to think this was perhaps just a few minutes before death. Not ill. But in five minutes, ten minutes, a couple of hours, whenever the brain next put it all in motion . . .

Had all my life been working towards this, all heading for this senseless finish up? It seemed very silly. I laughed. An end worthy of Charles's philosophy. I'd been thinking a lot about Charles's philosophy lately.

My head was hot. I smoked two more cigarettes, trying to cool down. When they were done it would be time to make a last attempt.

I got my shoes off and tied about my neck. Then a wry idea took me and I unhitched them and threw them round the hump of rock. They landed safely in the bushes. I wondered how long they'd last up there in the wind and the sun. Maybe a bird would nest in them, or the spiders find their dark corners useful. Pity they weren't the shoes Alix had sold me: that would have been symbolic.

Well, this was it, I thought. Either I had to stay here until I fell off from fatigue or it had to be faced while there was still some daylight. An extra stretch of the foot, that was all. I got up and stuck my toe in the same place and began all over again.

I think really I might have managed it quite well if I'd been in a normal condition; but as soon as I got the other leg over and began to stretch out with it, the dizziness came back. It came in waves. It wasn't that I was afraid to die, but that I was afraid to fall.

I stretched and stretched, groping feverishly for a foothold. The extraordinary feeling I got in the dizziness was that I was almost on my back clinging to an overhanging roof of rock, and that it would be hopeless even to get a foot grounded on the other side because it couldn't help. I dug my nails into the rock and pressed my face against it, absolutely unable to move. The damned wind kept pushing and pulling, and I cursed it weakly and fearfully every time a strong gust came. It seemed to suck at me like a vacuum, out of the depths of the valley.

I clung like a fly and felt the rock moving up slowly under my fingers. The sky was circling round. I jerked my right foot out and found the rocky ledge at last. It wasn't any use because I was already falling with the cliff. The whole cliff side was toppling into the valley. I slid another inch or two as it swayed and I moved my right hand, then my left, pulling into the shelter of the other side. Left foot was numbed and slow to move. It dragged behind. I hurt my knee. Then I fell forward into the safety of the bushes.

CHAPTER TWENTY

SOMETIMES WHEN you go through an ordeal and come out of it all right you feel uplifted and thankful. That was the way when my eyesight came back. Other times the processes work differently. This was one of the other times.

There was no one about and I sat by the road for ages, tying my shoes – which wouldn't be spiders' nests after all – vaguely straightening shirt and tie and trousers. They were in a pretty bad state, but it was instinctive to do something about them. Dizziness was better away from the heights, but a headache remained and I was chiefly worried about that, afraid it was something to do with my eyes. No one passed, not a car or a bicycle or a walker. The sun had left the valley and the wind was dropping.

It would be nice to recall that sitting there out of reach of the cliffs brought me at least relief or satisfaction. I don't remember it. Everything tasted too bitter. The anger had gone and left this.

It seemed to me then that I'd failed in the one thing that mattered, indeed that I'd never had the least chance of bringing it off. Realising that was the one outcome of the attempt on my life: now I knew where I was. I'd failed where Alix was concerned, and because of that I'd somehow failed towards myself. All that remained was to tidy up the loose ends and go.

I began to walk up the road towards the Villa Lavandou. It didn't occur to me that there might be any further danger there. For a time the things I did were as if worked out and decided by someone else. It was all gone through by a stranger.

Not many yards on I found a rivulet trickling down the rocks, and I drank some of this and washed the blood and dirt off my hands. After sitting there for a good time I began to feel better.

As the villa came in sight I saw there were two cars outside, but neither was the Studebaker. There was an old chap working in the lavender fields, and he gave me a glance but no more. I was surprised at that. Either he took no interest in an unusual sight, or I was less unusual than I thought.

The sun had set now, and the first twilight was fading. There were two or three lights in the villa, one being in the long Renaissance room. I was pretty clumsy and reckless, but I did have a twinge of caution at this point, and made across the lavender beds towards this light, hoping to look in without attracting attention.

As I got near I saw there were about half a dozen people in the room, and the first one I made out was Alix in a chair. She didn't look as if she was enjoying herself. Armand Delaisse, sulky and flushed, was beside her, and Charles stood by the mantelpiece. They seemed to be arguing with a man who had his back to me. As I moved nearer someone tapped me on the shoulder . . .

I jerked round: a man had come up behind me: a policeman.

We stared at each other. 'Your business, please.'

'My name – Gordon. I came to see M. Bénat.'

'May I see your passport?'

I showed it him. He said: 'Will you come with me?'

As we passed across the window I think Charles saw me. This development was a shock, and I couldn't make sense of it. The policeman opened the door of the house, led me into the hall, told me to wait, while he went off towards the living-room. Bénat's usual servant put his head out of another room, his eyes scared and curious and faintly greedy, but he nipped back as soon as he saw me. Then another policeman came out of Bénat's office.

The first policeman came back.

'This way, if you please.'

Down the familiar corridor. There were six in the room. A stranger just inside the door, the three I'd seen, another man with his back to me. In the corner was the lorry driver who'd put me over the edge.

Alix said: 'Giles! . . .'

The dog began to bark, great hostile gulps that filled the room.

'Quiet, Grutli,' Charles said.

The other man turned his head. 'Come in, M. Gordon.' It was Deffand. I'd forgotten his existence. I made sense of it all now.

Alix said with a sort of pain in her eyes: 'What is it? What's happened to you, Giles? Are you hurt?'

Armand Delaisse had hardly moved. I could see my coming had shaken up all three of them. Charles's clever sallow face ... The lorry driver had gone a bit green. But it was Alix I was looking at.

She said again: 'What is it, Giles? Why are you – like that? *Tell me.*'

I heard myself saying: 'Sorry to be – late.'

She glanced at Charles and I think she jumped at once to the fact that he was somehow accountable. Her face changed, the last roundness went out of it; she looked like her brother.

Deffand said: 'You've hurt your hands. Have you been in an accident?'

'Well, yes.'

'Have you come by car?'

'I *came* by car.'

Charles moved to a cupboard, poured a glass of brandy. Deffand's eyes followed him. Charles brought the glass over to me. 'Sit down, Giles. You must be quite tired after your long drive.'

We looked closely at each other. His lip had a derisive, defiant droop. My coming had finished it. The game was up – and he didn't care a damn ... It was part of the hazard, part of an expected malevolence in fate, part of his theory, fitting somehow into the pattern he'd made for himself. He almost welcomed it, as a masochist welcomes pain. I found myself suddenly hating him for the first time. I could hardly keep my hands off his face.

338

Deffand said: 'No doubt you'd like some attention.'

Charles turned away and the moment was gone.

'I'm all right.' My knees were weak and I sat down. Alix didn't move; she was still staring at me. The quiet man by the door turned over a page in his notebook.

'Why did you come up here this evening?'

'Has anybody a cigarette? I smoked my last – on the way.'

Deffand passed me one and held his lighter, taking in my broken finger-nails and shaky hands. I wanted time to think. A quick decision now which would affect everything else. It was almost too much; my brain was too tired and slow.

'I came to see M. Bénat. Invited for six o'clock – things delayed me.'

'My God!' said Alix. 'My God!' And put her face in her hands.

Deffand glanced at her with a narrow preoccupied frown. 'What happened?'

I stared at the end of the cigarette.

Charles said: 'Well, go on, Gordon, tell us what delayed you.'

I looked across at him, thinking it out. 'I should have hurried if I'd known there was going to be a party.'

'I thought you'd be sure to know that.'

'I'm damned sure you thought nothing of the kind.'

Grutli began to growl again at my tone. I gulped at the brandy, felt it go warmly down. A policeman came in and spoke in Deffand's ear. He waved an impatient finger and the man went. Alix wasn't looking at me any longer.

Deffand said: 'As you'll guess, Monsieur Gordon, I'm here in a professional capacity. I explained my mission to you earlier this week.'

'Yes.'

'Perhaps you know I have taken certain steps since then.'

'I saw something in the paper this afternoon.'

'You may remember I asked you to help me then, and you refused. Your help would have been valuable, but you see we got along without it.'

Nobody spoke. Deffand lit a cigarette himself and began to blow smoke through his nose. 'I'll be quite frank with you. M. Bénat and his friends are under suspicion for the same sort of offence. Their connection with the Café des Fourmis has been suspected for a long time. A search is at present being made of this house and its contents. It may succeed or it may fail . . .'

'It has already failed,' said Bénat indifferently. 'The sergeant has just told you.'

Deffand squinted at the end of his cigarette. 'Perhaps you have had too long an experience to commit much to writing, Bénat.'

'During the war it was almost all word of mouth. No doubt fighting the Germans from across the Channel was a different matter.'

Deffand said: 'The point is, Monsieur Gordon, that I could arrest these people at once if I chose – but generally speaking time and trouble are saved by moving only on concrete evidence. So we again invite your help. I shall in any case make a clean sweep in the end. Evidence from you now would be largely a matter of saving time and trouble.'

There was a minute's silence. Armand Delaisse was staring at me in a queer way.

I said: 'You're mistaken in expecting me to be able to help you.'

There was a faint stirring in the room. Bénat bent to stroke the dog.

Deffand said: 'You know these people well.'

'I've been up here twice this year.'

'But you knew them last year also.'

'I was blind then.'

'You have spent several days with Mme Delaisse this week.'

'We were out for pleasure. Nothing more.'

Charles laughed. His face had that dark look, as if it were in shadow.

Deffand said: 'I should like you to understand that it need not necessarily be a charge dealing with the things we've spoken of. What I want is evidence against M. Bénat which will give me greater freedom to act as I should like.'

'How graciously you put it,' Charles said.

Deffand ignored him. 'Let me express this a little differently, Monsieur Gordon. I understand your interest in Mme Delaisse. You must be anxious about her position at the moment, and her future.'

'Possibly.'

'Then let me put a suggestion to you. If I get suitable evidence against M. Bénat now I will give you my guarantee that Mme Delaisse will not be molested at all. She'll be free to leave France or to go on living here if she chooses. She will cease to exist so far as I am concerned.'

I didn't speak.

'On the other hand, if I have to follow these inquiries to the end, it will be my duty to charge everyone implicated. So it would be in her interest to speak now.' Deffand looked at me dryly. 'If you fear further intimidation I can grant you a safe conduct.'

I said: 'I never have feared intimidation.'

For the second time Armand Delaisse glanced at me. He looked very puzzled.

Deffand blew another spiral. 'Well?'

I met Charles's gaze. Under the irony was a relentless pride. 'I don't like this situation any better than you, M. Deffand. But I've nothing to say that will help in the case.'

There was a short silence. 'I'm sorry you take this attitude.'

'I'm sorry I can't help you.'

'A foreign visitor to this country is entitled to expect special consideration. But it would be a mistake to think himself above the law.'

'I've never felt that.'

'Just what do you feel, then?'

'I think it would take too long to tell you.'

'I am here to listen.'

'Sometimes,' I said, 'private wars get out of hand, take precedence over – public ones. It would please me a lot to see Bénat go to prison . . . But it pleases me more to keep him out. I can't explain why.'

Charles said suddenly, contemptuously: 'I've no use for magnanimity.'

'I *know*.' That was just it. That was what I'd been trying to get clear in my own mind. He had no place in his life for the magnanimous. It didn't *fit*. And because it didn't fit he would find it intolerable. For courage and all the virtues of the jungle, for revenge and betrayal and all the vices of man . . .

He said again: 'Don't let me tempt you into any gesture you'd be likely to regret. Deffand implores you to help him.'

'No,' I said. 'There's nothing I want to say.'

'You see,' said Charles to Deffand. 'He's trying to buy nobility by withholding what he doesn't know.'

Armand Delaisse pushed his chair back with a sharp irritable movement. 'If this farce is over perhaps we can go.' It was plain enough he didn't care two sous what was going on between us; all he knew was that I was willing to keep quiet.

Deffand said: 'Have a care for yourself, Monsieur Gordon.'

'Can I go?' persisted Delaisse.

Deffand put out his cigarette. 'You can stay, if that's what you mean. I am going. But don't make any mistake, I shall be back. Tomorrow, if some of your friends will talk. Next week or the week after if they will not.' He breathed nasally. 'As for you, Monsieur Gordon, if I were you I should take the first train home. Come, Lemierre.'

I said: 'Are you going to Nice? Could I ask the favour of a lift.'

He looked me over, professionally, with contempt. 'It is possible.'

He went out, followed by the other man.

I looked at Alix. She hadn't shifted from her chair and she had her eyes down. She looked pretty bad. I thought bitterly, this is the last time I shall see her. It didn't seem to matter. I turned to go.

Armand Delaisse said in an undertone: 'One moment.'

'Well?'

'We were told – we understood you had given us away to the police – that that was why we had been raided.'

'Did you run the Resistance movement on wild guesses?'

'Immediately after your last visit here you were seen to go to the British Consulate. Next day your friend from the Consulate met Deffand at lunch. Then Deffand called on you. Two days later the Café des Fourmis was raided. That and your other interferences – can you wonder at our mistake?'

I stared at him, thinking over the sequence. The lorry driver had come across, was staring at me.

'It was no mistake,' Charles said. 'All this is a little bluff between himself and Deffand.'

Delaisse said slowly, rather angrily: 'No. That can't be true.'

I said to Charles: 'Delaisse may have believed I talked. You never did.'

'Oh? . . . Very positive.'

I said to Delaisse: 'Think it over for yourself. Bénat

344

had his own reasons for wanting to be rid of me. He made use of you to do it.'

'. . . What does he mean, Charles?'

'My dear Armand, if you care to believe this fellow . . .'

'No, of course I do not. But . . .'

I said: 'In a leader it's always the first sign of a moral rot, isn't it – the betrayal, the degeneration . . .'

Alix hadn't moved. They would be waiting for me outside.

'Why didn't you tell Deffand about it, then?' Charles said.

I saw it all clearly again for a second. 'I think it hurts you more to be under an obligation to me.'

He stared. '"To accept a benefit is to sell one's liberty." Isn't that what the old Romans said?'

'It may be.'

'You think I feel the same?'

'I'm sure of it, yes.'

He blew out an amused breath. 'Well, thank you for being absurd. I accept the benefit gladly, since I might certainly lose my liberty the other way.'

'Well, it's really exchanging one liberty for another, isn't it?'

'I'm intensely practical, my dear man. We'll argue out the principles another time.'

At any price I wanted to say something to get at him. I said: 'D'you remember that evening at the Wintertons' remarking that to you – and to some other people – there was only one God, Charles Bénat, world without end, amen?'

'Did I? Very intelligent of me.'

'Wasn't it. But what happens when Charles Bénat starts lying not only to his followers but to himself? Isn't that a sin against the Holy Ghost?'

It did seem to hit him somewhere. 'I don't think I follow.'

'Oh, well, it doesn't matter.'

'No, wait.'

I looked down at his hand till he took it off my arm. We stared at each other. Armand Delaisse was listening – so was the driver. A twist of annoyance went across Bénat's face.

I said: 'Trouble with setting up as a tin god is that you've *got* to live up to your own standards – whatever they happen to be. Other mortals can fall short of them – not you. It's the one condition. Otherwise it all makes nonsense.'

'D'you think I care what the devil you say or do?'

'Yes. Over this.'

'Well, you're wrong. Run after Deffand. Tell him what you please.'

'Deffand's not important. I've no intention of telling him anything at all.'

'No doubt you'll whisper it all in his ear on the way home.'

'I used to think you a man without illusions. It was a point of pride.'

'I've no illusions about you, Gordon.'

'No ... Only about yourself – since you've already persuaded yourself into thinking you can accept your liberty from me.'

'I don't accept my liberty from anyone!' he said savagely.

'What rot! You accept it from Delaisse, this other man and people like them, who do the work and take the risks ... You accept it from all sorts of simple decent people who play up because to them you're still Bénat of the Resistance, still a name to conjure with. They don't realise yet that it's changed – should be Bénat the Racketeer.'

'Simple and decent ... Nobody's simple these days, and very few decent. They trust me because I let them have luxuries they couldn't get otherwise, and bring a little colour and romance into their silly drab lives.'

'Yes ... the little tin god again. So you take favours as your right. But it's not the same from me. I'm the atheist, the disbeliever. In future you'll only exist by my good-will, and I know you're sham. We both know it at this moment. If you can't draw me into the illusion you can't go on believing in yourself.'

I hardly knew what I was saying, but he stared at me as if his interest was caught in spite of himself.

'As if Christ had been cut down by the Roman soldiers who realised he was *really* going to die, eh? . . .'

'I'm not going that far.'

'No ... Neither am I.' He smiled, his lip judicial, contracted. 'You've paid me the compliment of setting the stakes too high . . .'

'It's you who set the stakes,' I said. 'I was afraid they were rather out of your class.'

Just for the moment then, under his smile, he gave

me a look that wasn't easy to take. He was going to say something more, but there was a cough in the passage.

'M. Deffand is waiting,' said the plain-clothes policeman.

We hadn't much to say on the way down. Deffand took a justifiably poor view of my silence, and I was feeling ill again. He did suggest that one of his men should look at my scrapes and scratches, but I wouldn't let him. He didn't ask a single question about my car. When he let me off at the hotel he said:

'Goodbye, Monsieur Gordon. Take my advice.'

'Don't worry. I'll not get in your light again.'

When I got up to my bedroom I was sick, and every now and then I'd have a fit of shivering through the night. I'd doze off and wake up with a start thinking I'd gone blind and have to switch on the bedside light to make it all right. But I didn't dream of the climb once. When morning came the shivering had worn off, and after some breakfast I felt a lot better. I went round to a doctor with the reminiscent name of Foch, and he told me I'd had slight concussion and ought to take it easy for a day or two. Otherwise there was nothing wrong. Then I called in at the garage and reported about the car.

There was a fuss, as I'd expected. Three men with strained faces and talkative hands argued it out with me. Had I informed the police? How could it have happened? I put the blame on my eyesight and told them I wanted as little fuss as possible. Fortunately there was quite a bit of money to my credit at the bank.

When I left I took my passport to the station and booked a seat on the evening train for Paris.

I was getting out – cutting my losses and quitting. It hadn't really started yet, the ache about Alix. I'd been too shaken up for the ordinary feelings to begin. I knew I'd done the only possible thing. She'd made no move towards me last evening at all. After the first exclamations of horror she'd neither moved nor spoken. It was hopeless to attempt to break the tie.

But I was going to feel pretty bad about it later on.

I didn't go near either the Wintertons or John to say goodbye. If I saw John I should quarrel with him for saying anything to Deffand. If I saw the Wintertons they'd overwhelm me with kindness. It was a bit rude, but I'd have to write to them. This last day in Nice was better alone. The train left at six. It had been hopeless to try for a sleeper. With luck I might get one side of a first-class carriage.

Anyway it didn't seem to matter much. Nothing mattered any more. I'd been following a private mirage of my own, and the end was the desert one might have expected.

CHAPTER TWENTY-ONE

I THOUGHT I'd have a sleep in the afternoon, so went back to the hotel and lay on the bed and smoked.

After a bit I dreamed what I hadn't dreamed the night before. I dreamed I was on the cliff again, among all the rubble, with the fissure I'd got stuck in just below me. But when I looked down Alix was caught in it and holding out her arms. She said: 'Don't let me go, Giles.' And I said: 'You're tied to Charles, not me. You're his sister, the same clan, the same blood, the same breath. You'll never be free.' And she said: 'Don't let me go, Giles. You promised. Don't let me go.' Then I left her there and got round the lump without difficulty and climbed to the top of the cliff. Then I woke in a great sweat to find the pain had started all right now.

I went out and walked round the town. It was a sultry day and busy in spite of the heat, and everyone was wearing the gay clothes of the season. I walked along the front and then up into the town. I thought: perhaps if I'd made an effort, perhaps if I'd gone across to her and argued with her again. Less than two days ago everything was all right – or it seemed so – it might have *been* so if I'd never let her go back. That's the way you chucked your life away. If you'd handled things rightly we might have been leaving together tonight. There'd have been trouble later perhaps, but at least we should have had our chance. In England, a thousand miles away, the old links . . .

Well, it was too late now. I was off on my own. The chance had gone. It was for the best. I tried to think myself into the mood of yesterday, to picture Charles and Alix up in their villa sympathising with each other over the police raid, discussing ways of preventing another, perhaps arguing over my part in it, she wishing to be grateful, he hating the sound of my name, Grutli at their feet waiting for the tit-bits. A united family.

Today I couldn't begin to think what had come over me last night. It had all seemed clear as anything, a sort of drunkard's clarity. I wasn't sorry I'd not turned him over to the police, but I couldn't follow the arguments I'd used on him, convinced then that I was wounding him in his tenderest spot, his intellectual self-esteem. They seemed as much nonsense to me today as perhaps they had to him last night. No doubt he would make a good bit of fun out of them when Alix had forgiven him for the attempt on my life.

I walked up the Avenue de la Victoire, and something made me turn in at the familiar café and sit down at the usual table. Sentiment. I ordered cognac and sat gloomily sipping it. I didn't know how long I sat there, but when I looked at my watch it was five. There was only just time to pick up my things at the hotel and get to the station. I hadn't the energy or the inclination to move. But if I didn't go today it was all to do again tomorrow. I was still suffering from shock, was stiff and bruised and could do with a day or two in bed. Should I stay? That was the coward's way. Better to make the clean sweep as intended.

Alix sat down at the table.

She said: 'I've been watching you for nearly an hour.'

She was pale as a sheet. I remember she was wearing grey, and that made her look thin and young.

I said: 'Where were you?'

'Over in that corner. I was there when you came in.'

At the sight of her something had turned over inside me. I wanted to say, oh, darling, I . . . And then it all froze again.

I said: 'What do you want?'

'I've been watching you, trying to come over and speak to you all this time. I hadn't the courage.'

'Courage again?'

She said: 'Listen. Can I talk to you a few minutes?'

Something made me say: 'I'll miss my train.'

Her eyes went very dark. 'Very well, Giles. I've no right – to keep you.'

I said: 'Hell . . . There are a million trains.'

She put her hand on the table, spread out her fingers in that way she had. 'Let me, please, say what I have to say – and then you can go. After you'd left last night I came down following you; but I couldn't go to your hotel – couldn't face you – I think you hate me now. I – stayed out all night – walked a lot. This morning I saw you go out to the doctor's. Since then I've been walking again . . .'

I stared at her. 'I don't hate you. Only I know now it's no use.'

'What's no use?'

'Expecting you to break away from Charles. It's too strong for me.'

Her lips curved down painfully. 'I broke last night.'

After a long time I said: 'Why?'

'Because I'm an idealist, a romantic – what were all those things you said? Because I expect too much of all the people I love. Fidelity from my husband, loyalty from my brother, friendship from my friends . . .'

'Dear God,' I said, with a sudden dreadful feeling of humiliation; 'and what did you expect from me?'

She didn't answer, but sat there looking at her hands. 'Yesterday morning – they told me about the raid on the Café des Fourmis; Charles said it was you. I didn't believe it. Only in the afternoon when you didn't come – and Deffand came instead . . . When at last you came and I realised what Charles had done, I saw then that you must hate me, for ever having any connection . . .'

I stared at her. 'It wasn't *that* at all.' I wanted to explain the things I was only just realising about my own feelings yesterday. Since I came back to Nice there'd been one idea in my head, one thought – *her*; it had gripped like a vice on everything; all the rest shoved aside. On Wednesday night her sudden giving in had left a vacuum: and the vacuum had filled up with all the doubts there'd never been room for before. If you argue

353

with someone for a long time, and then he suddenly gives way, it's common enough to feel for a minute, well, am I *certain* I'm right after all? It's the human reaction you can't get away from; the very vehemence of your own argument tells against you. That was what had happened to me. All these thoughts early yesterday morning . . . And my feelings after the attempt on my life. I wanted to explain this to her now, but I didn't seem able to find the words. It was a new experience for me.

The waiter came across, but I waved him away. I saw her shoes were covered in dust.

'Did you come down in your car?'

'No. I – left it there – telephoned for a taxi. It – was his car, bought with his money . . .'

'You've been out all night?'

'Yes. Oh, it doesn't matter. I felt I had to see you this once. Then I hadn't the heart. Then when you came in here . . . I'm sorry if you've missed your train.'

I said: 'Yesterday, over the phone, Charles said you were unstable, contradictory from day to day.'

She flushed. 'He's right, I suppose.'

'He's *wrong*.'

She looked out of the window, shook her head as if to get the tears out of her eyes.

I said: 'The instability's been in the people you've loved. Isn't that the truth? *Nothing else* at all.'

She searched my face. 'I don't know. I never have known.'

'Well, now's the time to put it to the test.'

She said with a sort of wretched determination: 'Yesterday you hated me.'

354

'. . . Yesterday I was nearly as jealous of Charles as he is of me.'

She tried to smile, but it was a failure.

I said: 'Listen, dear Alix. Listen to me.' But then I couldn't get any more out. I swallowed to clear my throat but it didn't help.

We stared at each other for a minute.

She said: 'I love you, Giles. And I want to cry.'

'Not here. Come on.' I put out a rather shaky hand to her.

'Where to?'

'Back to my hotel first. Have you your passport?'

'Yes.'

'Thank Heaven for that.'

She didn't move. 'But . . . are *you* quite sure again?'

I said: 'Dear God, and I might have caught that train.'

I took her back and rang up Maurice in Cagnes, asked if he could come over and pick us up. He said he could at nine. I told him it would be a long drive, but didn't say where. I didn't know myself yet. I wanted to be out of here as quickly as possible. It was a premonition. Alix had dark shadows under her eyes. It would be silly to underestimate what the break with Charles had cost her.

The people at the hotel accepted the change of plans phlegmatically enough. My room was not let, and I was welcome to use it, they said, until I left. A few minutes after we went up the phone rang. It gave me rather a shock, and if Alix had not been there I don't think I should have answered it. I went across with misgivings.

'Hullo?'

'Giles? This is John. I tried to get you earlier.'

'Confound you,' I said, 'for an interfering fool.'

He sounded a bit taken aback. 'You mean – about Deffand?'

'Of course.'

'My dear old boy, it wasn't of my seeking. He approached *me*. He was full of inquiries about you, wanted to know what sort of a reputation you had – all the rest. Apparently you'd been seen hanging round the Café des Fourmis. I told him no more than I could help.'

'Oh,' I said. 'I'm sorry. You see, I naturally thought . . . What's the trouble now?'

'Not trouble exactly. But I thought you might like to know. A fellow came in about five and told me that Bénat had given himself up to the police.'

Queer twist in my stomach. Alix was looking out over the balcony.

I said: 'On what – er – charge?'

'I don't know. You hadn't heard anything?'

'No. Nothing. Look, John, I'm leaving for England soon. If I don't have a chance to come round . . . Thank you for all your help.'

'Rather sudden, isn't it? Is everything all right?'

'Quite, thanks. You know I'd been intending to leave.'

'Ye-es. What's happened about Bénat's sister?'

'I'll write you from England, John,' I said.

As I put down the receiver she turned. 'That was John Chapel, the man from the British Consulate. You've heard me speak of him.'

Something in my tone made her look at me quickly, but she didn't speak. Over supper we tried to be normal, matter-of-fact, to discuss the details of a journey that wasn't properly decided yet. I felt no triumph, no satisfaction over the news from John – rather a discomfort, as if I were partly in the wrong, as if some good had gone to waste, some rich talent squandered in a world of poverty.

Abruptly I said: 'How did you leave Charles? Or would you rather not talk about it?'

She fumbled with a piece of bread. 'Sometime I'll tell you – not now. It was – awful. I said ... All the same it's like losing – some last link. With the past, you understand.'

'. . . Did you tell him you were coming to me?'

'I think he thought it ... Giles, why would you not give him away?'

I shook my head. 'I don't quite know. It all seems out of focus now.'

But was it, I thought? Some grains of truth in all the nonsense, some sting put into his pride that spread its poison, and would not be pulled out ... The last glance he'd given me had seemed to come out of the darkness of his spirit.

I looked up and found her watching me. She smiled with her eyes. No, I thought, she's the cause, what she said to him, her action in leaving him for good. The break would tear both ways.

Anyway, whatever brought him to do what he had done, it was something to feel that he could make no further move to separate us now.

WINSTON GRAHAM

'What are you thinking?' she asked.

'I like that frock.'

'You like all my frocks. I don't believe you are very discriminating, Giles.'

'Well, I always give you a reason. I like that because it reminds me somehow of our meetings last year.'

'I had it last year. Now it's too short. But I felt – when I left . . .'

While she was speaking a monstrous suspicion came into my mind. Charles couldn't separate us, but Deffand might. In a second the suspicion got out of hand. Was this Charles's way of taking up my challenge? Suppose he agreed he could not accept his liberty from me – and so gave himself up, *because* by so doing he could take Alix away from me again. Confession to Deffand – bringing in Alix – anything was on the cards – even a confession to last year's murder. Nothing was impossible in a certain mood . . .

'Sorry,' I said, in a cold sweat. 'I've just remembered I – have to phone.'

I ran up the stairs, got to the bedroom and tried to think. Marseilles. I rang up the airport at Marseilles. It took a few minutes and then a few more before getting through to the right official.

'No, monsieur, I regret there is no plane leaving for England before fourteen hours tomorrow.'

'None in the morning?'

'No, monsieur.'

'Is there any leaving for Gibraltar or Malta – or Cyprus?'

'. . . There is one leaving for Cyprus at thirteen hours.'

358

I chewed my bottom lip. 'Can you offer me *nothing* better than that at all?'

There was a slight hesitation. 'We have an Iraqi Airways private charter in from Baghdad, Nicosia, Athens. It will be leaving at six in the morning for London, but I don't think there are seats . . .'

Something in the voice made me say: 'For a consideration . . .'

'Well . . . I will see what I can do. Two seats, monsieur? Be at the airport by five fifteen . . .'

When Alix came in I was on the balcony.

'. . . Is there something the matter?'

'Yes, everything's the matter. I've got what I came for. Now I want to take it home.'

She came and stood beside me. 'Have patience, darling. I'm coming.'

We held hands almost without knowing it. The evening was cooling. There had been great banks of cloud over the city during the afternoon.

She said: 'Have you decided how we must go?'

'Yes. Marseilles, I think.'

She looked at her watch. 'The car should be here in half an hour.'

We didn't talk much then, but I think I prayed.

She said: 'I have no clothes, no money . . .'

'Do be sensible.'

She said: 'Is this our car? It looks . . .'

A car had stopped outside the hotel and a man got out. It was Maurice . . .

On the way out of the hotel I said goodbye to the proprietor, told him we were leaving for Monte Carlo.

Maurice came towards us with a smile and a bow, apologising for being early.

A big car came quickly round the corner from the lower end, accelerated towards us, seemed about to stop, then passed on. I let out a slow breath of relief. But there would be no proper relief for many hours yet. Not till after six tomorrow morning.

At the door of the car Alix paused, looked at me with a little turn of the lips, then round at the street, the houses, the shops and the sky. She took a deep breath as if filling her lungs with it. Then she got in. I followed her.

Maurice lit a cigarette and blew out a cloud of smoke. 'I don't think it will rain after all,' he said. 'The stars are coming out.'